The Many Mistakes of Amy Love

The Many Mistakes Series - Book 1

RA Hunter

Edited by: Paige Gadsby

Cover Illustration by: Jess Lang

Character Art by: Cryptid Queer

Publisher: Strange Digital Publishing

TO ALL THE FRIENDS WHO BELIEVED IN ME WHEN I COULD NOT

Foreword

This book is written in dedication to a person I think about and miss everyday, who never got the chance to grow up and see who he would become. I like to think he would be as loving and caring as the version of him I wrote here.

It's easy to think that being queer and the challenges we have faced is something long in the past, but sexuality, gender and identity are murky waters to navigate at any point in history, especially now, as we see a global shift black towards binary thinking, and ideologies. It's why we should never stop fighting for love, equality and acceptance of our trans and non-binary siblings. Trans rights are human rights.

The Many Mistakes series contains depictions of Autism and other disabilities in an authentic and at times raw way. These are based on experiences close to my heart and are not designed as a plot device but as a part of who the characters are.

Everyone has their own experiences and journey with disabilities and the trauma that can come with that. Our labels may be the same but disability can show in so many different ways. What I mean is, just because your sister's cat's nephew has a disability and acts differently doesn't make it better/worse – just different. While we are talking about the fun stuff, this book has graphic depictions of panic attacks, anxiety and trauma induced nightmares. If this is something you are going to struggle with, then maybe put the book down and come back to it later.

Searching Spotify or Apple music for 'The Many Mistakes of Amy Love' will lead you to the accompanying playlist, designed to be played in order to match the feeling of the book – or play it on shuffle, I cant stop you! You can find me across most social channels under some variation of 'RA Hunter' and you should 100% reach out, I don't bite – unless you ask very nicely.

Hunter ♥

Chapter 1

Amy

The feel of the cheap fabric seat under her fingers was repulsive, like the fibers were catching on the microscopic details of her finger prints. It made her skin crawl. Nevertheless, she gripped the arm rests tight as she looked out the small round window. Amy Love had never been on a plane before. She knew it was going to be loud, but she never expected it to be so loud. She hadn't booked a window seat; she hadn't booked anything but the cheapest one way ticket to Toronto. A chance at a new start and a new life. Somewhere that no one would think twice about her, a place where she could be whoever she wanted and not the person life had made her. She was leaving that person behind.

An old couple sat next to her and smiled in that way old people do when they see someone young they think needs help. They had insisted on giving up their window seat for her after striking up an awkward conversation as Brits did best in uncomfortable situations. Amy hoped they didn't want to talk to her the whole eight hours they would be in the air. She didn't much like people on a good day, and this wasn't a good day. Her thoughts were interrupted as the plane lurched forward, building speed and, by some miracle of engineering Amy couldn't hope to comprehend, it lifted into the air.

"It's OK, dear," the woman to her right said, gently patting Amy's arm. The feeling of the unwanted physical contact made Amy want to recoil, but she felt unable to do so instead she flashed a practiced smile back at the woman, not trusting herself to speak. "Once we are up in the air, it's all blue skies," she beamed back, clearly happy with her assistance.

Amy turned her head back to the window. London was quickly disappearing below her; individual streets became indistinguishable and the urban sprawl of the south of England morphed to one homogenous block stretching all the way out to the sea. From here the water was steel blue, vast and unforgiving; she could still smell the beaches she had grown up on, summers spent wasting time with friends on the shore – winters spent bracing yourself against the cold surf and spray. It was strange to think she was never going to see those places again, never going to feel the water against her skin. Almost incomprehensible that everything she had ever known was disappearing below her.

Toronto was a new start. It had taken her an extra year to get everything together: the money, the college grades and to secure a place studying biology at the university. When she had told her mother she was leaving, the woman had been as uninterested in it as she was everything else Amy did; their relationship was born out of court ordered relocation four years prior and had barely improved since. Blankets of apathy and resentment had piled between them over those four years, Amy choosing to never let people close to her, opting to bury herself in studies and dreams. It wasn't that her mother had been unkind; they just simply didn't want to spend time with each other. She had, however, been a vast improvement on her father, a man who Amy refused to ever think about. Just the thought of his existence caused panic and dread to prickle at the back of her neck.

Toronto was a new start.

Chapter 2

Ten Years Later

Amy's fingers flew across the keys on her laptop as she sat cross-legged on her office chair. The afternoon sun, cool and pale, stood in contrast to the warm glow from the side lamp, both casting long shadows up the walls of her living room. She wanted to get the latest data set recorded and uploaded before Jamie inevitably texted her asking where she was. Her PhD had been such a focus and driving force, taking up her time for close to four years. It was unfathomable to her that she would let anything get in its way, even her best friend – fortunately they worked together and he respected the research as much as she did.

No sooner had Amy input the last sequence than the soft alarm on her phone started to chime. Sitting back and stretching her arms above her head, her back and neck made a satisfying set of clicks. Reaching over to silence the alarm, she noticed several missed video calls from Jamie spanning the last thirty minutes. As she picked up the phone, she got a momentary flash of her reflection in the black screen, her piercing green eyes and flame hair in stark contrast to her pale skin – she looked like every celtic stereotype possible. Having spent most of her childhood being teased about it in school, she had come to accept her looks. Sliding her fingers across the screen, she called Jamie back, a bright picture of the two of them at graduation many years ago filling the screen before it was replaced by a slightly older real life Jamie.

He was a tall slender man with dark brown glossy hair that he kept long and floppy. In his youth, he had spent years dying it black and straightening it to death; it appeared to have caused no long lasting damage as he still had a full head of hair. He still kept it long and sweeping and was forever shaking the mess out of his eyes. Amy knew what he was wearing even though she couldn't see it under his lab coat: he always had on black skinny jeans and a band t-shirt. Whatever memo the rest of the generation got regarding emo fashion, it had never reached Jamie; she suspected it would eventually come back round and he would gloat that he was a trend setter. Most importantly, he was beaming at Amy, his eyes sparkling even via the pixels of a video call.

"Hey! I have been trying to call you!" He smiled at her through the phone. He and Amy had been friends for almost ten years, they met at a University doing their biology undergraduate. She was the awkward queer English exchange student and he was the out of place gay – unsurprisingly they hit it off straight away. Now they were as inseparable as ever with Amy three quarters of the way through her PhD and Jamie the lab technician at the university.

"I know, this is me calling you back." She laughed at him. She noticed he was still at University, the unmistakable background of his lab tech office filled with storage boxes and files behind him. "Why are you still at work? I left hours ago!"

"Because it's my job, Amy! " He rolled his eyes in mock annoyance. "I don't get to come and go as I please, unlike all you lot." He waggled his finger in her vague direction. "Plus I know Professor Arden is still here and he always leaves a mess – and I *don't* want to have to deal with that tomorrow."

"Ok, ok." Amy smiled as she moved towards her kitchen, flicking on the kettle. "I just wondered if you were hanging around to try and see Todd..." She raised an eyebrow at the phone as a blush crept up Jamie's face. His lack of response told her everything she needed to know – she made a note to mock him about this later. "Are you still coming over? Or are you going to sit in the lab all night hoping for tall, dark and handsome to come say hi?" She busied herself making a cup of tea. She didn't need to look at Jamie to know he was probably bright red.

"I'll be there in an hour." He huffed with all the indignation of someone being called out, he disconnected the call as Amy chuckled to herself in the quiet kitchen.

"Are you sure you are going to be ok here alone over the holidays?" Jamie looked worried over the steaming cup of coffee in his hands. He was leaning against Amy's kitchen counter as she finished the last of the washing up from the Chinese he had arrived with. He was concerned; it had been years since Amy was alone for the whole holidays – not since their first year of undergrad when she was the only student in dorms over the break. Every year since, she had gone back to Jamie's, where they welcomed her like any other family member. Unfortunately, this year the thing keeping her in the city was work. She could theoretically monitor the experiments remotely, but the idea of something going wrong and being unable to fix it gave her an icy feeling of dread. Amy was so close to finishing with this part of her research she didn't want to risk it, even for a week of homemade food. Family time was not something there had been a lot of growing up. She didn't have loads of rose tinted Christmas memories she was trying to replicate – it was lovely going and spending time with a family of people that loved and cared for each other. It was beautiful how they had welcomed her as one of their own – but simply put she wouldn't miss it if she didn't attend one year.

When Amy had first told him that she wouldn't be coming with him at Christmas, he said he would stay too, but his mom needed the help back home. Jamie was the oldest of 5 and Amy was never going to stand between Debbie and her boys – especially at Christmas. He had eventually reluctantly agreed. Amy suspected he was more sad about the situation than she was. She knew he found being back home in rural Ottawa difficult, with a large conservative family to match. Amy was a great buffer for prying family members.

"I promise you will still have a lab to come back to! I'm only coming in to take readings and record data. I won't even be using your fancy test tubes." Amy smiled over her own cup of tea, as she settled at her kitchen table having finished the last of the dishes. He was understandably protective of his labs; not only was it his responsibility to keep everything in working order, but if anything damaged or interrupted some of the experiments, it could be years of important research lost. The protectiveness didn't just extend to the materials in the lab but to his friends and family too; it was something she loved and admired about him.

"And I will hold you to that promise!" He waggled a finger jokingly in Amy's direction "But you know that's not what I meant! It can get pretty lonely round here over the Christmas break." A look of concern crossed his face. He was also right; Amy knew exactly what he was getting at, she just didn't want to talk about it. She was more than capable of entertaining herself for the break; and if she kept things as she planned there would be no risk of her anxiety getting the better of her.

"Todd is working the holidays too, I am sure we will bump into each other on campus and he will drag me for a coffee. I also have a pile of books and movies that I have been saving for some peace and quiet." Amy smiled, trying to reassure her friend that she really would be ok. She didn't want to admit she was also trying to reassure herself.

"Talking to the campus security guard doesn't count! However toned his ass is," Jamie said, looking off wistfully dreaming of Todd's ass – the same ass he had been lusting after for the last several years. "Will you at least come to the party tomorrow night? I know you are not an 'out out' kind of person, but you will have a good time, I promise!"

Amy rolled her eyes at his use of the painfully English phrase; he picked it up from her years ago and it made her chuckle every time she heard his thick Ottawa accent say it.

Each winter just before Christmas, Jamie threw a massive pre Christmas party. Over the years, they had become somewhat legendary within the queer community; they started out as a safe space for people to hang out with like-minded people and found family before having to head back home for the holidays and deal with their traditional families who weren't always the easiest to be around. As the years progressed, they evolved into the must-attend event of the season, regardless of your impending holiday plans. They soon grew too large for the small campus bar and moved to a downtown club.

"Ok ok ok, I'll come, as long as you promise to stop saying 'out out'!" Amy raised her arms in the air in mock surrender. Maybe it would be worth going out before everyone headed off for the holidays.

Amy had never been. She wasn't much of a clubbing person; they were loud and full of people, and she preferred her company in a smaller more intimate group setting. After moving to the city she had spent a lot of time expanding her social circle; she had a D&D group that met every few weeks, she attended some fitness classes at the local YMCA and she got involved with activism at the University student union. But this time, she was tempted by the party, given how solitary the next week or so was going to be – maybe it would be nice to go out before everyone headed off until the New Year.

"Fuck yes!" he squealed. "I promise you it will be worth it!" Trying hard not to spill his coffee on the floor, Jamie did a little wiggle which made Amy roll her eyes as she flashed a smile at him. There was no way he was going to let her back out of the party now she had finally said yes – it was about time she got out a little and embraced the queer nightlife of the city. He expected his best friend to get cold feet at least three times before he even left tonight – but she had said yes and he was determined to hold her to it. Looking over at her, Jamie was always floored by how unaware she was of her own charm; striking looks and outwardly-winning personality were a well-crafted mask that very few got to really see behind. Many times over their decade of friendship, he had come to smooth out situations Amy had walked into without her own knowledge – he could never understand how someone so intelligent could be so clueless with people. Sipping his coffee again, he mused on what trouble Amy was going to get into next.

Chapter 3

Laura

Work was going slowly – painfully slowly. Laura wanted to be home and getting ready for her night out. She knew her housemates were already in the party mood – well most of them, Zoey wasn't coming – as usual she feigned that she had too much studying to do. Laura was so ready to let her hair down and have some fun with her friends. They had been going to these pre-Christmas parties for a few years after Ali helped the organizer find a new venue – ever since they had been a staple of their social calendar.

Laura stole another look at the time on her phone: it was almost 4.30, only another 30 minutes before she could pack up her laptop and leave the office guilt free. Jason was sitting opposite her, deep in some coding problem he had been struggling with all day. His nose scrunched up in frustration as he tapped his fingers on the desk, his shaggy dirt blond hair ruffled and messy from the repeated motion of running his hand through it.

"Want a hand there?" Laura asked. She had finished all her tasks several hours ago, and there was no point in starting something new so close to the end of the day and the weekend.

"Urgh please!" Jason rubbed his eyes in frustration. "This code just doesn't work and I can't figure out why." He gestured at the screen, filled with lines of code.

"Coding is just like women, Jason." Laura smirked at him as she got up and walked round the desk to look at the lines of code. "You just need to know how to read them." It had been a long running joke between the pair that Laura was much better with women than he was.

"As my chronic single status shows you, I am clearly no good at that either." He half-jokingly shoved Laura's shoulder as she flicked her fingers across the keyboard. With satisfaction, she pressed enter and watching all the lines of errors messages magically disappear one by one. "You're so infuriating! And you get more women than me!" He huffed with a smile on his face.

"You know the offer is still there to come tonight if you want. I can be your wing woman – help you with two problems in one day." Laura was laughing now, a sense of satisfaction washing over her, improving her mood instantly.

"No, I am not about to be shown up by you twice in one day! My ego couldn't take it!" Jason batted Laura away until she returned to her side of the desk. Jason was a big sweetie and she loved him for it. She knew there was a person out there for him – he just needed to stop overthinking it. "Besides, I have to look after my niece," he added, turning his attention back to his computer.

Laura studied him for a moment – it always amused her how much he was searching for 'the one'. It was one of the main differences between the two of them. Laura wasn't interested in relationships; she went with the flow and often found someone to keep her company for a night or two. She liked this set up: no strings, no complications and no feelings – not that she was against a relationship, she just wasn't looking for one. Not when there were so many amazing people to get to know. Jason on the other hand was all about serious serial monogamy, he was on all the apps and went on blind dates – but they never seemed to work out.

Thoughts turning to tonight, Laura was hopeful she could lose some of the tension she was feeling around the holidays ahead; an attractive woman would be the perfect way to do that. It was unusual for her to be alone over the whole holidays. For the last few years, it had been a mix of housemates and her best friend Emily – but this year Emily and Zoey were going back home for a tentative family reunion, and Munaza wasn't working so was taking the few free days off to see family. But with everyone out of town, it meant she had the apartment to herself: free to watch movies and cook whatever she wanted whenever she wanted. It also meant the rule about 'no overnight guests' would be suspended – and she intended to make full use of it. Looking back down at her phone, she saw the apartment group chat had woken up and more than a dozen messages littered her screen. Swiping across the screen, she busied herself in coordinating outfits and timings while waiting for 5pm to finally roll around.

Chapter 4

Pre Christmas Party

Amy let the hot water cascade over her body. Despite living alone, she had always relished the solitude and thinking space she got from being in the shower. Several times over the last twenty-four hours, she had debated texting Jamie and pulling out of the event tonight – but instead she had messaged Rachel who had talked her round every time. She knew how important tonight was to Jamie, and she had always felt a pang of guilt for never going and supporting him, especially when she loved the drive to his parents the following day, hearing all the gossip about people she had never and would never meet. But this year, she was going to experience it all for herself, for better or worse.

Hopping out of the shower, she walked across her modest living space. It wasn't anything fancy, but it was hers and she could have it exactly as she wanted. The space was split between a comfy couch that had seen better days and her desk, the walls lined with rows and rows of books. Toweling her hair dry, Amy headed into the bedroom, frowning at the three outfit choices laid out on her bed.

Much discussion last night had been focused on what was appropriate to wear tonight. Jamie had humored her for hours as she fretted over what was the right look. In the end, she had narrowed it down to these three options, each with their own pros and cons. The final factor was going to be texture: could she handle the seams and itchy labels for the night? did the material make her skin crawl at the slightest touch? All these small details changed from day to day. It was infuriating to say the least, but when you had lived your whole life like it – it was just something you got used to.

Running her hands over the leather jacket hung on the end of her four-poster bed it felt cool and smooth to the touch, perfectly acceptable for the weather and the occasion. She had wanted to wear her favorite green jacket - but Jamie had looked horrified at the thought of her wearing it. True it was shabby and a little patchy – after all, it had been darned several times with love – but it was her comfort blanket and she was never going to give it up. Amy stared at the three neat piles of clothes, ruling out the skirt instantly – she didn't think she could handle tights tonight.

Settling on fitted black jeans and a white t-shirt with her leather jacket and heeled boots, she quickly finished drying off and got dressed. Standing back and looking at herself in the mirror, she was happy with the look; her pale skin didn't look out of place against the contrasting black and white, whilst her hair gave the much-needed splash of color as it fell long and full of natural deep waves over her shoulder like a glossy auburn waterfall. Her hair had been an untamed mess up until she got drunk enough one night to give herself a retrospectively terrible undercut that was fortunately fixed by Rachel the following day. Removing all the bulk had transformed her bushy unruly mess to a manageable series of deep waves and curls that require very little effort to manage – much to Amy's relief.

Walking back into her living space, she picked up her keys and discreet ear defenders; the little rubber buds were a lifesaver and made busy spaces endurable when it was impolite to use noise canceling headphones. She took one last look around her studio flat before heading out the door. Rachel and Jamie had agreed to meet her a few blocks away so she wasn't walking into the venue alone. It was little gestures that really showed how much her friends cared: walking into a place full of people she didn't really know was nothing short of torture. With one last tap on her pockets to check she had everything, she flicked off the light and headed down the stairs.

Chapter 5

Christmas Party

The music was loud. The vibration of the bass rattled through Amy in a not totally unpleasant way. The ear plugs were doing their job and keeping the sound muted. In the past, she would have been embarrassed to be seen using them, but fortunately they had become a bit of a fashion accessory. Amy wasn't opposed to loud music, but it always made her feel cut off from conversations. She had to work extra hard to listen to people and it just always made her feel a little detached from the rest of the world – even more so than normal. That's not to say she wasn't having a good time; she had to admit that it was nice to spend some time with people before her week of solitude. She knew most of the people in the group – she had been hanging out with Jamie and Rachel long enough for their friends to become her friends too. Group cinema trips, casual dinners, lazy Sundays in the park had all become a semi-regular part of her life and she was glad of it; that combined with the group chats meant she felt like she was really part of a community.

As with any event like this, friends had brought along

friends – and they brought more friends – until the place was filled with someone that knew someone, that knew someone, who inevitably knew someone else who was attending. Whilst Toronto was a fairly large city, the queer community was still comparatively small to the total population, meaning odds were at least one person in every friendship group knew someone in another. Amy had been introduced to a handful of new people, but she couldn't remember any of their names – another barrier of the loud music and foreign environment. As she leaned against the bar sipping her second drink of the night, she watched Jamie and Rachel on the dancefloor; he was in his element, swishing around the packed dancefloor like a pro. The lights flashed in time with the music, the walls covered in a technicolor of light refractions off the large disco ball hung high from the rafters. Amy took a moment to really look around the space, an old building – well, as old as they really got this side of the ocean – this had probably been a mill or a factory less than 200 years ago. The club was on the top floor, the lower floors hosting a selection of small business and studios perfected for the artistic community of Toronto. The bare brick walls and high vaulted iron beams were the perfect backdrop for a night of revelry and dancing, all adorned with a mirage of pride flags and moving lights. Jamie had been so excited when a friend of a friend had found him this spot. It came with a large dance floor and bar as well as a rooftop area that worked perfectly for quiet conversations.

Amy looked back at her friends. A smile crept across her lips as she watched them. They were dancing with Rachel's friend Emily, who Amy had met a handful of times before – she seemed nice but they had little in common. The song ended and the group made their way to stand with Amy by the bar, each taking the opportunity to have a drink and catch their breath, excitedly chattering about the artist they had just danced to. Amy had nothing to add so she kept quiet – content in the atmosphere.

"Having fun there Amy?" Rachel smiled at her. Rachel was far more outgoing than anyone had any business being. Amy and Rachel had taken a while to warm up to each other but now they were thick as thieves. Amy rolled her eyes at Rachel; this type of conversation was well worn over the years. Rachel would worry Amy wasn't having fun because she didn't go and dance, or because she sat on the edge of the party. In truth, Amy preferred it this way: she got to enjoy people and their company but didn't have to be the center of attention.

"Just like the last time you asked, Rachel, I promise, I'm fine." Amy nudged her with a shoulder as she smiled. "I'm having a really good time, I'm really glad I came out." She shot a smile at Jamie who beamed back. The three of them went back to their conversation, something about the song that was currently playing they didn't care for. Amy went back to her drink.

A few minutes later, Emily excused herself from the group, she returned with someone Amy didn't think she had met before – she was sure she would remember this woman. She was undeniably stunning in a way that took Amy's breath away. Her dark hair framed her face with eyes deep blue like exotic waters that captured her for just a second and held her hostage under their gaze before carrying on round the rest of the group. Her smile shimmered in the changing colored lights of the club making her look almost ethereal.

More people had joined them now, taking a break from the dance floor to greet the newest member of the party.

One by one, the new guest was introduced to people; her smile was so natural as she hugged and introduced herself to everyone, working round the circle.

Amy was not a big fan of hugs. For a fleeting second, she felt ice cold and the social expectation of giving one to a stranger – so she stood where she was and waved, flashing a brief smile. The woman tilted her head slightly to the side and shot back a smile that gave nothing away. Her cool blue eyes met Amy's and gave off a friendliness that Amy didn't think was possible. As quickly as it happened, it passed and the woman was on to the next member of the party, exchanging smiles and hugs again. Amy let out a breath she hadn't been aware she was holding.

As she made her way around the group, pausing to chat with a few of Emily's other friends, Amy couldn't help but steal a look at the new member of the party. She was around her height and the woman's olive skin was darker than her own, evident even in the dim light. The white cropped top exposed her delicate midriff, accentuated by her pale baggy jeans hanging off her waist.

Amy had not been subtle as she checked out the newest member of the group, as Rachel leaned in and whispered into her ear. "That's Laura, she's meant to be a lot of fun, you should go and talk to her" She pulled back giving Amy a wicked smile and placing her hand on Amy's back, giving her a gentle push.

"You know full well I am not going to do that." Amy smiled back. She could think of nothing more embarrassing than introducing herself to someone new, especially when that person was deep in conversation with other people. She looked down at her glass, realizing it was empty and took this as the perfect excuse not to engage with the new party member. "But I will go and get myself another drink. Do you want anything?"

"She won't bite!" Jamie leaned over rolling his eyes. "Well, maybe she will if you ask nicely," he said loud enough for others around them to turn their heads. Seeing Amy blush and shift uncomfortably in her shoes made him shoot her a more genuine smile. He could never understand how Amy was so content being a wallflower, but he loved her regardless. "Anyway Amy, thanks for the offer, but I'm going back to the dance floor!" And with that he pushed off from the bar grabbing Emily and Rachel by the wrists pulling them to join him. A few others got up and made their way on to the dance floor once more – disappearing into the vast mass of moving bodies.

Amy made her way towards the bar, ordered herself another drink – the third and last alcoholic one of the evening, she thought to herself. Looking back at the packed dance floor, she decided to go and check out the roof. She liked these spaces at events, often frequented by smokers and people drunkenly making out. Amy liked it up here because it was quiet. She could stand and people-watch without the loud music making her whole body vibrate.

As she opened the door she was greeted by an ice cold breeze. The heaters on the roof kept off most of the December cold, but it was still a distinctly cooler place than the bar, with the wind whipping off the bay and snaking through the sky scrapers. She moved to position herself with a good view of the Toronto city skyline, with the distant lights of the tall buildings twinkling like urban stars. The rest of the roof – which had less than a dozen people chatting in small groups scattered across it – was a continuation of the same red brick and iron beams, the edges covered in what Amy assumed was fake ivy to help soften the space.

Scanning the array of people Amy noticed Laura was also up here. She was engaged in a conversation with a man Amy didn't recognise. There was nothing unusual about that – the event had grown over the years and now not even Jamie knew everyone who attended. From this distance, she couldn't make out more than her basic features; the dark hair and white crop top were unmistakably her.

Amy may not have been good at talking to people, but something she had grown to be good at over the years was reading body language. Even from this distance, it was clear Laura wasn't having a good time with her new friend.

Chapter 6

Knight in Shining Amy

The signal in the bar was terrible. Laura knew she had at least one message but it wouldn't load. After saying hi to the people she knew with a flurry of hugs and quick introductions to the people she didn't, she made her excuses and headed to the roof where hopefully she would get enough signal to read whatever messages had made her pocket vibrate non-stop. Stepping out onto the rooftop, with the city stretching out in front of her, she couldn't deny the view was amazing from up here. From this spot, she had a perfect view of downtown and all the older parts of the city, the new high rises jutting out in the distance, highlighting everything she loved about her home city. There was always something magical about the skyline. They had been blessed with a few days' respite from the snow leaving the clear sky behind an impenetrable inky black. The temperature was resolutely hovering around freezing and her breath blew out great plumes of vapor, as the cold air bit against her cheeks. It made her long for warm summer nights.

Laura had been to this bar a few times with Emily, but this was the first time she had come to this rather legendary holiday party. She had met Jamie and Rachel a few times before; this was one of the largest friendship groups on the queer scene in the city, so everyone knew someone who knew someone. In fact, she had met almost everyone before, but she couldn't ever remember meeting the beautiful redhead who had awkwardly waved at her inside though – maybe she was new to the city. Laura made a mental note to try and talk to her at least once tonight, maybe even get her number.

Taking her phone out of her pocket, she saw that it was the apartment group chat that had been pinging away all night. Zoey was heading off first thing in the morning for an early flight so was making her goodbyes now. She had also used this as an excuse to not come out tonight – Zoey was good at coming up with reasons not to go out, but after a brutal first term on her MBA and with a stressful family Christmas looming, Laura could cut her some slack.

This was the first year Laura was going to be alone over Christmas; she had been home the first few years she had lived in the city but recently she had taken a more lowkey holiday season with her housemates. Ali worked retail so rarely got the time off, and Munaza didn't celebrate so rarely went anywhere; however, this year both of them had plans to be out of the city. She wasn't thrilled about being alone over the holidays, but she wasn't going to let it get in her way. She had things planned to keep her entertained – Laura was determined not to put herself in a bad mood. As she typed a quick goodbye to Zoey, a man she didn't recognise slid up next to her.

"Hey sexy!" he said with a little too much confidence as

he leaned over her, one hand against the wall near her head. While not an overtly threatening move, it boxed Laura into a conversation she had not agreed to have. His smile was cocky and far too big across his face, something Laura suspected came from the alcohol he stank of.

"Hi," she replied curtly. He was standing closer than she wanted. She had no idea who he was, and she didn't want to find out.

"You don't have a drink," he stated, licking his lips and looking down at her hands. He took his time looking her up and down, his eyes raking over her body, a deliberate move he wanted her to see, before tilting his head back up to look at her face. The feeling of his eyes on Laura's body made her skin crawl, violated by just his look. "Maybe we should head inside and I can get you one?" he continued, leaning in closer to her as if he was telling her a secret. The hot stickiness of his breath on her skin was vile.

"No thank you, my friends are waiting for me an – " Laura started trying to move away from him. She had to slide further along the wall to try and move round him, but as she did his other hand came firmly up to her arm, squeezing just a little too hard. She bit back a sound, not wanting to give him the satisfaction of knowing he was hurting her, the only place to look was his face, she closed her eyes turning her head as far away as she could, hoping it would hide some of the panic she was feeling.

"Awww come on, they won't mind you having one drink with me." He leaned a little closer. His words were firm and authoritative – he was expecting Laura to come with him. "Who knows we might really hit it off." He leaned in even closer, his face almost touching hers. She kept her eyes closed tight so she didn't have to look at him any longer. The panic set in deep, coiling in the pit of her stomach. Ice shards felt like they were puncturing her insides, spreading through her veins, twisting as they went. His grip on her arm tightened; the smell of the stale beer on his breath made her feel sick.

At that moment, Laura felt someone else by her side. Now it was impossible for her to get away, the fear began to rise into her chest, the ice shards pricking the bottom of her lungs making it almost impossible to breathe. It had been a long long time since she had felt threatened in public. She was always careful to go out with friends and tell people where she was, but at that moment she realized no one knew she was up here, no one was going to come and look for her.

"Oh My God! Laura!" A loud, unexpected voice came from the new person standing to her side, making Laura jump – it sounded feminine and smooth. Laura searched her mind, trying to place the voice but she didn't recognise this person at all. They sounded friendly and playful, a stark contrast to the man gripping her tight. "The lads and I have been looking everywhere for you!" Laura was so confused, struggling to keep up – what lads was this female voice referring to? The only guys she knew in their party were Jamie and a few others she couldn't remember the names of, and she doubted they would have come looking for her so quickly she could only have been gone for, what, fifteen minutes? Laura's inquisitiveness got the better of her. She slowly opened her eyes hoping it might give some clarity to the situation, but it only raised more questions. Stood to her side was the auburn haired woman that waved at her downstairs – she couldn't even remember her name, she wasn't even sure she had been given it. A wave of relief washed over Laura as this woman looked at her with a massive painted smile that did not stretch all the way to her eyes. Those eyes. Laura was captivated by them even in a moment of panic. The earthy green color was enthralling and comforting like they might hold the world's greatest secrets.

The man shifted slightly, moving back, pulling Laura out her thoughts. He clearly did not want to meet these 'lads' that had been mentioned. "Come on." An arm came up to her side and gently started to pull her away, the warmth from the woman's hand was soft and reassuring. "We can't celebrate graduating from the Police Academy unless we are all together!" the woman practically sang at Laura, who continued to look baffled. But the radiating warmth for the hand on her arm was helping, the ice was retreating from her lungs.

"You're cops!?" The man moved back even further, his eyes going wide. Suddenly it was as if he couldn't get far enough away from Laura.

"Yep!" replied the redhead, still light and airy. "Would you like to join us?" She flashed him a wicked smile, one that this time did go all the way up to her eyes. A clear look of warning flashed across them as she uttered, "Or are you going to fuck off and leave my friend here alone?" Her voice dipped lower with a threatening edge. She took a step closer to the man, putting herself between him and Laura. She was a good foot and a half shorter than him, and unless she was hiding some sort of super strength or mastery of martial art prowess – there was no way she could take him on in a fight.

"No, no, officer I – " he backed away even more, his arms up in the air as if he had been caught red handed. "I think I am going to go home."

"What an excellent idea," the woman sang back, all

hints of malice now gone from her voice as she sent the same smile at him. "Have a great night!" He was almost off the roof completely now; she sent a small wave in his direction as he disappeared around the corner and out of sight.

Chapter 7

Call Me Maybe

Laura's brain was struggling to process what had just happened. Everything had gone from zero to one hundred and then back to zero even faster. She was full of emotions and adrenalin and all she could do was look at the back of the woman's head standing in front of her; the faintest smell of cherries clung to the cold air around her. This total stranger had stepped in to protect her – she didn't even know who Laura was and yet she had come over to help.

Amy waited until the man was long out of sight before she turned around to look at Laura. She looked a little pale and shaken, her eyes were wide and it looked like she had forgotten how to breathe, her beautiful lips parted as she let out fast shallow breaths.

"Are you ok?" Amy said slowly and calmly. "Take some slow deep breaths ok, you're safe. He's gone." Instinctively Amy put a hand on each shoulder applying a little pressure, and looked straight into Laura's eyes. Now was not the time to notice they were as blue as the deep sea and strikingly beautiful. Nor was this the time to notice the small smattering of freckles across her skin, the dark lashes framing her eyes were the same deep chocolate as her long hair.

"I uh, I...," Laura trailed off, she didn't know where to start, she had so many things she wanted to say but her brain refused to make the connection to her mouth. Amy kept looking at her, a furrow of concern across her brow. "Your accent?" was still all she managed. She hadn't noticed before, but there was a definite clipped edge that was starkly different from the local Canadian drawl. Laura closed her eyes and took a deep breath trying to focus her thoughts. A few moments later, she opened them feeling a little more composed, cursing herself for making such a stupid comment.

"Oh, yeah, erm, I'm English actually, been here over a decade but still sound like a minor royal." Amy chuckled sheepishly, her eyes flickered to the floor, a warm wash of embarrassment crept up her chest and across her neck. "I'm also not a cop. Just to clarify." She let go of Laura's shoulders and took a small step back giving the woman some room now that it looked like she wasn't going to have a panic attack. Amy buried her hands in her pockets, struggling to know what to do with them now she was no longer holding Laura. "I didn't introduce myself downstairs, it was so loud. My name's Amy." She forced herself to stop staring at the floor as her hand came up to rub the back of her head – a nervous habit she often tried to hide.

A silence fell over them both for a moment as Amy gave a weak awkward smile at Laura. Laura didn't have the space to admit she found it kind of adorable – so much had happened so fast her brain was finally starting to catch up. This woman, Amy, a total stranger, had just saved her - Laura didn't want to think what from. All she knew was that in that moment she was beyond grateful.

"Well, in that case, thank you Amy. Can I get you a drink?" No sooner had the words left her mouth than she saw Amy already had half a drink in her hand. She instantly felt slightly stupid for everything that had just happened.

"You can later if that's ok?" Amy said, casting a quick glance to her partially full glass, tipping it up slightly to add emphasis to her words. "Are you ok? Do you want me to get you a taxi home? Or get someone from down stairs to be with you?" She paused then added "Or we could stay up here, chat for a bit if you like?"

Laura realized at that moment that she wasn't ready to be alone, or to go back downstairs: the thought of all the people and the noise was more than she could currently cope with. She sent her a small smile and nodded. "Yeah, are you ok to stay here with me for a few minutes?"

"Of course," Amy beamed back; this time the smile was genuine, as she gestured to a bench with a view of the city skyline "Shall we go sit?" She started to walk backwards and held out her hand for Laura to take, which she took instinctively, still in a bit of a daze. Amy's hand was soft and warm, her fingers wrapping round Laura's palm instantly made her feel better. She also couldn't ignore the bolt of electricity that emanated from the skin contact, glad that Amy was facing the other way and couldn't see her blush. As they sat on the bench, a silence fell over them as they both took in the cool night air and the view of the city sprawling out in front of them, their shoulders resting against each other.

Laura took the time to study Amy, now she wasn't full of icy panic. This woman was stunning. Her boots made her an inch taller than Laura, her casual black jeans hugged in all the right places and the tight white t-shirt left exactly the right amount to the imagination. The look was finished off with a casual leather jacket, giving Amy this magnificently sexy and mysterious vibe that Laura was instantly drawn to. Her red hair sat in beautiful deep waves that fell effortlessly and artfully in long layers around her stopping just below her shoulder, highlighting the undercut at the base of her neck. Amy's whole look was either well crafted or Laura suspected Amy had no idea what it did to people. She guessed the woman probably broke hearts that she didn't even know existed. Amy was definitely her type. As if reading her thoughts Amy turned her head to look at Laura, throwing a half smile and giving her another flash of those expressive sage eyes.

"Are you doing ok?" she asked, a hint of concern laced her smile. This woman was sweet as anything as well as sexy, Laura noted, quickly helping her forget about what just happened, and it made her want to get to know Amy a lot more.

"Yes, thank you. You didn't have to come save me back there, you only met me like five minutes ago." Laura tried to keep it casual, adding a forced laugh.

"Why wouldn't I?" Amy asked, looking slightly puzzled, her eyebrows pulled into a small furrow. She genuinely would have done the same thing for anyone that looked like they were in that sort of situation, whether she knew them or not. It hadn't even occurred to her to not step in. "I sometimes forget to think before I act, I kinda put my foot in it sometimes," Amy started, surprised with herself for this uncharacteristically honest confession. "I would rather interrupt a cute date and make a fool of myself than think of the alternative that could happen." She felt very self conscious and exposed. She didn't talk to many women she found attractive – truth be told she didn't talk to many new people at all – and her conversation skills felt rusty.

Fortunately Laura seemed to be as easy to talk to as she was gorgeous. "That sounds like the voice of experience," Laura said playfully. She was on the verge of having a good time with Amy.

"I am going to choose not to comment to save my own embarrassment." Amy half laughed, feeling the heat rise in her neck again. She was rusty yes, but she still wasn't going to admit to anything embarrassing. "So, who do you know downstairs?"

Laura noticed the change of subject, and desperately wanted to go back and find out more. She felt there was a cute but potentially embarrassing story hidden there, but she was very much enjoying being in Amy's company and didn't want to push. "I'm here with Emily and Ali, they dragged me out before they all headed out for the holidays. Emily's my best friend and I live with Ali, I think she helped Jamie find this place." Laura looked up at the sky, not wanting to think too much about the empty flat for the next week. "What about you?"

"Jamie is my best friend, he has been trying to get me to come for years, I think he feels guilty that I am going to be working over the break without him here."

"First solo Christmas in the city?" Laura asked. Knowing someone else was here alone made her feel a little better, especially if they were this cute.

"Yeah, but I am a lot less bothered about it than he is. I normally head to his family for the holidays." Amy chuckled and shrugged it off. "I am a lot more ok in my own company than he is, he thinks it's on par to torture – I'm almost looking forward to it."

"I wouldn't say I'm looking forward to it, but I'm glad I'm staying in the city," Laura replied, also tipping her head to look at the sky. The stars were faint against the city's light pollution, and only a few were visible. "I guess England is a little far to travel for like a week?" Laura felt Amy stiffen slightly next to her, but she was unsure if it was the cold or something she had said; she had been trying to find out if Amy was likely to be around long.

"You can have my number if you like," Amy said without even thinking, then silently cursed herself for sounding like a child in a school yard. She had been so quick to want to change the topic away from her homeland she just said the first thing that came into her head. "You know, in case you want company or anything." Oh god, Amy thought, that sounded a lot like the offer of a hook up, and given the way Laura had just raised an eyebrow, she clearly felt the same. She was at the risk of babbling again. She used all her strength to just smile and keep her mouth shut, willing the blush that was creeping up her neck to fade.

Laura was surprised at how forward Amy was, given they didn't even exchange a hug in the bar. This was unexpected, but a very welcome development. She slipped her phone out her pocket, unlocked it and handed it to Amy. Who took it gingerly, carefully putting her number in and handed it back. She was sort of expecting Amy to present her phone to fully exchange numbers – but she had never even reached for it. Laura decided not to read too much into it.

"I think I could do with a drink," Laura announced after a brief silence. "But if it's ok with you, can we keep this to ourselves? I don't want to cause drama or ruin anyone's night." She got up from the bench and looked over at Amy, whose expression was unreadable.

"Yeah, if that's what you want." Amy smiled as she stood up. Both women made their way back down stairs where their friends were indeed waiting. Jamie shot Amy a very excited look that made her roll her eyes. The man was way too excited to see them together, he was going to be very disappointed when he found out that nothing happened.

Chapter 8

One Night Without Amy

The rest of the night passed without much note. Laura did a lot of dancing and a lot of drinking, exactly as planned, barely leaving the dance floor for more than a song or two. Amy did a lot of people-watching; if she was being honest with herself she was doing a lot of Laura watching – out of concern, she told herself, but that was a thin excuse and she knew it. There was something captivating about the way she moved to the music, so carefree and open, it was intoxicating – hypnotic to watch. Jamie had tried repeatedly to get some gossip out of her about what happened upstairs, but Amy remained tight-lipped and said they had barely spoken, just bumping into each other on the way down the stairs.

Emily was quizzing Laura in much the same way. She knew Laura had a reputation for picking up women at the drop of a hat, but this was strange: they had looked so close coming back to the group but there was no flirting, no hint of a passionate make out session on the roof – in fact it was like they had barely spoken at all. Emily wasn't sure if Laura had noticed that Amy was watching her; the redhead was definitely looking at her friend more than was acceptable for people that didn't have a connection.

As the night slipped into the early hours of the morning, Laura – with a mix of bravado and alcohol – was feeling bold and she couldn't get Amy out of her mind. The feelings of gratitude had given way to far more impure thoughts, remembering the electric feel of their hands together, the protective, strong way she had stood in front of Laura. Plus her whole look was just doing it for her. She had noticed Amy looking her way occasionally, their eyes had met a few times and they had shared an intense look that made Laura's core flush with desire.

Laura was no stranger to one night stands – in fact she did it often, she enjoyed the physical connection and release it gave her without any of the dating baggage. Laura decided the next time she noticed Amy was at the bar or off getting some air, she would make her move.

Amy looked down at her empty glass. She had switched to non-alcoholic drinks some time ago, the buzz wasn't the same but she was having a good time nonetheless. Putting her glass on the table next to her, she realized she was getting warm again; she took the opportunity to retreat to the roof for some cool air. Catching Jamie's attention, she gestured to him that she was popping out for a moment. He waved and continued dancing. Amy made her way across the bar to the door.

Amy was no longer standing with her back to the wall. While Laura had been dancing, she missed Amy slip out and now had no idea how long she had been gone. Emily must have noticed her searching for Amy as she bopped into view

"Looking for someone?" she sang with a giant smug smile across her face as she continued to dance to the music "Maybe an English rose?"

"Urgh, don't ever say that phrase again!" Laura rolled her eyes back at her friend.

"Fine." Emily mockingly huffed "Well I guess you don't care that she just headed up to the roof then – alone" Laura didn't even bother to reply, opting to stick her tongue out and leave the dance floor as quickly as possible.

As the cold air hit her face, Laura realized she was probably more drunk than she had originally thought. She made a mental note to take a break from shots for the rest of the night. The buzz was great. But she didn't want to push it any further, opting to enjoy the carefree way she felt right now. Being too intoxicated to perform was no fun for anyone. She did however want to have a chat with the redhead standing with her back to the rest of the roof looking out over the city: the way she was so nonchalantly leaning on the railing as if there wasn't a care in the world was drawing Laura in. Confidently she slid in next to Amy, flashing her a winning smile as she propped herself against the wall to get a better look at her profile.

"Hello again, my knight in black leather," Laura said, looking purposefully at Amy. To her surprise Amy wrinkled her nose at the comment.

"I think I prefer Amy." Laura's comment had made Amy bristle, she didn't want to be seen as some heroic character for just doing the decent thing.

"Well, in that case, we meet again, Amy," Laura said, slightly lower and with a hint of seduction laced in, she gently barged her shoulder into Amy's. "How has your night been? Any further need to play a police officer?"

"No." She smiled, turning to face Laura. "No further need to don the badge and keep the mean rooftops of the city safe. Also, yes I am having a good time – thanks" They were less than a foot apart. Amy could feel the confident aura radiating off Laura; she wore it well.

Laura took a second, she was yet again struck by how extremely attracted she was to Amy. When their eyes met, it felt like a jolt of electricity; the lights on the roof made the green shimmer. Laura raised her arm and ran her fingers slowly down the front of Amy's jacket zipper, before slowly entwining her fingers with Amy's. The woman visibly blushed in response as Laura moved a fraction closer. "I wondered if you would like to get out of here with me," Laura purred "My place isn't far from here. I still owe you a thank you for earlier." As soon as the words left her mouth she realized this was not going to go the way she wanted or expected. This sort of move would normally have people eating out the palm of her hand – but Amy's expression had gone cool, her body stiffened, her eyes narrowed, the sparkle had vanished.

"No," Amy said firmly and took a step back, ending the physical contact that up until a few moments ago had been all she could think about. Now she was angry; she didn't like where this was going. She didn't help Laura earlier expecting something in return, and most certainly not in exchange for sex. Not that Amy was against casual hook-ups, she had had them in the past and enjoyed them; she was pretty sure she would have enjoyed it with Laura – a lot.

But Laura was slightly too drunk, her emotions could still be all over the place; most of all, she didn't want this to be a thank you shag. In fact this whole interaction had kicked some memories in her head that she very much wanted to stay quiet. "I think you are very attractive, and I am sure we would have a great time. However, I am not sure I like the connotation that sleeping together is some sort of thank you gift." Shit. That had come out a little blunter than Amy had intended. She tried to soften her voice and added, "Your emotions are probably still all over the place; that amount of adrenalin can make us do things we might regret later. I respect you too much as a person to exploit that."

Laura's mouth was open slightly; she was shocked. Ten minutes ago, she was certain of what she thought was going to happen, but now she didn't think that could have been further from the truth. For the second time tonight, Amy had thrown her a curveball, and it was taking her a minute to recover. She hadn't said she didn't want to – even if she had said it, Amy's physical reaction told a different story – in fact, she had said they would have a great time. So where was the problem? Everyone was a consenting adult, Laura had ASKED for this, she was in control. Laura pulled herself together. She had been turned down before and there were never any hard feelings. She flashed a winning smile at Amy, whose expression was blank, giving nothing away.

"Thank you again. Looking out for me twice in one night." Laura reached forward, closing the distance and resting a hand on Amy's arm.

"That's ok," Amy replied, as she turned her head to look at the skyline again she couldn't help feeling the pang of regret in her quick no. She really did find Laura attractive. "You have my number if you want to hang out over the holidays."

It was all she could think to say. She wanted the conversation to be over and to head back inside. Anxiety was building up inside her, she wanted to drown it out with music, and maybe some more alcohol.

Laura watched as Amy, in a swift movement, stepped back away from her and went back inside. Something in her demeanor had changed; it was small but it was there, just behind her eyes. It made the woman even more intriguing to Laura – plus she was right, Laura did have her number if she wanted to see her later. Which felt very much like an invitation for a holiday hook-up. Laura smiled to herself heading back inside.

Amy couldn't focus. She regretted saying no to Laura, even though it was the right thing to do. She was definitely jealous of the woman Laura was currently making out with on the dance floor. That could have been Amy – but she blew it. Clearly she had been wrong and it wasn't a thank you as Laura had framed it, she just wanted to have fun. Not that she felt like she would be the best company now; she had definitely not managed to shake the anxiety that crept over her like moss. Amy knew what it was and where it came from but that never made it any easier to shake. The alcohol hadn't done anything to lift her mood, in fact it had made it worse. Kicking off from the wall she was leaning against, she scanned quickly to see if she could see Jamie and Rachel to say goodbye before she left. Neither looked to be on the dance floor or at the bar, so she decided to text them and head home.

Laura looked over to the wall Amy had been standing against most of the night since they returned from the roof, a little saddened to find her gone. She extracted herself from the arms of the woman she met at the bar an hour or so ago, shimmying over to Emily.

"Did you see where Amy went?" She had to practically shout over the music, pointing at the wall where Amy had been.

Emily looked over Laura's shoulder to where she was pointing. "No." Then looked at the woman her friend had been dancing with for the last hour, slightly amused to see she was in dark jeans, a white top and a black denim jacket - something Laura had clearly not picked up on. "I can ask Jamie if you're worried." It was a big city, and it was an unwritten rule that everyone had to check in with someone when they were leaving.

"No, no it's fine! I guess she went home!" Laura said a little too quickly as a blush flared across her cheeks, knowing full well her friend would have noticed. "I should probably get back to my..." Laura tilted her head to indicate the woman she had been dancing and making out with. Emily raised an eyebrow with a coy smile as she turned back to dancing.

Walking back over the woman she had made the object of her attention for the last portion of the night, Laura pulled her closer, using her denim jacket for leverage and went straight in for a deep searing hot kiss, leaving nothing to the imagination. The woman reciprocated in kind, pulling her in closer. A familiar feeling of anticipation spread between Laura's thighs.

"Would you like to head back to my place?" she asked. The woman nodded without question and after they made their goodbyes to their respective friends, they headed out.

Chapter 9

Lonely Christmas

Laura swiped across the brightly-colored movie posters on her TV screen. She was already bored of everything on offer to watch. Lounging on the couch for the fourth day in a row was definitely losing its charm. She should be enjoying the fact she had the apartment to herself, but it felt cold and empty without anyone else in it. It was the twenty-sixth of December and this was definitely the worst day so far: boredom was setting in and she was getting restless. Emily, Zoey, Ali and Munaza weren't back until New Year's Eve, when they had all planned to hang out together for their traditional New Year's celebration.

The apartment wasn't big, considering four adults lived across its three bedrooms, single living space and moderate-sized kitchen. Laura was lucky she had her own room. Zoey and Ali shared; they had roomed together in college so didn't mind too much, they also paid less rent. Munaza took the smallest room that they all suspected had been created by the landlord to increase the occupancy, in a move probably breaking several property codes and standards. Living with so many different personalities presented its own challenges. Zoey was very particular about the communal space remaining clean and tidy at all costs which had caused friction in the past. They had a very strict set of ground rules and everything worked out fine. For all its flaws, the space was home, filled with love and laughter most of the time. Except right now it wasn't. It was deathly silent and boring. Laura threw herself back on the cushions, letting out a massive sigh as she did. Lying staring at the ceiling she almost cursed herself for being so stupid – the rule was no unexpected overnight guests when people were home – but there was no one home.

With a new found sense of purpose, Laura picked up her phone and flicked across her apps; what she really wanted was someone with her in the space. She was a people person and was starting to go crazy after this length of time on her own. She opened her contacts list and scrolled down thinking about who would be around and who she might like to see, her finger and eyes drifting past most of the usual suspects – some women who she had had several nights with but none of them felt like the kind of night she wanted. Then her eyes settled on a new name, one that took her a moment to place: 'Amy L'. Opening the contact details showed that she had never had any communication with this person, but as her eyes passed over to the date the contact was added, everything became clear. This was the mysterious and sexy English woman who had turned her down on the roof last week. Her heart skipped a beat. She had felt an instant connection with this woman, regardless of the circumstances of their meeting. Amy had made it clear she was definitely around and at a loose end this week too.

Without thinking too much about it, Laura sent a quick

text to Amy. The message was delivered and read almost immediately, a reply came almost as fast. It wasn't long before they had agreed to meet at a bar about thirty minutes from Laura's house for a drink. Laura put her phone down and went off to get ready, a new bounce in her step, making sure she had left enough time to straighten up the apartment before heading out the door.

Amy looked over the messages once more, trying to work out any meaning that she had missed in the brief text conversation. She was painfully aware that she didn't always pick up on social cues and that went for texts as well. She was a little worried she had replied too fast, and that it might give the wrong impression – not that she was sure what the right impression was.

Unknown: Hi, it's Laura from the roof top last week. Hope you are having a good holiday?

Amy: Hey you! I am doing ok, just reading and chilling out. How about you?

Laura: I'm ok, wondered if you fancied meeting up, maybe tonight?

Amy: Yeah that would be cool, you do owe me a drink after all ;p

Laura: I do indeed! How do you feel about Limelights, they do some pretty good cocktails.

Amy: Sounds great, I can be there about 8pm if that works for you?

Laura: Perfect, see you there.

She decided it all looked perfectly innocent, that this really was just meeting someone for a drink. If she was being honest with herself, she couldn't decide if she was happy about that or not. After getting home from the party, she had a long think about how everything went down with Laura – she decided that if the woman contacted her she wouldn't be against a hook up, but was glad she had said no on the night.

In fact, if Amy was being honest with herself she was also feeling pretty lonely, more than she was expecting. She lived alone which she liked, but going to the lab every day and the whole university being so quiet had really hit her harder than she was anticipating.

Laura had suggested a bar Amy didn't recognise, it was about thirty minutes from her flat and after a furious amount of googling and looking at pictures, she felt she could manage the space: it looked intimate, a perfect location to get to know someone. Extracting herself from her armchair where she had been sitting reading, she stretched and headed to the shower to get ready.

Amy was feeling good about herself. Less than an hour later, she was heading out the door towards the metro. She had decided not to go for anything too dressy; they were only meeting in a bar for a drink, a drink with a potential friend. She had opted for classic black jeans and a black top, nothing too fancy but something that would work in almost any setting. Paired with her usual green jacket – it had been her go to for almost as long as she had been in Toronto – ex-army surplus lasted a lifetime, she had been told, and given its age, she was inclined to agree. Given the climate of the city, it was her go-to – even if she was teased by Rachel for looking like a member of a sad British rock band from the 90s. It was without question her comfort blanket – like a suit of armor she could shrug on in most weathers – it had been lovingly patched up in several places over the years, and it had definitely seen better days. But people could pry this jacket out of Amy's cold dead hands – however hard Jamie and Rachel tried.

Chapter 10

Come to my House

Laura arrived at the bar first, as she had expected too. LimeLights could be a little tricky to find, its doorway tucked in a corner off the main street. It was one of the reasons she liked it here: small and intimate, you could really get to know someone without distractions. Normally they had live music playing, but given the holidays they had opted for a DJ. She took up most of the stage, her blonde hair bobbing hypnotically to the beat of the music. Opting not to sit at her usual spot on a central table but instead going for the bar stools against the wall at the back, she felt Amy would rather be here, away from the noise.

Once she realized she was going to be here early, she texted Amy and asked what she wanted to drink, along with a copy of the drinks menu. Amy had again replied almost immediately with a spiced rum and coke, something so simple; given all the fancy drinks on offer that Amy had gone for a relatively standard drink made Laura chuckle. The feeling of anticipation was almost consuming her, the fizzle of attraction bubbling inside her chest as she returned to the table with the drinks. She realized she really did want to get to know Amy better. Physical attraction was good, but it was nice to have something a little deeper, especially as Laura hoped they would be going back to hers after a few drinks.

Amy was bang on time, almost to the minute. She walked in the door and scanned the space looking for Laura; she found her almost instantly sat at the back of the bar, nice and secluded. She smiled as the butterflies fluttered in her stomach, both the anxiety she felt walking into somewhere new, but also the excitement at seeing Laura again. It was easier to get a better look at her here, without the lights and crowds of people in the last. She was in a dark blue dress that fell off her shoulders and hugged her chest and torso before stopping midway down her thigh, her jacket draped elegantly across the back of her chair. Amy cursed to herself – she was definitely more dressed up than Amy. A familiar wave of embarrassment washed over her, anxiety prickling at the base of her skull, but it was too late to turn back: Laura had seen her and thrown her a wide brilliant smile.

"Hey," Amy said as she slid into the seat opposite Laura, assuming it was hers by the drink sat in front of it, hoping none of her anxiety bled through into her body language.

"Hey yourself," Laura beamed back, sliding Amy's drink across the table. In this light she could really see the green of her eyes, combined with her auburn hair that gave Amy an effortless beauty she suspected the woman was oblivious too.

"Thanks for the drink." Amy took a sip of the cool fizzy drink, it was welcome as her mouth was feeling particularly dry. She would love to blame it on the cold outside but she knew it was all down to the woman in front of her. "Did you have a good time at the party?"

"Yeah, I had a great time, well, once we got past the business at the start." Laura decided to leave out her hook-up, not that she was ashamed but she didn't want to give the wrong impression. "I was sad I didn't see you leave though." Laura's eyes flitted down to Amy's mouth; her pink lips were deeply kissable.

"Yeah I had to be in the lab early the next morning, so I bailed. I'm really glad you had a good time," Amy lied. She didn't think it was fair to say she left because Laura was making out with another woman and it made her irrationally jealous.

"A lab? What is it that you do?" Laura took the opportunity to change the subject; besides she really did want to find out more about Amy.

Conversation flowed easily over the course of several drinks. They found they had similar interests in films and TV shows, although Laura was saving the next instalment of the female detective show everyone was raving about for when her housemates came back. Amy had talked about her work at the university, which had enthralled Laura – even if she didn't really understand everything they spoke about, she found it endlessly charming how passionate Amy was. Before too long, a bell rang behind the bar signalling last orders.

"Would you like to come back to mine?" Laura purred as she moved her hand across, laying it over Amy's. Neither woman could deny there was a spark when they touched. Amy noticed this was a similar move she had seen Laura use last week, not that she particularly cared if it was a well-worn and tested method – they had been growing closer all evening.

"Yeah that would be great." Amy was so close to saying no, letting the nerves get the better of her. She chewed on her bottom lip, trying not to stare at the fingers caressing hers, the sensation was almost too much to bear and yet she didn't want it to stop.

"Excellent, it's not far from here if you don't mind the walk – or we can get an Uber if you want to speed things up." Laura moved to get up, pretending not to notice the nerves in Amy's voice.

"The walk might be nice," Amy replied, pulling her jacket over her shoulders before following Laura out the bar.

The edges of the sidewalk were still piled with gray snow and ice after several more days of snow had fallen across the city. They walked mostly in silence as their hands brushed against each other several times, neither of them brave enough to take the lead, both enjoying the sparks flying between them. As they entered the building making their way up in the elevator, the excitement in Laura grew. This was going well: she was having a good time and a woman who she was extremely attracted to was coming back to her unusually empty apartment. At least she could guarantee this time that the place would be tidy and free of nosy housemates; she slid the key in the lock and a wave of confidence washed over her – she finally had Amy where she wanted her.

"I am afraid I don't have much in the way of drink here," Laura shouted from the kitchen across to the couch where Amy was sitting. "I have some vodka or red wine."

"Actually water would be great, if that's ok," Amy replied. She wasn't in the habit of mixing drinks and now didn't feel like the time to start. "Do you share the place with many others?" Amy asked as she looked around at the eclectic mix of styles. She knew Laura had housemates and that they were away for the holidays but no more than that.

"Three others and myself. It can get a little crowded at times, but I love them all like sisters." Laura walked over to the couch and handed Amy the drink, before sitting with her. Amy was occupied looking at the books on the shelf.

"And I assume all the baking books are yours, given how great this place smells?" Amy turned her head smiling at Laura. Laura leaned over and squeezed Amy's leg, keeping eye contact with her the whole time.

"Baking is not the only thing I like to do when I have the place to myself." She gave Amy a look that left nothing to the imagination. Or so she thought.

"Yeah, I live alone and my place never smells this amazing," Amy lamented, turning her attention to the rest of the room.

Why isn't Amy making a move? Laura thought to herself; she had given all the hints, subtle and otherwise, she had done a fair amount of lingering hands and looks, she had even invited her back to her place for another drink. Yet the redhead was firmly not picking up on the neon signs being placed in front of her. It looked like Laura was going to have to make the first move. She placed her drink on the coffee table and slid across the couch, lifting Amy's drink out of her hand and placing it on the coffee table next to hers.

Amy's eyes met Laura's, with an unexpected amount of confusion at the new closeness between them. Laura placed her hand on Amy's cheek, noticing how smooth it was. Amy turned her head slightly into her open palm. Their faces now held mere inches apart, the energy between them was impossible to ignore. The feel of her warm breath across Laura's cheek was sending her heart-beat racing. But still the woman didn't move in to kiss Laura, but equally she didn't move away. At this distance, Laura could see the beginnings of a blush spread across Amy's nose and cheeks. It was adorable. With a small smile Laura leaned in and placed her lips against Amy's; they were warm and soft with the faintest hint of spice leftover from the rum. The fireworks that had been slowly smouldering all night finally lit, Laura felt them all go off inside her as Amy reciprocated the kiss, her lips moving against Laura's in ways she had spent all night thinking about. After a few minutes they pulled apart – Amy was definitely blushing now, but smiled as she looked deep into Laura's eyes.

"Th..that..that felt really good," Amy stuttered as she fiddled with the cuff of her jacket, looking down to try and hide the redness of her face.The faintest hint of vanilla and lavender that accompanied Laura at this close a distance was intoxicating.

"Wanna do it again?" Laura half joked as she pulled Amy in closer for another kiss, this time with more pressure, which she was pleased to find Amy reciprocated. In fact, Amy did more than reciprocate, as her tongue flicked out and ran across the edge of Laura's lower lip, causing a wave of goosebumps to ripple across her skin. From there, the passion only increased, lips and tongues clashing in a fit of desire. Before Laura could even process how they got there, Amy was lying next to her on the sofa both women pressed together, hands roaming, pulling each other closer. Laura moved to position herself on top of Amy, straddling her, her thighs wrapped around her hips as she leaned down allowing Amy's hands to work their way down her body.

This felt amazing, Amy felt amazing; it was like she knew exactly where to put her hands to make Laura's pulse race.

It was at that moment that Laura was acutely aware of her dress, how it was stopping Amy's hands from touching her bare skin; this was something she needed to rectify. Immediately. Shifting off Amy's hips and standing in front of the couch, Laura looked down at Amy as she reached to pull the zip on the side of her dress, slipping it off and letting it fall to the floor around her feet. The sight of Amy lying on the couch with one arm propping her up to get a better look was intoxicating. But nothing was as satisfying as the look on Amy's face: her eyes darkened, filled with undeniable wanting, her lips parted in a mix of shock, desire and happiness. She couldn't help but stare at Laura's form now exposed, the golden brown skin remained even across her whole body, perfectly accentuated by pure white lace underwear.

Amy had sat up on her elbow to take in the sight of Laura removing the dress, once it was gone, Laura retook her position straddling Amy's hips, leaning down to take Amy's lower lip playfully in her teeth. A desperate moan escaped, before they once again locked lips and she continued to devour Laura, one hand firmly placed on Laura's waist, the other buried deep in her hair. The tension between them crackled, as Amy's hands freely moved across Laura's skin, where her fingers pressed they left a well of heat, adding to Laura's building need to have Amy as close as possible. Laura rocked her hips into Amy's, taking the small amount of friction, using it to edge her closer. She didn't think it would take much for Amy to tip her over the edge, one well placed hand on her wet core and it would be impossible to resist. But Amy was teasing her, refusing to put her hands anywhere that skin was not already exposed, it was driving Laura wild. The feeling of Amy's fingers brushing the edge of her lace lingerie on her thigh was all consuming.

It wasn't long before Laura broke off the passionate entanglement, unable to wait any longer. Taking the opportunity to catch her breath she leaned back, noting the swollen lips tinged a darker shade of pink from all their heavy making out.

"It's getting late," Laura said, low and husky as she ran her hand up Amy's arm. Standing up, she allowed Amy to move to a more natural sitting position.

"Oh, yeah it is." Amy said looking at her watch which informed her it was past two am. "I should probably get going then." Amy stood up. She was so close to Laura they were almost touching, the electricity between them was as strong as it had been when they were on the couch.

"If that's what you want." Laura closed the distance between them, placing her lips on Amy's neck, feeling the shiver run up the woman's spine gave her immense satisfaction. She was going to enjoy tonight, she had already enjoyed what they had shared so far – but it held such promise for the rest of the night. The desire to know how Amy tasted was almost all she could think about, well, and the idea of Amy's mouth pulling her to climax.

"Well, as you said it's getting late, and I am sure you have other stuff you want to get on with tomorrow, and I didn't bring anything to crash on the sofa in." Amy nodded towards the couch, as she moved around Laura to get her jacket. Laura was too dumbfounded to stop her. Did this woman who had been running her fingers across the lace on her inner thigh, really think she would be sleeping at all – let alone out here in the living room?

It all became clear in Laura's head a fraction of a second

too late. Amy had her jacket on and was looking at metro times. Laura followed her to the door of the apartment, still in shock as to how they had gone from making out to this in less than five minutes.

"I had a really great time." Amy smiled at Laura, reaching with her fingers to brush Laura's lips. The electricity was still palpable, sending a spark through Laura that made her breath catch.

"Yeah, me too," Laura replied in a daze, unable to fathom what was happening. "Let me know when you get home safe please?"

"Of course! Night!" Amy smiled back as she turned the lock and slipped out the door, heading off towards the elevator.

What the fuck just happened!? Laura screamed internally as she leaned against her front door, where only moments before the woman she had spent the last few hours making out with had stood, and so casually left. She couldn't remember a single time in her life where she had been left this frustrated. All the tension was coiled in her ready to be released, released by Amy – who had just left, without a second thought. She was pretty sure Amy didn't regret what had happened, that it was something she had also wanted – it had certainly felt like she wanted it.

Stomping down the hall towards her bedroom, turning off lights and tidying as she went, Laura kept running through things in her head – had she misread the signals, she didn't think so. She was pretty confident Amy was into her, people don't make out for that length of time and not be into the other person. Changing out of her – very nice, but wasted – underwear, Laura tried to remember the last time she has felt this much for someone. She wasn't against dating it just hadn't organically happened in a long time.

Amy was interesting and they had chemistry, given the way her body was still aching for the woman's touch, Laura felt their connection was undeniable.

Lying in bed, painfully alone and still exceedingly turned on Laura tossed and turned unable to sleep. She sat up as her phone chimed; it was a message from Amy.

Amy: home safe, thanks for a great night. x

Laura threw her phone across the room in frustration. Why was she sitting in bed feeling like a horny teenager. Clearing her head, she decided on the practical solution and reached into the drawer in her side table. A few minutes later her physical desire was taken care of, but it paled in comparison to the orgasm she knew she would have got with Amy.

Chapter 11

What do you Mean She Left?

"What do you mean she left?!" Emily almost shouted down the phone, she had left it late to call Laura, not wanting to interrupt her hot date.

"I mean she left! I took my clothes off and she fucking *left*!!" Laura repeated with exasperation. She was lying like a starfish in the middle of her very empty bed after a night full of explicit dreams, all revolving around Amy. Sadness flooded Laura when she had woken up alone in bed, still frustratingly unsatisfied.

"Wow, that's a new one." Emily chuckled. "Are you sure you didn't give any mixed signals? Say anything stupid?"

"Like I said, I was sitting on her in my – very nice – underwear. We were making out, it was hot and it was definitely going somewhere. I hinted that maybe we should move things to the bedroom. And she left!"

"Laura, can you remember exactly what you said?" Emily pressed.

"Urgh! " Laura almost screamed down the phone. They had been going over this for almost an hour, Emily switching between being helpful and laughing at her misfortune. "I said it was getting late, which is pretty clear code for come and fuck me in my bed pease."

"Ok, yes that's how I would take it, but what did *she* say?" Emily had a feeling that Amy was very much into Laura but was being a little safe in regards to personal space.

"She agreed it was getting late. Said she would leave. Put her coat on and left. She left me in my underwear -- who does that?!" Laura flipped over in bed to bury her head in the pillows, mortified to even be sharing this story with her best friend. She had never been turned down by a woman twice, and never in such an embarrassing way.

"Ok, so she agreed it was getting late, she told you she was going to go – then what did you say?"

"I said if that's what she wanted to do then fine." Laura's voice was now muffled in her pillow.

"Laura, babe – did you think to tell her that you wanted her to stay?" Emily let out a sigh of mock exasperation.

"Well... no... I thought that it was kinda obvious," Laura huffed. She really didn't see how any of this was her fault. "It's ok before she left she told me she had a 'really great time.'"

"Right, so at no point did you verbalize with your big girl words that you wanted her to stay," Emily said in a matter of fact tone. There was a long pause on the line. Emily smiled to herself at the complete ineptitude of her best friend.

"...no..." Laura said, pouting to herself.

"Then maybe you should text her, invite her round tonight and be explicit this time that you want to fuck." Emily couldn't help but laugh this time. It had been a long time since Laura had let anyone get under her skin. It was about time someone gave her a reason to feel this exasperated.

"Fuck you," Laura said playfully down the phone.

"No Laura, fuck Amy! Go on. Go text her! I expect a full report with screenshots this afternoon!" Before Laura could even argue Emily disconnected the call. Still chuckling to herself, it wasn't long before she had several messages from Laura, with the agreed screenshots.

Chapter 12

Third Time Lucky

Amy was standing outside Laura's building for the second time in twenty-four hours. The butterflies she'd felt yesterday had come back in full force; this time the anticipation and anxiety was mixed with a hint of shame. She clearly had got it wrong last night, another mistake. But here Laura was giving her another chance to get it right – that was probably more than she deserved. The texts had been direct to say the least. Leaving Amy to think that maybe she had misjudged the situation the night before. She knew they had been doing a decent amount of flirting at the bar, and she had really enjoyed the make out session on the sofa. Looking down at the text, the message now was crystal clear.

This woman was beautiful. Laura looked like a goddess with and without her clothes on, and for some unknown reason she wanted to be close to Amy; she wanted more than to be close. She explicitly wanted to have sex with her. Right now. This was her chance to prove she was more than the awkward shy nerd that she suspected many people viewed her as; someone who avoids parties and large crowds in favor of test tubes and books. This was an opportunity to spend time with a woman that appeared to not only like talking to her, but also wanted to get to know her intimately. She would be a fool to turn this down.

> Laura: I think you should come back and finish what you started last night.

If the message itself wasn't explicit enough, the accompanying photo of Laura in some very skimpy black lace underwear was. The image was enough to make Amy go weak at the knees and her head to spin. Laura was confident, attractive and it looked like she was into Amy. She knew she would be a fool to let tonight pass.

She readjusted the bag on her shoulder, hoping it wouldn't come across as too forward; she had included some basic overnight items, her laptop for work tomorrow and a spare shirt. At worst she would be taking the bag home with her later today, at best she had everything she needed for the following day at the lab.

Taking her phone out of her pocket, she could see she was still a few minutes early; she didn't want to appear too keen so she filled her time by checking some other messages. The group chat had been active today as people discussed the plans for New Year's in a few days. As usual Rachel and Jamie were trying to convince her to come out, and as usual Amy was sitting on the fence. She was probably going to go – she liked her space and spending time with Laura had been fun, but she missed her friends.

Pocketing the phone, Amy took a deep breath and rang the buzzer for Laura's flat. Instantly, the door clicked and she made her way up to Laura's apartment. Amy hesitated before knocking on the door to the apartment. She was filled with anxiety; she was, in her defense, always filled with anxiety.

Any feelings of her overnight bag being too forward evaporated instantly as Laura opened the door in the same black underwear from the photo and an open silk gown. Nothing was left to the imagination. Amy didn't even try to stop herself raking her eyes over the form in front of her.

"Wanna come in?" Laura whispered low and husky, the same way she had last night, a twinkle in her blue eyes. "Or are we going to do this in the corridor?"

Amy opened her mouth to respond but Laura's hand flew towards her, grabbing fistfuls of jacket and pulling her inside. The apartment was much darker than the brightly lit corridor; it smelt even better than yesterday.

"Have you been baking again?" Amy breathed in the warm sweet scent, it made her think of families and Christmas festivities – not hers, but ones you see on tv commercials, the ones selling you the idea of perfection.

"Yes, I made confetti sugar cookies this afternoon," Laura sang, still holding on to Amy's jacket, inches away from her face. She could feel the cold outside air clinging to her clothes. "And if you're good, and don't leave me again – then I might let you have some."

"Oh yeah, sorry about last night." Amy felt the knot of anxiety in her stomach twist. She had really misread that whole situation and was feeling awful about it. Her hand instinctively went to the back of her head as she looked at the floor. "I ah, sometimes don't always get the memo, and yeah last night, well I didn't get the hint."

This Amy was cute, Laura thought to herself as she watched the redhead trip over her words in an attempt at an apology; the awkwardness was endearing. Finally letting go of her jacket and leading the way towards the kitchen,

Laura had made sure that the space was as inviting, and as mood appropriate as possible, with low light coming from a few lamps and candles dotted across the kitchen and living area, while small LED strip lights set a soft pink tone in her room - ready to be explored later.

"You can take your jacket off and hang it on the hooks there." Laura gestured at the rack. "Feel free to put your bag wherever and lose the shoes." She was enjoying coming across as a little more assertive than the night before. Laura was used to being the one in control, but this was a new level of directness even for her, something flickered inside at this new commanding tone – something she would have to investigate in the future. Amy sheepishly nodded and followed the instructions, giving Laura a wave of satisfaction.

Amy was standing near the breakfast bar facing Laura, she looked nervous, but oh-so-expectant. The look in her eyes did something to Laura, reminding her vividly of the way her body had ached for Amy after she left last night; she was determined not to let tonight end the same way. The desire that had been bubbling away in Laura's core all day rose back up to the surface. She moved to close the gap between them. Laura put her hand up to cup Amy's face, pulling her into a deep kiss, igniting her with the same passionate intensity as before. Pulling out of the forceful kiss, she moved her lips to Amy's throat, teasing and running her tongue across the bare cool flesh, satisfied with the reaction Amy gave, the goosebumps tactile under her tongue.

"I hope it's clear now what I want," Laura whispered as she made her way back up to Amy's ear, gently pulling her lobe with her teeth.

"I think I got the message this time," Amy said playfully as she moved her hands to Laura's hips pulling them in closer. Their mouths crashed back together, as if they hadn't taken an almost twenty-four hour time out; all the sensations returned, as the two women fell together again.

Amy could feel the high table pressed against her lower back. It was a welcome anchor as she used her hands to explore Laura's skin again; it felt like fine silk under her finger tips, impossibly smooth. Laura had one hand buried in Amy's hair, the other was resting on her chest. She could feel her heartbeat through her shirt.

A nagging feeling was brewing deep in the back of Amy's mind. Laura was being more forceful this time. She liked it but it came with the familiar cliff edge that rested just out of her mind's eye; she really didn't want to ruin this after last night, she knew this was her third and definitely last chance with Laura.

She needed more control.

So she took it.

Moving both hands to Laura's exposed, well-crafted ass, she flicked the tips of her fingers under the thin black lace – sending shivers down Laura's spine, causing her breath to catch slightly. Deep blue eyes met her own, a swirling mix of ocean tones stormy and filled with lust, begging Amy to push further. Amy smirked as she slowly dragged her nails to Laura's upper thighs. Laura went weak at the knees, Amy could feel it as she pressed against her, her weight shifting in response to her actions. This was the opportunity she was hoping for. In one smooth, swift motion she lifted Laura up, turned them round and placed her on the edge of the breakfast bar. Now she was the one firmly in control.

It happened so fast Laura could barely register it at all: the sparks from Amy's fingers against her flesh, the quick movement and then the cool wood of the table underneath her. She instinctively wrapped her legs around Amy for balance, pulling her closer with fistfuls of fabric at the waist, using the other to keep their mouths together. Looking deep into Amy's eyes, she saw everything – the lust, the desire, the wicked determination – but she could also see something else, something hidden at the back, something she knew she wasn't supposed to notice.

But she didn't have time to think about any of it as Amy moved a hand up her inner thigh, now spread wide, straddling her on the kitchen table. Fireworks clouding her vision from just this simple touch, Laura wanted nothing more than to feel Amy's skin against hers. It was suddenly the only thing she needed. She began to work her way under Amy's shirt, feeling along the edge of her jeans, slowly tentatively moving up until her full palm was resting on Amy's ribs, just below her bra. As if in response to her exploration, Amy snaked her fingers further up Laura's inner thigh, brushing her hot wet center over her panties. All Laura could think about was how she needed Amy to touch her, to really touch her, as a moan escaped her mouth causing Amy's lips to curl up into a smile.

Amy was enjoying this, a lot. It was different to last night – she couldn't say how but there was something in the air. She chalked it up to pent-up frustration left lingering from last night. She slowly moved her fingers across Laura's wet core; the only thing preventing her from sliding inside her was the thin layer of lace. It left nothing to the imagination, and it clearly drove Laura wild. Using her spare hand she began to tease the edge of the lace around Laura's hips, pulling it slightly, indicating it was soon time for them to come off. Taking the instructions without the need for words, Laura put both her hands on the table and leaned back, giving Amy a view so breathtaking she couldn't even put it into words. She slid the lace undergarment off Laura's legs and discarded them on the floor at her feet. Now there was nothing stopping her doing whatever she wanted to Laura, a bolt of ice slid down her spine, causing her to freeze momentarily. Anxiety threatened at the edges of her vision.

"Sure this is what you want?" Amy said, looking directly into Laura's eye, breaking all forms of physical contact to help get her attention.

"I can't believe you are asking me that!" Laura replied. Reaching out and grabbing Amy's shirt to pull her closer again.

But Amy didn't move, she needed a clear answer before she continued. "Are you sure you want this?" Amy reiterated firmly.

"Oh my god yes!" Laura almost shouted with exasperation. The look on Amy's face indicated she was satisfied with the response, as she moved closer and picked up exactly where she left off.

The euphoric sensation once again exploded across Laura's body; that paled in comparison to the way she felt when Amy rested her thumb on her clit. She was so sensitive, both wanting desperately for the feeling to never stop and at the same time needing the release she had been climbing the walls for. Amy set about a slow, deliberate motion of running her thumb over and around Laura's clit, it drove Laura wild! She pulled again at the tshirt, bringing her closer, needing to feel as much of her as she could. Their mouths once again met in a feverish dance, tongues and lips exploring each other. Small moans of ecstasy escaped Laura's mouth, which just encouraged Amy more. Moving her unoccupied hand to Laura's chest, Amy pushed softly, indicating for Laura to lie back; once the woman had complied, Amy dragged her fingers down across her midriff, around round her hip. She could feel the tension. She knew it wouldn't take long for Laura to finish. Part of Amy wanted to keep her in this space of wanting, the other part of her wanted to taste Laura.

The urge to taste won out, Amy moved her thumb away from Laura's now-swollen clit, causing the dark-haired woman to whimper before she gasped in satisfaction at the feeling of Amy's tongue purposefully and slowly replaced the movement of her hands. A smile tugged at the edge of her mouth at the sound.

"Worth the wait, princess?" Amy uttered without skipping a beat, the smile still pulling at the corner of her mouth. Her tongue continued its path across Laura's slick wet core ending every stroke at her swollen clit. This felt like more than just sex, this was like unraveling a mystery, finding every movement that pushed Laura closer to her edge.

"Amy," Laura moaned, her voice horse and low drawing out the sound involuntarily. She didn't have time to process being called "princess" as Amy's fingers unexpectedly slid inside her. Laura's back arched away from the cool countertop, her head tilting back – trying to take as much of Amy in as she could on the first stroke. Stars began to prickle the edges of her vision, she was so close, she couldn't stop it even if she wanted to.

The orgasm rushed through her, emanating out from her core. Her back arched further as her hips thrust into Amy's hand and mouth, drawing every last moment of the sensation from them. Her hands clawed in vain on the cool wood underneath her as she bit down on her lip to prevent herself from screaming.

Amy felt all of it – every nerve impulse and muscle twitch. What she didn't feel she heard, as Laura tried to grab on to something, anything to anchor herself in the moment. Amy slowly slid her fingers away from Laura's folds, standing up to take a look at the sight of a totally spent Laura, still in her silk gown and lace bra panting for breath, spread over the breakfast bar. Amy watched her breathing slow, the rise and fall of her chest become more even, her eyes closed in a desperate attempt to reduce stimulation.

"Do you need a hand?" She offered after a few moments, as she held out her hand to Laura, who took it and used it to pull herself up to the sitting position. She looked a little wobbly, so Amy put an arm under her legs and one around her shoulders, carefully picking her up and relocating her to the couch. Before she went back to the kitchen area, opening cupboards in the hunt for a glass.

Laura opened her eyes a fraction as Amy moved her from the counter to the couch. She was grateful as there was no way she could have stood up. The faint smell of cherries clung to Amy's hair from her shampoo. Laura would be lying if she didn't find it comforting. She was struck by how kind Amy was, to go from fucking someone in their kitchen to placing them on the couch in a display of aftercare not often associated with one night stands. No sooner had Amy placed her there than she retreated back to the kitchen, Laura could hear doors opening and closing, then the sound of the tap running. Moments later Amy returned with two glasses of water and two cookies, one in her hand and the other already in her mouth.

"These are really good," Amy said round a mouthful of sugar. "Please eat and drink some water." She motioned to the glass and cookie on the coffee table in front of Laura. Both women sat in silence for a moment, until Laura realized she was very underdressed compared to Amy. She hadn't even realized that Amy was still fully dressed, but now they were sitting so normally, it was making her feel exposed.

"Either you need to take some clothes off, or I am going to have to put some on." She looked into Amy's moss-green eyes, hoping she picked up on Laura's desire to continue this. The eyes gave away nothing; it was almost unnerving to Laura how guarded Amy's looks could be. Fortunately the blush that crept across her nose and cheeks did give her away. Laura smiled, leaning forward and placing a kiss on Amy's lips. Laura was shocked at how easy this had all been. Well, not getting Amy to her fuck her; but now she had there was no denying their chemistry, they worked well together, they had similar interests and Amy was great eye candy.

"Maybe this time we could get as far as my bedroom?" Laura's words had the desired effect and the blush only deepened as it spread down further across Amy's face. Stealing another kiss, Laura stood up and took Amy's hand. Leading her towards the bedroom.

Chapter 13

Your Bed, Your Rules

Amy was relieved to see it was darker here than the living space. She had blindly let Laura lead her to her bedroom, which was just as fascinating as the shared spaces; here you could really see who Laura was, with big art prints on the walls and a bookshelf so full it looked like it was being held up by the books itself. The soft pink LED strips that topped every wall bathed the room in a glow that helped put Amy at ease. Under her feet there was a thick shag rug, Amy wasn't sure she could cope with the sensation of the fibres on her feet for long, and was deeply thankful she still had socks on.

While she was distracted by the room, Laura moved and started placing kisses on her mouth. This felt different; this felt tender and full of emotions. This wasn't going to be like the kitchen Amy realized - this had the potential to mean something. That thought should have made her stop and take a breath, but she was distracted by warm smooth lips and the fluttering in her heart.

"Can I?" Laura asked softly as she pulled at the edge of Amy's jeans, motioning that she wanted to take them off.

The pent-up frustration was gone; the fire inside Laura was now smoldering, and this time she wanted to savor every feeling.

Amy's mouth was so dry she couldn't talk. She just nodded as Laura's fingers made quick work of the button and zipper before sliding her hand inside and down Amy's front, stopping only when she felt how turned on Amy was. A gasp caught in her throat as she grabbed a fistful of Laura's hair and her waist at the same time. Locking eyes with Laura, the passion was undeniable. Laura was applying just the right amount of pressure and movement to make Amy's mind go into overdrive, full of anticipation and wanting. Laura could feel how wet Amy was even through her underwear. It was undeniably sexy.

Snaking her hand round to Laura's back, Amy found the clasp of her bra easily, and just as easily undid it. Following the path where the bra was moments before, Amy ran her thumb over Laura's nipple; it reacted instantly to her slight touch. Laura's kiss deepened, the new sensation adding yet another layer of intimacy neither wanted to acknowledge. They stood like this for several minutes, both lost in the feeling of the other and the slow build of their own pleasure.

"I know we made it to the bedroom, but do you think we could make it to the bed?" Laura whispered in Amy's ear. She could hear Amy's heart stop. "But, I do need to let you know about the no clothes policy. Which means these – " Laura pulled against the denim of Amy's jeans, " – and this would need to go away." Laura ran her hand over Amy's t-shirt.

"Your bed, your rules,"' Amy stated with a wicked smile pinching the corners of her mouth. Her voice conveyed a confidence and belief in herself that was distinctly lacking.

Onside she was so filled with panic she could barely move as she took a step forward, pushing Laura towards the bed, sliding off her jeans.

Laura had the privilege of removing Amy's t-shirt, pulling it over her head in a swift motion and discarding it on the floor, having no idea how unusual this was for Amy, how unlike her it was to have anyone get this close to her – to touch her like this.

Once on the bed, things became more feverish again, hands and mouths having new exposed flesh to explore, as Amy worked her mouth across Laura's sensitive nipples and Laura ran her hands across all of Amy's milky white skin. One dipped low between Amy's legs, back to the same rhythmic stroking she had done before.

"Can these come off now too?" Laura tugged on the edges of Amy's boy-shorts. They cut off beautifully at the top of her thighs. But before she could get an answer, Amy's hand found its way back to Laura's center, her hand firmly on the top inner of Laura's thigh, leaving her thumb stroking her clit once more. Laura moved in closer to Amy, losing her focus, using both her arms to pull Amy in closer, to feel more of her body pressed to her. Taking cue from Laura's reaction, Amy pushed herself in between Laura's wet folds. Laura dug her nails into Amy's flesh out of shock and satisfaction, rotating her hips into Amy's wrist movement, edging herself closer to climax. The movement was hypnotic, the rocking of Laura's hips pulling Amy's fingers in deeper, desperately wanting her to go faster, to bring that release to her.

Amy didn't give in. She kept the rhythm steady and methodical, kissing exposed flesh as she went. This time it was different; it wasn't feverish like in the kitchen, it had emotion behind it. Both women pressed together, taking the time to explore and discover each other, all while Amy pushed Laura closer and closer. Amy curled her fingers round, causing Laura to roll her eyes back with pleasure bringing one hand up to the back of Amy's head feeling the short bristly undercut. She pulled Amy's head back to hers, the need to have her soft lips against her own was unbearable. Laura could still taste herself on Amy's tongue mixed with the sweetness of the cookies. It was intoxicating.

Amy could feel Laura getting close again, she took the chance to look into the dark blue eyes only inches away from hers. They called to her like sirens out at sea, a hint of danger lurking in their depths swirling with arousal and anticipation.

Laura had never had someone watch her so intently while fucking her. It should have been off putting but it wasn't, it felt sensational, like Amy had taken back all her layers and was really looking at her. It added another dimension to this climax, made it more intimate, caring, personal. All these thoughts and feelings flowed together as she came for the second time that night, Amy held her as the orgasm slowly worked its way across her body, only stopping once Laura couldn't take anymore, then choosing to plant kisses across her mouth tenderly while she caught her breath. This was something she had never experienced before. It was more than a quick fuck or fooling around, it had meaning.

Both women flopped back in bed, taking in the coolness of the sheets against their bare skin.

"I am not sure I am going to be able to bake in the kitchen again and not think of you fucking me on the breakfast bar," Laura mused, running her fingers idly over Amy's arm.

"I am not sure confetti cookies are going to ever taste

quite as sweet," Amy offered in return, lifting a finger to her lips, remembering both the taste of the cookie and Laura.

"It might be a while before I get the chance to bake much again," Laura lamented. "Everyone gets back in a few days and it's much harder to find the time or space to bake then." Another thought crossed her mind. While her housemates were fine with occasional one night stands and brief encounters, they had quite a firm view on repeat visitors. Laura's heart sank a little – she really didn't want this to be a one time thing.

"Then I should enjoy them while I can." Amy leaned over and placed a kiss on Laura's forehead, such a small gesture but it caused warm ripples across Laura's face.

"That goes for me too – they are not huge fans of unexpected guests," Laura added, looking up at Amy, silhouetted softly by the light.

"Well then I guess I should make the most of that too then." Amy half chucked as she placed another kiss on Laura's forehead. A yawn escaped her mouth, quite unexpectedly. "I should probably head off, it's..." Amy looked at her watch the little numbers glowed in the dark telling her it was gone at two in the morning. "Shit, it's very late."

"Then maybe you should stay?" Laura suggested. She wasn't unused to people staying in her bed, but she rarely wanted someone to stay as much as she wanted Amy to at this moment.

"That's really tempting. I can hop on the metro here and get to the lab relatively easily." Amy had already looked at these logistics not out of presumption but optimism.

"I do hope that's not the only thing that's tempting," Laura whispered coyly into Amy's ear as her hand once again started to wander across her milky skin. They continued to tenderly explore each other's bodies with their hands, as their tongues danced together. But it wasn't long before they both yawned again and agreed to get some much needed sleep.

Laura lay next to Amy reaching out to graze her fingers across her thigh. She was met with Amy's fingers wrapping round hers.

Maybe Laura was being oversensitive after a very long night of fucking, but it really felt like she had a connection with Amy, something she knew she wanted to explore. With only a few days before her housemates returned, she decided to take every opportunity she could to spend more time with Amy. In or out of her bedroom. It only took her moments to fall asleep, the steady low breathing of Amy matched her own as their fingers remained entwined under the covers.

Chapter 14

Nightmares on Sadness Street

Laura felt like she had only been asleep for moments, but looking at the clock showed her it was almost 5am. She had awoken with a start, taking a minute to get her head straight. A mix of the night's activities and her blossoming feelings had left a pleasant ache across her body that wanted to pull her back to sleep.

Then she noticed the reason she was awake: Amy was curled in the bed next to her, shaking. Her face was tucked into her chin, her arms defensively over her head. Laura reached out and touched Amy's shoulder, but her reaction was like someone had touched Amy with a cattle prod. She screamed, a high pitched, unmistakable scream of terror; one that caused Laura to feel that terror seep into her own skin.

"Please stop, please no, please don't, no no please," Amy pleaded, her eyes screwed shut, still deeply asleep. It made Laura's blood freeze in place. Whatever Amy was having a nightmare about, it sounded like she was pleading for her life.

"Hey, Amy it's ok – it's just a dream." Laura reached

over to touch her shoulder again, this time giving it a little shake.

"Please don't, I promise I wasn't, no please, please please p –" the last word getting caught in Amy's throat. Whoever she was pleading with in her nightmare, they were not stopping.

"Hey. Amy. Wake up." Laura shook her a little firmer this time, her words louder trying to cut through the terrified mumbles still coming from Amy.

Amy's eyes snapped open as she gasped for air. Even in the dark, Laura could see the panic and pain; whatever was going on, it felt real to Amy. She waited a few minutes for Amy to calm down and regain her bearings, the green eyes almost shimmering in the darkness. Both women lay in silence. Amy faced the ceiling, unblinking, willing her breathing to get under control. If there had been enough light in the room Laura would have seen the tear escape. She didn't dare look at Laura, who was propped up on her arm, looking over at her with confusion, wonder and fear. Amy wanted nothing more than the ground to swallow her up. This is why she didn't do overnight visits – this is why she lived alone. She felt anxiety curl round her lungs like tentacles of icy darkness, mingled with the shame of her actions she felt like she could barely breathe.

"Do you want to talk about it?" Laura asked as she placed a hand on Amy's shoulder, her skin slightly cool to the touch.

"No," Amy shot back. Laura's hand on her shoulder felt like it was the weight of the world, crushing her, pushing her into the bed. She had almost forgotten what it was like to have someone else there when it happened, and she most definitely didn't want to talk about it.

"Ok...," Laura was a little taken back by the bite in

Amy's tone. This was clearly not something they were going to discuss – and she had to respect Amy's boundaries. Looking down at the English woman, she could barely make her out in the darkness, but the memories of a few hours before meant she knew every inch of her. She was surprised about how protective she was feeling: she wanted to envelope Amy in the biggest hug and not let go until she felt better – probably a little over the top for a one night stand.

"I should probably head off to the lab. I have a lot to do today." Amy started to move out of the bed, wishing she didn't have to leave the warmth inside. It had felt safe, and that was in part due to Laura. Chasing that thought out of her mind; she didn't have the mental space to really think about what that meant. She decided to switch to autopilot, make the right noises and deal with the fallout later; better to distract Laura from asking too many questions.

"It's five in the morning Amy, can't it wait?" Laura sounded exasperated. This felt like Amy was running away. This wasn't a feeling she enjoyed, they had agreed only a few short hours ago to do this again, but Amy fleeing her bed at five in the morning didn't feel like something someone did if they wanted to come back. As if Amy had sensed Laura's concern, she crossed back across the bedroom, now almost fully dressed and planted a tender kiss on her lips – god they were soft, Laura thought. "Let me know when you get there. Ok?" she relented.

"Sure, but I can't text you from inside the lab, it's got a hermetic seal, so I can't take anything in that might contaminate the samples." Amy smiled one of her winning effortless smiles at Laura, a second distraction in as many minutes. "And I am stealing some cookies when I leave." Amy stuck out her tongue in jest as she left the bedroom. Laura could hear her moving round the flat before the final click of the front door and then... silence.

It was early and Laura had had less than three hours sleep, but even in her sleep-deprived haze, she could feel her heart ache for Amy to return. Laura shifted over in the bed to where Amy had been sleeping. The pillow smelled faintly of cherries, just like Amy's shampoo. Before she could stop herself, she was holding the pillow tight and taking in the scent, trying to imagine Amy was still there.

She caught herself, now wide awake with a shock of adrenaline. This was not a new feeling, but one she hadn't had in a while. She really wanted to see her again; but it was more than just a physical desire, she wanted to get to know her, she wanted to know everything about her. She would be lying to herself if she didn't admit she was curious to find out what had just happened to cause Amy to leave.

Laura tried to get her thoughts together. She wasn't against wanting more; people made assumptions on her dating preferences based on her sexuality, but enjoying casual sex didn't mean she wasn't interested in more. Had Amy started as a hookup? Laura didn't think so, in fact, Amy turned her down in the first place. A smile filled Laura's face as she thought about that night, how Amy had appeared out of nowhere to rescue her from the guy at the bar.

Picking up her phone, she scrolled back to the first few texts. They were completely innocent. If anything Amy had been the one to flirt first. Yes, they had come back to her apartment, but they didn't hook up then either, so Laura was pretty certain this was not a hook-up, until she got to yesterday's message and picture – that was definitely a booty call. She smiled to herself as she stretched out on the bed, drifting back to sleep.

Chapter 15

Instant Coffee

Amy pressed her pass to the sliding doors. They slowly opened and she slipped inside with a gust of cold morning air. A combination of mid-winter and the holidays meant Toronto was like a ghost town. This early in the morning, the dark clung to her clothes like a deathly shroud, pulling all the warmth out of her. Amy wasn't against the quiet, and the solitude of her walk to the lab had given her time to clear her head and calm down. She was deeply embarrassed about the nightmare, and how she had all but run away from Laura's bed. The wounded look in those deep blue eyes had stung, mixed with the confusion she was clearly feeling after so little sleep – Amy almost felt bad for masking her feelings so she could escape.

Walking up the stairs, Amy toyed with the idea of texting Laura, but she assumed the woman was asleep again curled up in her warm bed – a place Amy would really like to be again.

It had been years since she had stayed the night in someone's bed. Sure she had had flings and dates, but nothing had gone quite that far. Was it a new feeling or something so long dormant she barely remembered it – Amy couldn't tell.

In fact, Amy was surprised at how good it had felt to be close to Laura. Everything felt natural; there was no hesitation, they had enjoyed each other's company both in and outside of the bedroom. Amy let her mind wander to the soft skin that had been under her only hours ago, how responsive Laura had been to her touch, every flick of her tongue and caress of her fingers replayed over in Amy's mind. The way she looked when she lay on the kitchen counter completely undone by Amy's actions was something she never wanted to forget.

A wave of pleasure swept over her as she remembered the feel of Laura's hands on her skin, and the feel of Laura's hand as it snaked down the inside her jeans. The touch had been magical, so full of promise and passion. The way Laura's fingers ran over the material of her underwear, teasing Amy. It was all she could think about as her mouth went dry and her core pulsed with unfulfilled anticipation. Amy tried to push the thoughts out of her mind. She had work to do.

Placing her bag and phone in the locker, she took off her jacket and hung it on the peg where her lab coat rested. The building was empty and sterile, the low hum of the fans rumbled on. There was nothing to distract her from her wayward thoughts. Amy closed the locker and rested her head against the cool metal. She needed to focus on the day ahead, not the night's activities - or the way Laura had made her feel. She had so nearly let Laura touch her, the desire in her had been almost maddening, but she couldn't bring herself to let go – anxiety always pricked the back of her head and threatened to ruin the moment.

"This is early, even for you." A familiar voice came from the doorway. Todd was standing with his shoulder resting in the frame, his night shift still several hours away from completion.

"Yes, I... I couldn't sleep." Amy shook her head trying to get her mind to focus on the day ahead. "Once I have taken some preliminary readings and checked on everything, do you want a coffee?" She smiled in his direction, hoping it wasn't written all over her face that she was thinking about shagging Laura.

"Sounds good. I can run to the place at the end of the road once they open in a few hours if you like?"

"Perfect." Amy nodded at him before disappearing into the lab.

The next few hours passed painfully slowly. The data collection was a slow and tedious job on a good day, and today wasn't a good day. She still couldn't get the thought of Laura out her mind: she wanted to text her, to see her again, feel her, fuck her. Amy would catch herself drifting to thoughts of what they could do together, to each other, scolding herself every time for letting fantasy rule her brain. By the time it came to get coffee with Todd, she was grumpy and frustrated.

Leaving the lab she grabbed her phone and laptop out of her locker, walked towards the breakout space on the ground floor to see Todd waiting with two large steaming takeaway cups. Glancing at her phone she could see no messages. Trying not to be disappointed, she reminded herself it was also barely eight am – and that she was the one who left in the middle of the night.

"Why the frown, Dr Love?" Todd chuckled as he handed her one of the steaming paper cups and sat on one of the low empty seats.

"I am not a doctor, as you well know Todd. I still have to finish the research and write up my findings before I can even think about submitting for that," Amy said matter-of-factly as she blew onto the steaming liquid.

"Yes yes I know. But it won't be long and then you better get used to it!" Todd continued to chuckle. "And don't think that gets you out of answering my question. I know you did not arrive before six am just to get work done." He looked at her with his large chocolate eyes.

"Can't we just pretend that I have a really good work ethic and was really keen to get these data samples down?" Amy pleaded with him.

"Not a chance."

"Damn it." Amy huffed in mock annoyance. "I went on a date last nigh –"

"Oh *wow*!" Tod cut her off, almost jumping out his chair. "You went on a date? And it didn't end until the very early hours – that means it went well, right?"

"Yeah, I think it did. She was really nice and we had a good time at a bar then we ended up back at hers and..." Amy trailed off, suddenly embarrassed. Not at the sex part but the fact she did leave so abruptly. "But she had an early shift so we called it a night," she trailed off, hoping he wouldn't see through her lie.

"Oh yeah? That's cool!" Todd looked impressed. " Gonna see her again?" He looked coyly and raised an eyebrow over his coffee at Amy.

"I don't know, we didn't make any arrangements or anything." Amy looked down at her very silent phone. "And she's not messaged me or anything."

"Ok, but have *you* messaged her to say what a great night you had?"

"No." Amy felt the wave of embarrassment return. Was she supposed to have texted already? She was really unsure about etiquette in this situation. Laura had been pretty confident and straightforward with what she wanted last night; Amy had assumed Laura would continue to take the lead if she wanted to see her again.

To keep herself busy, she took a sip of her drink. These coffee hang-outs with Todd had become more frequent over the holidays, but she had always made time to sit and talk to him over the years. She knew he was working here while he was building up his personal trainer business and that he wanted a big family like the one he came from. Jamie had had the biggest crush on him for the best part of three years. She couldn't count the number of times he had tried to work out if Todd was available, but his sexuality had eluded her – and much to Jamie's frustration she hadn't pressed the topic much.

"Amy... you need to text this woman." Todd interrupted Amy's train of thought.

"Isn't the rule you have to wait three days or something?" Amy protested. "I don't want to come across as desperate."

Todd laughed. "Amy, you haven't stopped thinking about her all morning."

The blush rose on Amy's face, all hope of remaining cool, lost. "Fine." Amy relented "But not until lunch, it's not even nine am." Todd didn't protest as he chucked at her.

The rest of the morning passed a little faster. Back in the lab, Amy started to hit her rhythm; focusing on the work was much easier after the caffeine and the chat with Todd. As noon approached she felt her stomach rumble, a tell tale sign that she needed to take a break. Turning to Jamie's desk, she rooted through the drawers, finding a selection of instant noodles and chocolate complete with a note telling her to eat them when she forgot breakfast. Amy smiled. She knew Jamie had been worried about leaving her over the holidays – he knew her too well.

Taking the noodles down to the staff kitchen area, she popped them in the microwave and absentmindedly scrolled her phone, sending a message to Jamie thanking him for the noodles, then one to the group chat to catch up on New Years plans, before she left her finger hovering over Laura's messages. She scrolled up a few messages to look at the photo Laura had sent asking her to come over. Just looking at it brought back all the feelings from the night before. She rested her elbows on the counter as she watched the cup spin round the microwave for a few moments. She needed to text Laura, but what? Something fun? Sexy? Flirty? A string of apologies – she really had no idea where to go from here.

After over thirty minutes of writing, deleting and re-writing a message while she ate noodles, Amy finally settled on a message she felt reflected the mood from last night.

> Amy: Hi, what are you baking today? I still can't get the sweetness out of my mind.

She hated it the moment she sent it, instant regret filling her lungs, but it was too late. She sat alone, not daring to look at her phone to see if she had a reply. The embarrassment was almost to much to bear- this is why she didn't date people. Communication was complicated and full of easy places to make mistakes and fuck it all up. Packing up her lunch things and heading back up to the lab, Amy's phone buzzed in her pocket. Reluctantly, she picked the phone out of her pocket and looked at it before throwing it in her locker. She was surprised to see it was a message from Laura.

Laura: Why don't you come over tomorrow and find out?

Amy: I wasn't really talking about the cookies princess

Laura: I know! My place tomorrow at 6?

Amy: Perfect.

Amy flopped on to her sofa later that afternoon, a productive day behind her and another meeting with Laura organized for tomorrow giving unexpected butterflies. She wasn't sure of the details or the exact parameters of the visit back to Laura's –the word date hadn't been mentioned but it definitely felt more than friends hanging out.

Looking at her watch she saw it was coming up to five pm now, unlocking her phone she scrolled down to Jamie's number and dialled. He picked up on the second ring.

“Heeeey kiddo, how's it going?” he practically sang down the phone.

“I just got in, actually, I was at the lab *all* day.” A wave of tears washed over Amy as she realized it had been almost twelve hours since she woke up and even then it was only a few hours of sleep.

“Did you manage to speak to Todd at all?” Hopefulness rang through Jamie's voice.

"I did, but he *still* gave nothing away – I think you are just going to have to ask him outright."

"Yeah, no. I won't be doing that – I would be mortified if he was then not interested and I had to see him everyday for the rest of ever." Jamie could be so dramatic when he wanted to be; this time was no exception as he virtually wailed down the phone, causing Amy to giggle. She had missed her best friend, in fact, she was really missing everyone right now.

"I can't believe you lot are all away at the moment." Amy tried not to sound too morose. "I have no one to help me navigate the dangers of texting sexy women."

"Excuse me, WHAT?" This time Jamie actually did shout down the phone. "What have you been getting up to and with who? I swear we go away for five days and all of a sudden you are the hottest woman in Toronto."

"Well, in all fairness, there are not that many women here right now," Amy stated. "And actually it's just the one woman. One from the party before the holidays?" Amy tried to play it cool. She hadn't had a chance to talk to Jamie about Laura yet; he was away with family and she didn't want to interrupt. She knew how his mom was and how stressful it could be with all his brothers in one house.

"Laura?" Jamie offered. "Dark-haired Laura? Like the sexiest woman in Toronto?"

"Yes."

"Laura that you turned down in the club, for reasons I still don't really understand."

"Yes." Amy laughed.

"You are so out of your league." He laughed back, no hint of malice in his voice.

"I know." Amy sighed even though she couldn't get the grin off her face

"Tell me everything." Jamie demanded.

Despite Jamie's millions of questions, Amy didn't in fact tell him everything. She left out the creep in the bar – Laura had asked her to keep that one quiet and she intended to keep that promise. She also left out the more explicit sex details.

"Right, so just to clarify – you left her naked in her apartment?" Jamie had listened to the whole story before interrupting.

"Well, she was in her underwear," Amy tried to explain, knowing full well how stupid it sounded.

"I don't think that's the win you think it is, kiddo." Jamie was somewhere between shocked and amused by the whole situation. "Just wait until Rachel finds out about this!"

Amy groaned – she was never going to live this down. "Look! I went back last night and fixed my mistakes." She tried to protest.

"Maybe you are not a complete loss after all then." Jamie laughed. "The fact that she agreed to see you again, let alone fuck you after that is frankly impressive." He stopped laughing, his voice becoming more serious. "But that doesn't explain why you were in the office before six am today. What happened?"

Amy became quiet, Jamie was the only person that really knew about her anxiety and its causes. "You know what happened."

"I suspect I know what happened, but I think you should tell me. You can't hide from it forever, you know." Jamie was using his reassuring voice. Amy hated how much safer it made her feel.

"I had a nightmare. She asked if I wanted to talk about it but I obviously didn't and I left." Amy sounded deflated; she felt deflated. "But it's ok because I texted her and she wants to meet up again tomorrow night." Amy tried to sound bright. "So I must be doing something right."

"Just be careful, Amy." Jamie wasn't falling for her fake brightness "Whether it's this girl or the next, you are going to have to let someone in – or it won't just be their heart you break, but yours too."

Chapter 16

Good Girls Save Water

For the third time in four days, Amy stood on a cold wintery dark street looking up at Laura's apartment. The building was a matrix of warm glow from lights and TV sets flickering against the walls. She couldn't believe she was about to spend another evening with the same woman; this was something she just didn't do and definitely did not do in such quick succession – but she put that down to the holiday season. Fortunately for Amy's sanity there had been some more texting, and some more flirting that had given the night context. This was a movie and dinner, helping Laura enjoy her final night alone in the apartment before everyone came back home tomorrow. Laura had made it quite clear, with more delectable photographic evidence that she wanted to enjoy *all* aspects of her empty apartment tonight and Amy wasn't planning on disappointing her.

As she had come straight from the lab, she hadn't had time to shower, but Laura had assured her she could grab one before they ate. This made the bag on her shoulder even bigger and more presumptuous than the one from the night before – but she tried not to let herself worry too much about it. Laura had offered explicitly in writing, so she wasn't overstepping.

Amy rang the buzzer and the door clicked. Making her way up the elevator, she felt the worry building, rising with the floors. The mix of anticipation and anxiety tied themselves together in knots, her fingers fiddling with her bag strap.

The door of the apartment was already ajar, and the most amazing smells were emanating from the inside: sweet warm baking, Amy supposed it was meant to smell like home, or some fond childhood memory, but to her it smelt like promises. With a deep breath, she pushed open the door.

"Hey." Laura sounded delighted to hear Amy arrive, her hair lazily thrown over her shoulder. "If you want to hop in the shower now is the perfect time." Laura turned to look at Amy, ocean-blue eyes filled with lust. "but if you leave the bathroom door unlocked I can't promise I won't join you in there." Laura watched as Amy's face slowly morphed from shock into a goofy grin, the now familiar blush creeping across her nose giving away her feelings.

After discarding her jacket, shoes and bag – minus her change of clothes and wash bag, Amy silently made her way to the bathroom. She loved how direct Laura was, even if it did scare her a little. Thinking for a moment, Amy decided to leave the door unlocked. The intentions for her visit were clear even before she arrived. This was nothing outside of the realms she was expecting to happen – she had anticipated eating first, but that wasn't a good enough reason to turn away what she was being offered in the moment. The air filtration in the lab always made her skin feel overly dry. The best feeling ever was a hot shower when she got home, showering at someone else's was almost as good, showering with someone else – well that could only make things even better.

Folding her clothes up in a neat pile she turned on the shower, waiting a second for it to heat before she stepped under the stream. There were very few feelings better than this, or so she thought until she felt the change in air temperature that signalled Laura was also in the room with her.

A wave of panic came across Amy. This was the first time Laura was going to see her completely naked, and in such a bright space. She closed her eyes and twisted so Laura would see her back first in some vain attempt at modesty. Panic soon subsided when she felt Laura's warm lips on her neck and her hand sliding across her back; in fact, for a split second, Amy lost all thoughts.

Laura had taken a moment to enjoy looking at Amy before moving in closer. The expanse of pale milky skin was inviting; she couldn't wait to touch all of it, first with her hands and then with her lips and tongue. She had a whole night planned out in her mind, and this was only the start. The reaction to her lips on Amy's neck only increased the yearning deep in her core, feeling that showed no signs of disappearing when Amy turned round and took her mouth in hers with just enough force to make Laura melt. Taking the opportunity to pull Laura closer Amy put a wet hand on the back of Laura's neck as the other found her nipple and gently ran her nails over it. Amy pulled away from the extended kiss for just a second, her eyes meeting Laura's, her green eyes almost glowing with wicked flickers of arousal.

"Turn around," Amy commanded, it was soft yet left no space for questions. Laura – in a surprise even to herself –

did as she was told, again slightly shocked by how forceful Amy was, and delighted by how turned on it made her. Her body and face now inches from the white bathroom tiles, she placed both her hands flat on the cold wall to brace herself. Amy pressed herself against Laura, causing her body to lean into the icy porcelain tiles, a satisfying gasp emanating from her lips at the touch. Amy leaned close and whispered in her ear, "Should I fuck you now princess?" as she teased her teeth across Laura's ear lobe.

Laura couldn't work out how the nickname had made her feel the last time Amy had used it; she was so preoccupied that it had got lost in pleasure. But this time there was no question how much she liked it. The lazy way Amy rolled the word "princess" off her lips, sounding just a little condescending in the clipped English accent, all while putting her firmly in her place.

"Yes," was all Laura could manage as Amy's hand ran down her back and across her ass applying just enough pressure with her nails. The anticipation was almost unbearable. Fortunately, she didn't have to wait long, as Amy pushed Laura's legs apart and then pushed her finger inside. She slipped in easily, a small smile pulling on her lips at how wet Laura was from such a small action. The smile grew when she saw Laura's face in profile, her eyes closed and lips slightly parted.

Sex in the shower was something Laura had experimented with before, but this was different; she was pinned and powerless and it felt every bit as amazing as she had been led to believe it could be. The sensation of Amy's breast pressing against her back and the cool tiles in front combined with the hot water falling on her back and face was a conflicting collision of temperature and textures that Laura had not anticipated – but was very much enjoying. It just heightened the pleasure ripping across her body, all from Amy's slow deliberate movements. She wanted to turn round and kiss her, pull her in closer but as she went to move, the pressure of Amy behind her increased. "Where do you think you are going, princess?" Amy almost purred in her ear, words falling in the same rhythm as her wrist. "You move when I say you can move. Understood?"

Laura nodded. She couldn't form the words; this was not the shower she was expecting -- she didn't even think Amy would leave the door open, let alone take her like this.

"No, Laura, I need you to use your big girl words." Amy sounded amused under her thin layer of condescension.

"Yes, Amy," Laura barely whispered the words, stuck behind her lips, her mouth inexplicably dry given the hot water falling over her face.

"Good girl," Amy purred as she rewarded Laura with another finger sliding deep into her begging cunt. Laura whimpered, she thought being fucked on the breakfast bar was going to be the best sex of the holidays, but this shower was giving it stiff competition. Any thoughts she tried to string together unraveled; all her concentration was being focused on the quickening movement of Amy's hand, her hips rotating as much as they could with her legs spread apart and her body pressed into the wall.

Amy could feel Laura getting close; the way she moved, the tension in her whole body, it was electric and mesmerizing – and Amy couldn't believe she was the one causing this reaction. Watching Laura closely, Amy saw her biting down on the corner of her lower lip, the other side of her face pressed into the cold white tile, her eyes closed – totally lost in the moment. There was nothing else in that moment besides Laura's own pleasure, and Amy was the one doing it to her. Laura tightened around Amy's fingers, her breath caught and she parted her lips to let in a ragged breath as her knees attempted to give way under the ferocity of her own orgasm. The only thing holding her up was the weight of Amy pinning her in place.

Once Amy was sure Laura could stand, she planted a tender kiss on Laura's exposed shoulder as she stepped back, giving Laura space to turn round. Blue eyes looked up at her, the edges of pleasure still lingering. Amy couldn't help but lean down and kiss those lips, the water from the shower flowing over both of them, wrapping her arms around Laura to help steady her and keep her warm. They remained like this under the water for several minutes, not exchanging a single word, lips and tongues doing all the talking for them.

Pulling away from her, Laura looked up, finally able to form independent thoughts again. "Hungry?" was all she asked as she wrapped her arms around Amy's neck, bumping their noses together, surprised at how tender the moment felt.

A small nod in agreement from Amy and they were both drying off and getting ready for dinner. Amy was grateful she had thrown some comfy clothes in her bag, she had worried they were too casual for the evening, but she really didn't want to put her jeans back on. When she emerged from the bathroom in a white shirt and gray sweat-pants with her damp hair braided down her back Amy was pleased to see Laura in an oversized hoodie and small shorts, giving an excellent view of her legs.

"It smells amazing here." She let herself inhale the sweet smell of fresh baking and was alluring and mouth watering. She didn't realize how hungry she really was, now the smell of a pasta dish being prepared had cut across the sticky sweet smell. She sat herself down at one of the tall chairs at the breakfast bar, smiling to herself remembering the last time she had been here.

"Thank you, but you are going to have to wait for the butter tarts, they are still in the oven. I made Carbonara, I hope that's ok." Laura kept her back to Amy, busying herself with pots and pans on the cooker top. Amy was sat exactly where they had fucked just a few nights ago, and Laura had struggled enough to concentrate in the kitchen today with that memory without needing to see Amy sat there.

"I am sure it will be perfect." Amy beamed as she watched Laura float around the kitchen. "I am not much of a cook and would probably live off noodles if I could." They existed in silence for the next few minutes, Amy watching Laura as she prepared what looked like the best meal Amy had had all week.

"I was thinking we could eat on the couch and get the movies started," Laura said as she dished up two bowls. She really couldn't sit next to Amy at the counter and focus on the food or the conversation.

"Sure." Amy smiled and started to move things around, amazed at how natural this felt, how normal to be in another person's space, just existing. She took herself over to the sofa and sat down, tucking her legs underneath her and fumbled for the remote, they had already discussed what they planned to watch – terrible nineties action films had been their agreement.

Chapter 17

And Just Like the Movies

Discarded empty dishes on the coffee table and well into the second act of the most aggressively nineties action film later, Amy was struggling to concentrate on anything other than the beautiful woman sitting next to her. Laura was sitting with her legs crossed at the other end of the sofa, engrossed in the film, so at home in her skin and her space. She wasn't sure if she was supposed to be making a move or not. Amy felt drawn to Laura, wanting to be closer to her but not wanting to come across as needy or clingy. She began chewing the inside of her lip in frustration. This wasn't a sex date exclusively and she didn't want to give Laura the impression that's all she wanted. But the other woman's body looked so inviting, she wanted to run her fingers up her exposed thighs and beyond. Amy pulled her eyes away from Laura, and back to the TV.

As if by telepathy, no sooner had Amy looked away than Laura looked at her. Seeing the nerves across Amy's face made her heart warm. There was something cute about the slight furrowed brow and chewing of her bottom lip that made Laura want to reach out and touch her. In fact, now she thought about it, it was all Laura wanted to do. She wanted to feel their fingers entwined and Amy's body next to hers.

"Tart?" Laura said, causing Amy to break her trance with a small jump and look over at Laura in bemusement.

"Excuse me?" Amy tilted her head.

"Butter tart; would you like one?" Laura clarified with a smile as she paused the film, collecting the plates before heading back to the kitchen, not waiting for a response.

"That would be uh yeah, cool, yeah thanks." Amy stumbled over her words as she watched Laura once again emulate a domestic goddess in the kitchen. Putting dishes in the sink and placing the sweet pastries on another clean plate, Laura walked back across the apartment, placing the plate on the table in front of them. This time when she sat on the couch she deliberately sat much closer to Amy, so close they were almost touching. Out of the corner of her eye, she could see Amy looking her up and down, clearly admiring the view.

"Can I help you with something?" Laura playfully turned her head to Amy, blue eyes finding wide green as they snapped up from where they had been so clearly looking at her legs. The response from Amy did nothing to diminish the amusement Laura was already feeling as the redhead stammered and blushed like a child caught stealing a cookie. Laura laughed, taking a tart and placing it in Amy's hand before turning the film back on and directing her attention to the screen again. It was deeply endearing how shy Amy was; like they hadn't fucked only a few short hours ago in the shower, or spent a good chunk of a night fooling around before.

If the ground could have swallowed her up right now,

she would have let it. The blush across Amy's face was deep and as red as her hair and she had never been so thankful for someone turning the other way, directing those dark blue eyes somewhere else. She put all her nervous energy into eating the pastry placed in her hand. It was deliciously buttery and sweet – sometimes she missed the flavors of England, and this had a hint of home to it, that made it even sweeter.

Both women ate in silence as the film played on; any awkwardness Amy had felt slowly evaporated, not that she could take her eyes off Laura for more than a few moments. Now the woman was even closer, the urge to touch her was almost unbearable. Laura shifted in her seat and her hand brushed against Amy's on the sofa, sending a fizzle of electricity across both women; but neither of them made any effort to move away, leaving their fingers touching, enjoying the electricity that sparked between them.

The nervous energy coming from Amy was so strong Laura could almost see it. Amused at the reserved nature of the woman who had so confidently taken control on several occasions, this continued juxtaposition of her actions just added to Laura's desire to get to know her better. This woman had pinned her to a wall, done unforgettable things to her, called her a good girl and then fucked her senseless but was now apparently too sheepish to hold her hand.

Moments like this, felt like she got to see a bit of Amy that many didn't; she had no proof of this, but whenever they had been in public Amy had come across as shy but charismatic, like she had her shit together. Then in the bedroom she had come across as someone who took charge and took what she wanted. But this Amy sat next to her, this felt genuine – a little vulnerable – and Laura really liked it.

Deciding to put Amy out her clear anguish, Laura moved her fingers to intertwine with Amy's. A brief moment of stiffness – almost too quick to notice – came before Amy relaxed her hand into Laura's, all the while Laura could feel the intense sage green eyes on her, as a smile threatened to spread across her face.

It was these moments in dating that Laura loved: the finding out about each other outside of the bedroom, finding if you fitted together in life rather than just sexual chemistry and compatibility. Everything was full of promise and exploration, an energy almost impossible to explain as you got to know someone new. Not that they were dating; they hadn't actually discussed what this was, but then it was probably too early for that. Laura knew her feelings and where she wanted this to go: she didn't feel like this with anyone she had hooked up with – well, ever. Her thoughts were interrupted by Amy, who slid closer, resting her head on Laura's shoulder and wrapping her free arm around Lauras. Now it was her turn to feel surprised, she hadn't expected Amy to get closer, she had wanted her to, sure – but given the shy demeanor she assumed she would have to instigate further. The smile threatened to tug at her face again, she could feel Amy's heart beating fast in her chest, her breaths shallow, she could also tell that Amy had not put her bra back on after her shower – now a different feeling waved across her body and settled in her core. How long could she keep her hands off Amy?

The credits began to roll on the movie. Amy had stayed almost rooted to the spot since she had shifted to lean on Laura, fearing any movement would give the flutter in her heart a chance to take over her whole body and send her down an anxiety spiral. She wasn't sure what had possessed her to move closer and cuddle Laura's arm; it wasn't exactly normal behavior for a hangout and was the farthest thing from cool she could possibly be.

The warm pressure of Amy's body had remained welcoming and once her heart beat had slowed, Laura felt the woman relax. Turning her head to look at the pale face on her shoulder, she got a stronger hint of cherries, a smell now permanently associated with Amy in her head. Amy tilted her head up, her lips only an inch from Laura's, the temptation to push forward and take them was all consuming – especially as Amy parted her lips slightly.

"Wanna put another film on?" were the words that came out of Amy's lips, but the look of desire in her eyes indicated they wouldn't be watching the film for long. Laura only nodded in response as she shifted to grab the remote and play the next title in the queue. When she leaned back, Amy had repositioned so she was now sat up straight again, her hand still firmly holding Laura's. Their eyes locked together, green eyes dancing with promise as Amy turned and placed her lips tenderly on Lauras, so lightly they barely brushed. Passion waved over Laura; her eyes closed for a second and when she opened them again Amy was back leaning on her shoulder. Instinctively she placed her head on Amy's, the side of her cheek resting on the top of her head.

"When do your housemates return?" Amy asked out the blue sometime into the movie.

"Tomorrow afternoon, I think." Laura responded by moving her head off of Amy's.

"Have you missed them?" She hadn't moved to look at Laura, her voice sounded far away, like she didn't really want the answer.

"Yeah, I have mostly, although it has been nice to bake whenever I want and get in the bathroom whenever I want. Do you have roommates at your place?" Laura realized she knew nothing about Amy's living situation.

"No, it's just me." Amy's tone gave nothing away. "The location isn't as good as this place, and it's nowhere near as big. But the space is all mine."

"Yeah, I think I want my own place sooner rather than later. I have lived with Ali, Zoey and Munaza for a few years and we all get along. But it would be nice to have visitors whenever I want." Laura looked over at Amy, hoping she got the hint.

"Well, we should make the most of it now, then." Amy moved her hand from where it was wrapped around Laura's, and snaked it up to her neckline, using the material to pull her down into a deep long kiss. Instinctively, Laura moved so she was facing Amy, letting go of her hand and placing it on the back of her head, pulling them in closer. The movie was now firmly abandoned.

Fooling around on the couch with Amy was fun, unlike the last time when it had all been leading to one very specific outcome and laced with tentative exploration. This time Laura knew how Amy felt under her fingers, and she wanted more of it. She had one hand under Amy's top, slowly running her fingers over her erect nipple, teasing it with her fingers as she used the other arm to brace herself against the arm of the sofa while her hips pressed into Amy's open legs lying underneath her.

She could feel every stroke of Laura's fingers across her sensitive skin, a rhythmic pattern that she matched with the rotating of her hips. Amy's hands were equally occupied, one inside Laura's hoodie holding the back of her neck, fingers buried in her dark hair; the other around her waist, her thumb brushing the underside of her breast. Taking a rare moment when their lips were not clashing to nip at Laura's lower lip caused Laura to open her eyes, perfectly framed by falling dark hair as she looked down at Amy. It caused her heart to skip a beat.

She never let herself be this vulnerable – she always took the lead – and it was an equal mix of terror and sexual desire that kept her here in the moment. The feeling of Laura on top of her was so alluring and yet she felt completely safe. This was different to every other time they had been together – that had been about sexual relief and raw physical desire. This... this was more than that. She could almost completely ignore the cliff edge that sat at the back of her mind.

Chapter 18

Back to the Bedroom

They had at some point moved to the bedroom; Amy couldn't say when. Mouths and hands had roamed, teased and tasted their way across each other's bodies for the entire second film and the credits, before Laura had taken the initiative to head to the bedroom. Laura's legs were wrapped round Amy's hips as she straddled her lap, still kissing, but this time there was a lot less clothing in the way, all flesh exposed and ready to be explored. Amy could feel the heat emanating from Laura's core, feel the anticipation building, feel her want for Amy – it was intoxicating.

Moving her mouth away from Laura's swollen nipple where it had been occupied for several minutes she looked deep into Laura's eyes, searching for permission before taking this further. The eyes that looked down at her were so dark they were almost black; passion and yearning burning behind the shimmering midnight blue. Amy took this as permission to slide her fingers into Laura's awaiting aching folds. This was the first time since they kissed on the sofa that she had made contact with the center of Laura's desire, it took her breath away how much this woman wanted her. Amy could feel everything; how fast Laura's heart was beating, every breath she took, the movement in Laura's hips, pulling Amy's fingers in deeper, her body begging Amy to take her to the edge of ecstasy that had been promised all night. She placed her other hand deep in Laura's hair, keeping their bodies close together, Laura moved both hands up Amy's back, pulling them closer – her nails dragging down the soft skin, destined to leave scratch marks. All the teasing had meant that Laura was not only ready for her but could barely think of anything else but the feel of Amy inside her. This was no longer a want but a need.

Laura was getting closer and closer with every stroke, she moved her hips faster into Amy's hand, barely able to contain herself. She threw her head back, causing her back to arch. Amy took the opportunity to move her lips down to the edge of Laura's neck, pressing her teeth into the soft flesh, noticing the red and faint purple blooming there from many hours of attention. In response Laura moaned, tightening her grip on Amy's hair, continuing to pull her closer. She hoped Laura wouldn't mind the marks that would be staining her body for the next few days.

"Amy," was all Laura could breathily moan as the orgasm that had been building finally escaped, a sound so primal Amy felt it deep in her own wet core. Laura felt like she was floating and falling at the same time, tingling with euphoria all over her body. After being edged by Amy for hours, the climax was like nothing she had experienced before; it clung to her threatening to never end as Amy drew it out of her, curling her fingers to reach the most sensitive areas.

Amy wrapped her arm around Laura, offering some

stabilization, letting her catch her breath, before she flopped forward, her head buried in the crook of Amy's neck. She could feel the heat coming off her, the beautiful light sheen of sweat across her flawless skin shimmered in the faint light. Sat like this, Amy could feel her heartbeat slowly return to normal.

"I got you princess," Amy soothed, wanting to reassure Laura that she was safe and could take all the time she needed to put herself back together. After a few minutes she shifted to look Amy square in the eyes; a look danced across the reflective blue, one she couldn't place. It was clear this time it had been different, more than just a simple fuck – that was not the kind of orgasm you got when you didn't also share an emotional connection. Amy rested her head against Laura's chest, taking in the moment. She couldn't remember the last time she had shared something so intimate with someone. Worryingly, she realized she didn't want it to end, the familiar cliff edge at the back of her mind lurched, not letting her relax and enjoy the moment. After a few minutes, Laura moved off Amy's lap, rolling to lie down in the bed next to her. Amy followed; now facing each other, she planted a kiss on Laura's lips. It was tender, soft and Amy hoped it would help hide the panic that was building in her mind.

"You ok?" she asked, tenderly, but all Laura could do was smile and nod, her brain still floating somewhere unable to connect thoughts and words together. Amy smiled back as she shifted on to her back, pulling the sheets over them both; the air now chilly they were not pressed together. Amy gestured with her chin to the space under her arm, inviting Laura to curl up into her side. She didn't wait to be told twice and settled her head onto Amy's shoulder instinctively wrapping her arm around Amy's middle.

The warmth of Amy, the comfort of her soft skin, and the steady hypnotic rise and fall of her chest was quick to send Laura to sleep. It had been a long long time since she had been this close to someone. Sure, people had stayed the night after sex, but never this close, never this intimate. The last thing she remembered before her mind drifted off was the slow stroking of Amy's fingers on her arm.

Amy felt Laura drift off, her breathing regulated, her muscles relaxed but her arm remained in place across Amy's torso – pinning her in place. It felt amazing to be this close to someone, to have this level of closeness – Amy hated to acknowledge that she missed it, but as ever the anxiety pricked at the edges of her mind, there would be no chance of sleep tonight.

When Laura awoke, her bed was worryingly empty. Momentarily fearful that Amy had left without saying anything, she tumbled out of the bed, noticing it was cool save for the spot she had slept in. Grabbing the discarded hoodie still on the floor from last night, she ignored the pleasant aches she felt across her body, the reminders of several hours of physical exertion. It wouldn't matter how good she felt if Amy had left; it would have reduced last night to another hook up, a repeat of the time before, and that wasn't how Laura saw it. Trying not to run, she left the bedroom and headed towards the kitchen. She couldn't hear anything, which only made her worry increase. Maybe Amy was in the bathroom or maybe she had just snuck out at silly AM again.

When she did get to the kitchen, what she saw made the ice forming in her chest instantaneously melt. Amy was sitting at the kitchen counter working on her laptop, totally engrossed in whatever document she was reading. Laura couldn't help but notice the small furrow in her brow and the bottom lip that was between her teeth – it was frankly adorable.

"Morning," Amy said without looking up. "Sorry, I didn't want to wake you."

"That's fine." Laura padded over to where Amy was sitting. Running her hand over Amy's shoulders, she leaned in for a kiss on the cheek. She was surprised to feel Amy tense under her fingers. Now she was closer, she could see Amy's whole body was tense, an air of separation between them, and if she wasn't mistaken, Amy looked like she hadn't slept. She chose to ignore this as she cast her eye over the rest of the kitchen. Laura noticed it was spotless, a far cry from how she left it the night before. "Amy, did you clean my kitchen?" She leaned her elbow on the counter and looked directly into Amy's red rimmed moss colored eyes.

"Well, considering you did all the cooking, it only felt fair that I did the washing up." Amy's words didn't come with the confidence that reflected her actions last night. This was the shy tentative woman that lived at odds with the confident sexual partner Laura had enjoyed last night. But then she shot Laura with one of her effortless smiles, and Laura forgot any doubts forming in her head. "But I probably need to head off soonish, I have some anomalies in my data and I think I need to look at the samples directly in the lab."

Laura had not expected Amy to hang around all day; she knew that Amy had to go back into the lab – that was the whole reason she was here in the first place, but this felt weirdly abrupt.

"Of course. Would you like a shower before you go?" Laura motioned to the bathroom, keeping her eyes on Amy, she couldn't read her at all, her actions gave nothing away.

"That would be great, thanks." Amy smiled at her again. Closing the laptop lid and standing up from the stool, Amy grabbed her bag from the floor and headed to the bathroom, an unmistakable click of the lock signifying Laura was not welcome on this occasion.

Laura busied herself making coffee and packing up some containers for Amy to take to work, she hated food waste and knew the redhead was probably going to subject herself to instant noodles again otherwise. Once Amy came out of the bathroom, she was dressed and any air of hesitation was gone, Laura was once again looking at the put together Amy she met in the club.

"I put these together for you," Laura handed over the boxes to Amy, who looked dumbfounded at the clear plastic boxes now in her hand.

"For me?" Amy whispered, as she stared down at the hard plastic containers full of pasta and baked treats.

"Well yeah, if you want to take it that is." Laura started to worry she had done the wrong thing, the look on Amy's face was filled with confusion and that hint of something else Laura still couldn't work out.

"No one has ever made me lunch before." Amy looked up, locking eyes with Laura the green burning hot and bright; it was almost impossible to tell what she was thinking, but the words themselves came laced with an undertone of sadness.

Laura took a step closer to Amy, taking the containers back out her hand and placing them on the table next to her laptop. She had to tilt her chin just a little to make their eyes level, she cupped Amy's face with her hands and placed a simple kiss on her soft lips.

"Well then, I am glad I got to be your first," Laura said softly. She wanted to know why no one had ever made Amy lunch, she wanted to know what momentarily made her sad – but now was not the time to be asking questions like that, so she made do with a warm smile. Without warning Amy grabbed two fistfuls of Laura's hoodie, pulling her in even closer and crashing their lips together.

The kiss was deep and passionate; it was the kind of kiss that held promise for future encounters, more nights together, more moans and moments of pleasure. Laura felt herself melting into it and into Amy's arms that were wrapped around her, her body reacting to the fire in the kiss more than she was expecting; a lick of need plucked at her core.

"Have a good New Years," Laura muttered into Amy's neck, she was definitely getting one last smell of the cherry shampoo before Amy left. She didn't like the fact they didn't have a firm next date planned. She would have invited Amy for New Year's, but she didn't have time to run it past the rest of the group.

"Catch you soon princess." Amy smiled as she released Laura, moving to pack her things and the containers into her bag, she walked towards the door grabbing her jacket as she left.

Laura was left standing in her apartment, still in just a hoodie, suddenly very aware of her solitude, the mix of ache from yesterday's activities and the new pang of desire swirling inside her. Waking up and finding Amy sitting at her kitchen table working had felt wonderfully normal, something she could get used to. The thought was both electrifying and terrifying in equal measure. In fact, everything about last night had felt both new and exciting yet totally normal; sitting and watching films curled up together on the sofa, cooking for Amy, and the sex – Laura let her mind float to the sex. From the lustful shower encounter back to the far more intimate time in her bed, both had been perfect in their own way, and both were definitely repeatable. A nagging feeling came to the back of Laura's mind. Reassessing their time together, she noticed again that Amy had deflected any time Laura wanted to pay her attention – it had been done so masterfully that she hadn't noticed in the moment.

Making herself a cup of coffee and sitting on the couch, she replayed last night over in her head; Amy had instigated as much as she had, she had clearly been enjoying what Laura was doing. When Laura had moved her hands to Amy's wet center, she had been flipped over and ravished, or her hands moved and pinned allowing Amy full access to Laura's tender flesh. A pang of guilt for not making more of an effort to even the gratification settled in her stomach. She made a mental note to try and mention it next time they were together, maybe Amy was just shy – not that Laura could imagine why, her figure was like a Greek goddess, and she clearly knew what she was doing when it came to making Laura feel amazing.

They had spent quite a lot of time together over the holidays. It was unusual for Laura to have the spare time and the freedom in the apartment to see someone this frequently. Not that she had wanted to see someone as much as this for a very long time. Laura had been content with the single nights enough to have fun and release some pressure without anything complicated. But that didn't distract from the feelings she had when Amy was around:

she genuinely wanted to spend more time with her. Sipping her coffee, she let her brain picture what dating Amy might be like. She found herself smiling at the idea. More film nights and lazy sundays on the couch, nights out at bars and live music, introducing Amy to her friends and getting her to come along to their board game nights and day trips.

Laura was totally blissfully unaware that she had already started to fall for Amy Love.

Chapter 19

Happy New Year

Amy regretted everything about her evening. The label on her shirt was rubbing against her skin and she couldn't ignore it; she was having a sensory nightmare and was powerless to fix it. She stood in the club, the bright flashing lights bouncing off the mirrored walls creating a kaleidoscope of color. Amy looked down at her watch to see it was only 11.30pm, she groaned and tried not to roll her eyes. Still another hour before she could make excuses and leave. She hated going out on New Year's Eve; everywhere was extra busy and loud – but Jamie and Rachel had insisted given they had both been away for over a week. She wouldn't mind if that had meant she got to hang out with them, but they wanted to dance and let off steam after days trapped at family functions. The lack of sleep from last night had caught up with her, and despite a nap after being at the lab, it wasn't enough to lift her mood. He was feeling frustrated in more ways than just the sleepless night, her body's want for Laura was undeniable and lasting. Even a brief act of self-love hadn't done much to take the edge off. Midway through a yawn, her phone vibrated in her pocket, seeing the name cross the screen made her smile.

> Laura: Hey, just wanted to say happy new year. X

This was the first time Laura had ended a message with a kiss, and this really small detail made Amy smile a little more, before she tried to read too much into it.

"Oh look! Is our Amy getting another message from the sexy Laura?" Jamie teased, shouting loudly over the music. He and Rachel had come to take a breather from their manic dancing at the exact moment she had taken a look at the message.

"I swear, Amy, you refuse to even hook up with someone for literally years! And then in the space of a week you basically move in with this woman," Rachel teased nudging Amy's arm playfully.

"For a start, it's the first time she's texted me since I left this morning," Amy began, refusing to play into their lesbian Uhaul fantasy. "Secondly, I have seen her four times since the Christmas party, and one time included the party!"

"Yeah, and for you that's practically a marriage proposal Amy!" Rachel continued to joke. Amy was well aware of her reputation for being unobtainable – she maintained it was just British reservedness. It was a good excuse.

"Now, now Rach, we shouldn't get too excited! She turned the woman down once, and forgot to have sex another time." Jamie rolled his eyes in exaggeration.

Amy sighed, she was never ever going to live it down. "In my defense – she just told me it was getting late," Amy protested weakly as both her friends doubled over in fits of laughter. "And it was worth it, because she asked me to come back the next day, there were cookies!"

"Wait, wait, wait – this gets even better." Rachel wheezed trying to catch her breath. "She told you to come back and finish the job? *And* she gave you cookies?!"

"Well, technically she baked them," Amy interjected weakly, realizing this did nothing to help her argument.

"Wow, Amy, what did you do to bewitch a woman you turned down *twice to* invite you back for a third time and bake delicious sweet treats for you?" Rachel continued. "And we are still talking about Laura right? Tanned, sexy, dark-haired Laura who has whoever she wants whenever she wants?!"

"Yup, the very same," Amy clarified with a smile; she wasn't big on this sort of bragging but she was well aware of Laura's reputation. "And trust me, I don't get it either!"

"I swear, Amy, if you had any idea what people found so charming about you, you would be deadly." The light hearted chuckling still rang through Rachel's words.

"Come on, we can poke fun at Amy's useless sex life after we do the countdown!" Jamie pouted. "Come on Amy - you have to join us on the dance floor at least until midnight!"

"Yeah fine!" Amy mocked annoyance as she placed her empty glass down on a table and took out her phone to reply to Laura before the year ended.

Amy: Happy New Year Princess. x

Laura was sitting in her hoodie that still faintly smelled like Amy and sex, a glass of wine in her hand, trying desperately to deflect the conversation she was stuck in. Everyone had come home earlier that afternoon and they were now all together in the living area, finishing off the last of their Chinese takeout.

"So come on Laura, spill what happened at the party?" Ali pushed. She was doing long distance with her partner which meant she was extra invested in everyone's private life.

"You know what happened. I hooked up with someone." Laura was trying to play it cool, and failing.

"Yeah... then what? This place is way too clean for you to have not had them back here again – also you have been baking." Ali topped up her wine as she waited for an answer.

"Then nothing, I went back to theirs, and we parted ways as intended." Laura kept her mouth shut, she really didn't want to go into too much detail especially with all four of them at once.

"Then who have you been booty-calling over the holidays?" Zoey added, folding her arms with a smug knowing look across her face – Laura suspected Zoey knew a lot of what had gone on. Sometimes having your best friend and your housemate be sisters was a nightmare.

"It wasn't a booty call! We went on a date." Laura weighed up the possibility of giving just enough information to make them drop it. "I got her number at the party, but we didn't meet up until last week."

"And?!" Zoey pushed, barely containing herself. "I already know what happened, I just want to hear you say it."

Laura groaned as she took another mouthful of wine, cursing Emily as she did so.

"Come on Laura, you have to tell us now – it's not fair to keep secrets hidden," Munaza chimed in.

"*Fine!!*" Laura threw her hands in the air in mock outrage. "We met up and had a few drinks and I invited her back here, and we were making out and I had on really really *really* sexy underwear and literally nothing else. I tried to say we should move to the bedroom, but she got the wrong idea and left."

All three women burst out laughing at Laura's expense. "How does someone get the wrong idea?" Ali asked in bemusement around her laughter.

"I evidently wasn't very clear and I said it was getting late and she thought that meant I wanted her to leave or something? I don't know!" Laura was smiling now; the situation was much funnier now she had spent more time with Amy and she felt the subsequent sex had more than made up for the mistake. "I was literally straddling her with my tongue down her throat and she put her coat on and left!"

"Ok, so you cleaned the apartment in sexual frustration?" Munaza raised an eyebrow at Laura, not buying the story at all.

"Also for the record I don't know anyone on the planet that would assume you wanted them to go home in that situation" Zoey added.

"Emily had basically the same reaction you all just did, when I called her. She convinced me to text her the next day and be very clear about what I wanted." Laura decided not to include the photo she sent to Amy as part of her admission; her friends were great but they didn't need to know all the details.

"And was it worth the wait?" Ali pressed. She really needed to see her partner more Laura thought.

"And don't try and pretend you didn't then hook up. We can all see the hickey you are failing to hide under that hoodie!" Munaza chimed in, throwing a wink at Laura. She cursed herself for not making more of an effort to cover the mark Amy had left on her neck, but every time she saw it she got a flutter and a nice little reminder of how she got it. What her housemates also didn't need to know was it wasn't the only one – once she had finally got dressed that morning she noticed in the mirror a series of reddish purple marks, two around her breasts and another on her right inner thigh.

"Yes it was definitely worth the wait." Laura smiled at the memories each one conjured, her eyes drifting over to the kitchen counter where Amy had so thoroughly fucked her that first night.

"And are you going to see her again?" Zoey inquired. "If she's making you go all gooey eyed from one fuck session that she must be like Midas; and if you are not seeing her again – can I have her number!"

"No you cannot have her number!" Laura didn't feel much like sharing Amy with anyone at all, even though they had not got anywhere near to discussing exclusivity. "And for your information she came over again last night."

"Did she leave again?" Ali asked giggling into her own wine glass.

"No she didn't!" Laura protested. "I lured her in with baking and action movies."

"Woah woah woah, hold up" Zoey cut across the room, turning to look straight at Laura. "You are telling me this mystery woman left you frustrated, then gave you such a good orgasm that you invited her back, cooked for her then cuddled and watched a movie?"

"I never said we cuddled!" Laura retorted, giving up any hope of her housemates not dissecting every element of her holiday. "We did have a lot of sex, though." Zoey kept looking directly at Laura, eyes drilling into her. "*Yes,* fine, we did also cuddle a little bit." Laura gave up, nothing was sacred when it came to these women.

"Wow," Ali raised her eyebrows at this revelation. "Do we need to start looking for a new fourth person to split the rent with? I think I still have some packing boxes under my bed if you want a hand." Ali's words were cut off when the cushion Laura threw at her hit her square in the face. The room erupted in laughter again.

"Ok, but now it's time for the real tea," Zoey said, looking all serious for a moment. "Do you actually like this woman?"

Laura blushed and looked down at her drink. She wasn't sure she was ready to talk about anything like this with her friends, she was enjoying whatever was happening with Amy and she didn't want to jinx it. "Yeah, I think I do," she said more softly than before, still refusing to look at anyone in the room.

"Duh! It's clear you really like her because you baked for her!" Munaza threw her hands towards the kitchen. Laura shrugged and smiled, she couldn't deny it. "You never bake for us, and we live with you!"

"Sex must really be amazing then." Ali made an extremely lewd gesture that made everyone groan. "What?!" she protested. "It's not like Laura is denying it!"

"Urgh, *fine.*" Laura gave up. She was never one to hide her sexuality or her enjoyment of sex. "It was like the best sex ever, and no, I am not joking. I am not sure I have ever had anyone fuck me like that in my life." She paused for a second, not wanting to tell them they had had sex on the kitchen counter – Zoey would be so mad at her, even if she had thoroughly cleaned it after. "She just knew what I wanted and she delivered, it wasn't anything super kinky or debaucherous – it was just really fucking good." A silence fell over the room, Laura worried for a second that she may have given a little too much detail.

"Do we get to know anything else about this woman?" Zoey asked, her smug grin had returned, dancing across her eyes behind her glasses. "Like does she have an equally amazing in bed sibling?"

"I have no idea if she has any siblings." Laura rolled her eyes at Zoey. "She works at one of the universities doing some sort of biomedical research or something."

"Ok, that's super not useful information!" Munaza was getting exasperated with Laura "What does she look like? What's her name? You must know something about her!"

"Her name is Amy," Laura offered with a shrug.

"Amy?..." Zoey left a pause waiting for Laura to offer more of her name.

"I have no idea what her full name is. I also didn't ask for her social security number or tax code – sorry to disappoint," Laura shot back, regretting getting into this round of twenty questions.

"That name rings a bell, though," Zoey started, she sat forward putting her finger to the side of her head in an exaggerated thinking pose.

"Of course it does! Amy is like the most generic name in the world!" Ali interjected laughing at the scowl Zoey sent her from across the room.

"Is she friends with Rachel?" Zoey carried on, choosing to ignore Ali's interruptions and continued with her line of questioning. Laura at times hated how small the Toronto queer scene was; it was hard to meet someone and hit it off without knowing who their ex was or who else they might have hooked up with – not that Laura was put off by these kinds of things, she just hated how true the stereotype could be.

"Yeah I think she is, she was talking to her at the club that night, and they looked like friends." Laura shrugged.

"Redhead? English accent?" Zoey probed, her eyes growing more serious as she looked directly at Laura.

"Yes on both accounts." Laura raised her eyebrow at the new line of questioning.

"I think you want to be a bit careful there, Laura." Zoey screwed her eyebrows together. "She has a bit of a reputation."

"A reputation for what?!" Ali chimed in "For misunderstandings?"

"I hear people call her aloof and difficult to talk to." Zoey took a sip of her drink, she didn't want to put Laura off, but she equally didn't want to see her friend get unnecessarily hurt. "By all accounts she comes across as really charming and cool, but I don't know anyone that has even gone on a second date with her, which is suss if you ask me."

"OMG Zoey! I never believed you would be one to follow gossip!?" Laura hoped she came across as shocked and amused but really she was frustrated that her friend was already bowing to shitty rumors.

"No! But you know how small the community is. People talk! I am just trying to look out for you." Zoey refused to feel bad about her actions –she was only looking out for her friend. "She gives me bad vibes, that's all."

"Well I don't need you to all play Jessica Jones and start snooping on a person I have literally been on one date with and fucked twice!" Laura tried to keep her tone light but she could feel a harsh edge in her words. "And for the record she *is* really charming and has this weird cool vibe that I can't work out if it's super deliberate or if that's just her."

"Maybe it's the reserved English demeanor," Munaza added with a smile, which made Laura think back to the sex they had. Nothing about her had been reserved then for a moment she was lost in her thoughts, her body involuntarily reminding her how much she craved Amy's touch.

"Earth to Laura?!" Zoey's words punched through Laura's thoughts, startling her.

"Damn girl, you have really got it bad for this woman," Ali added, still laughing to herself. "At least tell me you have checked out her socials or something?"

Laura blushed; it hadn't even occurred to her to check out Amy's online presence. She had been quite happy in the little bubble the two of them had had over the last week. Salvation came not a moment too soon for Laura, in the form of her phone buzzing on the table, giving her temporary respite from more questions. Laura grabbed it quickly and busied herself opening the message, it was from Amy. The smile that spread across her face was unmistakable; it matched the skip her heart did.

"She just texted you didn't she?!" Ali squealed. "No one smiles like that at their phone unless they are fucking the person that text them." Laura couldn't even be bothered to deny it. She smiled and shrugged her shoulders before putting her phone down.

"Can we please talk about something else now? I refuse to end the year talking about this," Laura pleaded.

"Sure," Zoey said, her voice clipped. "But just be careful, ok?"

Chapter 20

Coffee and Tea

Amy screwed her face up, looking at the lines and lines of data on her laptop. There was something wrong with the measurements and she really didn't want to have to go and do it manually – it would take hours. Looking over at the clock on the wall, she saw it was nearly noon, and Jamie was still nowhere to be seen. Which she knew was down to the early hour he crawled into bed after ringing in the new year. This was not the start to the year Amy wanted; she hoped the long lab hours would be coming to an end soon – but given the current issues, she wasn't sure that was the case.

She tapped her foot against the chair leg, a nervous habit she did her best to hide around others, but as she was frustratingly still alone she indulged in the little self-soothing motion. After last night's sensory overload with the lights and music that felt so loud it rumbled her very bones, she could really do with a few days to herself or she was at risk of burning out. Frustration deepened as she remembered that not everyone felt like this – that most people didn't find a label on a top or the seam of their socks so unbearable that it would send them spiraling and unable to focus on anything else. It had taken years for her to come to terms with her own differences, and even longer to stop fighting them and accept that she was the way she was. Jamie had helped a lot with that acceptance, embracing her for who she was – not who she pretended to be. Instinctively, her mind slid to Laura, wondering if she would ever understand Amy's... unique challenges.

A cold bolt of ice shot across her body as she realized that meant she would have to tell Laura first – and she had no idea how the woman would act. But then, what was the need to tell her? They weren't anything – just a few very pleasant hook-ups – they had no plans to repeat it currently and there had been no discussion of moving it to anything other than casual.

Amy realized she had been staring at the data, and not focusing on it at all. Cursing herself for letting her mind drift to Laura – its current fixation – she shook her head and scrolled back up to look at the numbers properly.

It was another hour before Jamie slouched into the Lab, shrugging his lab coat over a very crumbled NIN t-shirt, the dark around his eyes a reminder of not only the celebration but the alcohol from last night.

"Afternoon," he mumbled at Amy, looking at her with bleary eyes.

"I was thinking of sending a search party for you," Amy said dryly, not letting herself get distracted from the readings she was trying to take, having given up some time ago and resorting to manual recording.

"Urgh, please, don't be so loud." Jamie leaned on the work bench next to her, head in his hands. "Why were you here so early?"

"Ten AM is not early," Amy protested as she filled in the final number from the sample she was looking at. "But since I have been here for hours and you look like death. Let's go get a coffee."

Ten minutes later, Amy was mesmerized by the steam coming off her coffee mug sat across the desk from Jamie, who was wedged in his office chair almost lying down with his eyes closed.

"Mom missed you; I think she would have preferred you at home rather than me!" Jamie lamented, refusing to open his eyes.

"You know that's not true," Amy smiled. "Did they like the gifts?" She had been worried about sending gifts with Jamie, worried that as she wasn't there in person, it would have been weird, but he had assured her it was acceptable to send them with her apologies.

"Don't pretend like you don't nail gifts every year! It's bad enough when you show me up in person but doing it when you are not even there is just rude!" He chuckled quietly, moving a hand to search for his coffee without opening his eyes. Amy could see the disaster about to unfold and intervene, grabbing the mug seconds before it was locked all over the desk. Jamie cracked his eyes open being unable to locate the coffee, only to see Amy holding the mug to his face, rolling her eyes in mock exasperation. "Anyway, enough about my boring family week – tell me how *your* holiday was?"

"Not a lot to tell, really," Amy sipped her drink, slightly too hot it burnt her tongue, but she was buying time – she wasn't sure yet how much she wanted Jamie to know.

"Worked here, read a little, caught up on some TV – you know standard things."

"Yeah sure, now give me all the gossip about Laura, no detail left out!" He narrowed his eyes at her, a playful glint in them.

"There isn't much to say really that you don't already know. We met at the party, we exchanged numbers, we met up a few days later, I went to hers the next day and then again just before you all came home." Amy had kept details brief, partly because Jamie had been at home and didn't have much privacy, but also because she knew her best friend would dissect her every movement in agonizing detail.

"So no. You will not be keeping this a secret from me Ms Love!" Jamie teased. "Not when this is the biggest thing to have happened to you in years!" Amy chewed the inside of her cheek; she was already hyper aware of how much time she spent thinking of Laura, and the time they had together and even more aware of how long it had been since she had been with anyone. Sure, there had been a few hookups but since the demise of her last relationship Amy had kept herself to herself – it helped avoid making more mistakes. She had pointedly not thought about how she was dangerously close to making more mistakes with Laura. She couldn't deny how at ease she felt around the woman – how unlike anyone else possibly ever, she wanted to spend time with her in a way that was both inescapable and terrifying.

"We met on the roof; there was this guy, he was bothering her so I asked him to leave." Amy paused; that was a close approximation of what happened, and didn't do much to break her promise to Laura about saying nothing. "We realized we were both here alone over the holidays and it made sense to meet up – for company."

"Company?" Jamie wiggled his eyebrows over his coffee "That's what you call it?"

"Well, it was just company the first time..." Amy tailed off, still mortified at how wrong she had read the whole situation. "She actually asked me back to hers at the party, but it didn't feel right, so I assumed she wasn't interested after I said no once." That was the truth, she had turned the woman down, regretted it instantly but never expected another shot after that. "I am aware how stupid that sounds retrospectively. " She huffed, a niggle of embarrassment resurfacing in the back of her mind.

"Yeah well, it sounds like she forgave you." He raised a single eyebrow. "So you went back the next day... and?" he probed. Amy had already filled him and Rachel in on the misunderstanding. He had laughed with her at the time but knew full well that Amy would beat herself up over hat mistakes for months – even though it clearly didn't have any long lasting or negative impact.

"She sent me a very, direct message inviting me back to hers." Amy felt herself smile at the memory of the message and the accompanying image.

"And...?" he pressed.

"And, we fucked," Amy stated simply.

"Did you actually?" Jamie's voice got a little more serious, making an effort to capture Amy's eyes with his own. Looking at her now it was clear that she wasn't masking, a rare privilege outside of her home. He noticed the involuntary tapping of her finger on the edge of her mug; he was going to have to tread carefully if he wanted to have an honest conversation with Amy about this.

"Well, I shagged her," Amy clarified trying to sound unfazed. "I left in the morning and carried on with my day. We have already been over this."

"Yeah we have, you gave me all the fun highlights. But the key card log said you were in the lab by six AM so you must have left hers super early." He hadn't told her about the alert he had set on his phone for the holidays; it wasn't just to check she wasn't spending all her time in the lab, or at least that was how he chose to rationalize it in his head. Amy's facial expression shifted, he could tell she was annoyed that he had accessed the logs, but he also wasn't going to let her derail the conversation by focusing on it. "Let's not get distracted by the outrage you are going to pretend to have because I monitored your lab time while I was away."

"Well, you know already that I had a nightmare and left. There isn't exactly much else to say." Amy's voice had the starting of a hard edge to it; Jamie didn't want her to retreat just yet.

"What did Laura say?" he probed calmy, hoping he sounded casual, looking at Amy's face he could see the flicker of sadness, maybe even regret, on her soft features.

"I didn't really give her a chance to say anything," Amy mumbled into her coffee cup.

"I see, but then you went and saw her again and you stayed the night?" He didn't want to dwell on the fact she had all but run out of Laura's home.

"Yeah, I did." A smile flashed across her face, tugging the corner of her lips as the memory of their encounter played like a sport highlight reel in her mind.

"Oh, I know that look!" Jamie set his mug down and fixed his gaze on Amy as she slowly turned red. "Now I need details!"

"Well, I got there, and needed a shower and she well... she came and had a shower with me." Amy stumbled over the words as the blush started to make her face burn. "Then we watched a film, and then we put another one on, but didn't really get much watching done, then uh, we went back to her bedroom and we fucked again."

"Damn, that sounds pretty hot." Jamie raised his eyebrow as he brought the coffee back to his lips. He knew Amy well enough that there was more to this story than the sex – he just needed to wait for her to open up. After a few minutes of silence he was rewarded.

"She made me a packed lunch for work." Her voice came with an air of confusion and hesitation. "And I don't know what that means."

"It means she likes you, you dummy." Jamie smiled warmly at his best friend; her brow slightly furrowed as she looked off into the middle distance. "And you didn't have a nightmare the second time you had a post-sex sleep over?" It was a long minutes before Amy replied, clearly weighing up her response.

"Well no," Amy shifted. "Because I didn't go to sleep."

"Ah." Jamie had wondered how she had managed to avoid it, apparently the answer was to just not sleep. "So now what?"

"Now what nothing?" Amy huffed, her leg bouncing under the desk, another clear sign she was getting agitated – one that she would have hidden around others. "We haven't really spoken since and we haven't made any plans."

"But do you *want* there to be more plans?" Jamie pressed again.

"I mean, yeah I had fun, she is fun." Amy trailed off clearly processing at the same time as talking, which from past experience meant that she had been avoiding thinking about it Jamie thought. "I mean, it's cool if it was just a holiday fling, but I wouldn't say no if she wanted to meet up again."

"She definitely wants to see you again Amy," Jamie rolled his eyes, always amazed at how clueless she was "She made you cookies and then sent you off to work with a brown-bag lunch." Amy's leg was still rhythmically bouncing, which abruptly stopped when Jamie pressed a little further. "Maybe next time you see her you could tell her a little bit about you?" Amy's eyes became laser focused on his, as they narrowed.

"We have done more than fuck, you know? We talked about movies and jobs and music and all the standard stuff." Her voice was measured, even to a fault.

"Yeah, I am sure you did, but she's not an idiot Amy – she is going to notice that she never gets to fuck you back." He didn't look away from her gaze, part of being someone's friend was telling them some uncomfortable home truths, and Amy needed to hear this. "And if she doesn't, then stop seeing her because you deserve better."

"She's not complained so far," Amy snapped back. "In fact no one ever complains." It was true, for the most part anyway. If she didn't spend much time with them, kept it casual and didn't let it get too far – no one really cared.

"Yeah? And you are happy like that are you?" Jamie threw his hands in the air with exasperation. "That's fulfilling is it?"

"Why does it matter?" Amy stood up unable to keep her anger from spilling out into her words. "Why are you pushing it? You dont normally care when I fuck someone." That wasn't strictly true, and Amy knew it – but it was out of character for Jamie to push quite so hard on the matter.

"Because Amy, I think you actually have a shot with this woman who clearly likes you and I don't want you to fuck it up because you won't tell her – " Jamie was abruptly cut off by Amy slamming her hand on the desk, her palms stinging from the impact.

"Won't tell her what?!" Amy's voice was raised. Jamie knew she would have nightmares about it later, he never heard her shout – it was just another stupid self imposed restriction. "That I am autistic?"

"Shut up, Amy, we both know that's not the issue here." But it would be a good idea if you actually told people you were different – so they could be there for you, he thought to himself. He understood why Amy didn't tell people; he saw the strain it put her under to mask constantly. But that didn't stop him desperately wanting her to let other people in. "What are you going to do now? Ignore her? Or just never sleep in the same bed as her?"

"I have data to record," Amy said flatly, the flames of anger now completely gone from her voice. Jamie knew he had got to her, as he watched her swivel on the spot and stalk out the small office.

"Sure, Amy. But if you're not careful, you are going to fall back into bad habits and break her heart – just like the others," Jamie shouted after Amy, as the door back into the lab slammed shut.

After a tense and lonely afternoon where Jamie did not come out of his office and she didn't make any effort to see him – Amy had headed home, the cold dark winter evening sucking out any warmth she had inside.

Amy poured herself a glass of clear liquid. It was rare she had a drink – it was always a gamble if it was going to kick off her nightmares and a subsequent panic attack, or nullify everything she was feeling. It was even rarer that she had a drink alone. But tonight she didn't care, Jamie's words had hurt – what was she doing with Laura? Why did it matter that she was denying herself? What business was it of his anyway? Knocking back the liquid it burnt her throat, not that it stopped her pouring another. She leaned against the kitchen counter, and exhaled.

Chapter 21

The Way You Taste

January was cold and dark; the temperature dropping in the new year always produced less snow than December which just added to its misery. It was like this every year, and every year it caught Laura by surprise. But this year she was really feeling it. She had spent a lot of time with Amy in their little bubble over the holidays and now she was back to normality, she missed it. It was always an adjustment to get used to living with so many people again after more than a week of blissful solitude – not that she didn't love them all, but only having one bathroom in the apartment was always a challenge. This combined with a new project at work meant she was leaving in the dark and coming home in the dark.

With all the long hours and Amy doing her own long lab days they hadn't had a chance to see each other at all. Laura reminded herself that that was perfectly ok and it had only been a week but that didn't stop her sulking about it. She wanted to spend more time with Amy, to get to know her outside of sex – not that she was ever going to turn down the sex.

As she trudged up the stairs to her apartment, she slid her key in the lock and let out a long slow breath. All she wanted to do tonight was eat pizza and watch TV in bed, and text Amy of course. But hanging up her coat and walking in the kitchen space, she saw Zoey alone working at the high counter. She had been avoiding alone time with Zoey since New Year's Eve, she knew if she spent any time with her, then she would want to know why she had such strong opinions on Amy. Laura hated having animosity with the people she lived with, especially with Zoey; they had known each other most of her life via her friendship with Emily.

Before Emily was Emily she was Eric, the destined-to-be high-flying lawyer set to inherit the family firm. But that had all gone when Emily came to terms with the fact she was, well Emily and started her journey to become her authentic self. They had been friends since junior year at high school, and Laura had been completely unfazed when in college Emily had finally come to terms with their gender identity. Unfortunately her family had been less than supportive, with only Zoey, her younger sister, standing by her. Zoey and Laura had gotten much closer over the years as the main support network for Emily – forming a friendship themselves outside of Emily. When it came time for Zoey to undertake her MBA in the city, it made sense for her to move in with Laura, dragging her college roommate Ali along for the ride.

Zoey herself was a powerhouse: nothing ever fazed her which was both admirable and terrifying at the same time. Her brown eyes, so dark they are almost black often hidden behind glasses, gave very little away, but she could be a real softie once you got to know her. Laura always felt kind of invincible with Zoey on her side, and hated being on the other side of her.

"Hey," Zoey said without even looking up from her computer, in the most neutral tone Laura had ever heard.

"Hey you," Laura said, trying to sound casual. "How's exam prep going?" Zoey was studying for a masters in Law in preparation to take over the family firm in the future, a far cry from the dreams she had growing up.

"It's fine." Zoey still didn't look up from the screen. Laura knew this was a perfect excuse for her to head to her room and not have a conversation, but she didn't move. After a few minutes Zoey stopped typing, took off her glasses and looked at Laura. "You want to talk about this now?"

"Want to? No. But I think we should." Laura shuffled nervously. She really liked Amy, but she trusted her friends, Zoey was yet to be proven wrong about a person. "I hate that I am kinda avoiding you – we are friends and we live together, and I don't want this to be weird."

"Ok, what is it you want to know?" Zoey wasn't prepared to offer any information she wasn't directly asked for.

"What did you mean, about Amy having a reputation?" Laura seldom felt as uneasy as she did right now, but she had equally never been warned about seeing someone before. Amy made her feel all sorts of things, but it was all new and fragile and she didn't want anything to get in the way of that.

"Ah." Zoey folded her hands together, every bit the perfect lawyer she was shaping up to be. "You need to know, my words came from a place of love, and they still do. I am not going to tell you not to see her or anything."

"That didn't answer my question." Laura narrowed her eyes. She hated lawyer Zoey.

"No, it didn't," Zoey continued, being slow and measured with her words. "I really was just looking out for you, and it's not like there are that many Amys, let alone English ones in the city's community. So I just asked a few people about her."

"So you took it upon yourself to ask around about someone – behind my back." Laura's eyes widened a little; she wasn't sure why her sex life was being granted such an analysis by her friends.

"You know no one can find her online right?" Zoey continued as if she was laying the facts down in court.

"It's not a crime to not want to put everything online you know." Laura felt the need to defend Amy's actions, the redhead was shy, and a bit of a nerd – not everyone had to be online all the time.

"No it's not," Zoey agreed. She let the silence grow between them, seeing the annoyance flicker across Laura's face. "I just don't want you getting really into this person and then she turns out to not be who you think she is."

Laura stayed silent refusing to engage in this stupidity.

"We are family Laura. Family looks out for each other. That's all I am doing. I know you and I know you want to see the best in everyone. But what do you actually know about Amy, who you are clearly more than crushing over?"

Not wanting to give Zoey the satisfaction of letting her know that she really did know nothing about her, Laura settled for a shrug and walked off. Zoey put her glasses back on and returned to her work. Both women knew this wasn't really over.

An hour later and Laura had a giant pizza and mind numbing TV to entertain her as she lounged about her bed. Unable to resist, she had also looked Amy up online, but realized she had no idea of her full name, or any screen names she might use. It had been a short and frustrating exercise, she also realized she hadn't had anything from Amy for over twenty-four hours, not that they made an agreement to talk every day – it was just a pattern they had fallen into. The last message in their chat glared at her, a large unanswered question from yesterday morning, left on read. Laura threw her phone back down on the bed. She didn't want to come across as needy – but she really wanted to talk to Amy.

One episode of her favorite binge rewatch and Laura caved. She crawled over to where her phone had landed and typed a new message to Amy.

Laura: Hi, hope you had a good day x

Hoping it came across as casual, Laura tried not to think about Amy not replying and leaving her messages read and unanswered again; the argument with Zoey was too fresh for her ego to take. Fortunately she didn't have to worry for long.

Amy: Hey you, sorry I didn't reply yesterday.I have barely been out of the lab. How have you been? How is the new project? x

Laura loved how Amy always took the time to ask how her day was, and to remember the things they had spoken about. It was a small thing, but Laura liked it nonetheless.

Laura: Work is S T R E S S F U L! But it will calm down in a few days, we are a new team and we haven't worked together before so it's all a learning curve for everyone

Amy: I am sorry it's stressful. I honestly don't know how you do it, I am terrible at working in a team

Laura: I don't mind it, I like working with people So what happened at the lab?

Do I need to be worried about an evil rage virus turning us all into Zombies?

Amy: We had a system failure and the server stopped recording the data, I had to do it manually and check all the old records. Sadly no chance of evil rage contagious from me. How is the flat now everyone is back?

Laura smiled to herself. Sometimes she forgot Amy was from the other side of the world, and they didn't always speak the same language, then she would say something very English, she found it cute.

Laura: That sounds like it was stressful too! The 'flat' is fine, I miss baking! But it's good to see them all again

Amy: I miss your baking too!

Wanna know what else I miss?

Laura: enlighten me

Amy: The way you taste.

Laura's phone almost fell out of her hand. She hadn't ever expected Amy to send a message like that. Her mind flooded with memories, she could almost feel Amy between her legs. She knew Amy was going to say something flirty, but that was downright filthy, and she loved it. Her mouth was suddenly very dry, she felt very awake. Her fingers hovered over the screen, as she weighed up her options for a reply.

Laura: I can't stop thinking about you. I wish you were here next to me right now.

Amy: Why?

Laura: So I could remind you how I taste.

Amy: Honestly, I couldn't focus on anything today, All I could think about was you. And now I'm a little drunk, a lot horny, and all alone. This feels unfair.

Laura: that does sound unfair

Laura hesitated for a moment. She hadn't expected Amy to be so honest about her feelings; this was the first time that she had admitted to missing Laura; it was also the first time she had ever referenced being turned on. She wanted to help further this, not wanting to lose the moment. It felt like Amy was breaking down her walls a little.

Slipping off her top, Laura took a very suggestive selfie. She had mastered the art of a sexy picture without compromising her modesty several years ago, giving enough ammunition to drive someone wild – but not showing too much that it would matter if the image was public. Without over-thinking it, she sent it.

Laura: Does this help?

Amy: If by help you mean make it even worse? Yes.

Laura: Good.

What would you do to me if you were here?

Amy: Fuck, you are driving me wild Princess.

Laura: you didn't answer me

Laura quite liked being more bold and confident, pushing Amy a little. Amy had so far always taken the lead, but she hoped soon she could switch it up and take the woman as she wanted. She wouldn't admit it but she had spent an almost unhealthy amount of time thinking about how she would fuck Amy, how Amy would unravel as she took her to the edge.

Amy: I would take your clothes off, and I would fuck you with my mouth until you couldn't take any more.

And then if I was satisfied you couldn't take anymore

I might let you thank me with your mouth.

She couldn't resist anymore, her hand was already teetering at the edge of her underwear. She wanted to touch herself at the thought of what Amy might do to her, but the fact Amy mentioned Laura touching her in return was possibly even more of a turn on. It was the final incentive she needed to push her own hand down into the wetness between her thighs. She could only imagine how her name would sound being moaned in pleasure with that English accent.

Laura: I am touching myself and thinking about you

Laura sent the message. A little wave of worry passed over her – she had never done this before, but she was touching herself and she was thinking of Amy. Sure she had masturbated and thought of others, but she had never told anyone. Continuing to work her fingers round her clit, dreaming of moss-green eyes, she felt her phone buzz next to her.

Amy: Good, so am I

That was all Laura needed: confirmation that Amy was as frustrated as she was, that she was also sitting somewhere playing with herself thinking of her. Eyes firmly closed, Laura pushed herself closer to climax, picturing all the ways Amy had touched her, all the ways she wanted her to touch her again. The feel of her mouth sucking on her breasts, the flick of her tongue across her needy clit, the scraping of her nails across her thighs before she fucked her into submission. She could almost hear Amy purring in her ear, "good girl." It took an embarrassingly short length of time before Laura was satisfied.

Amy was sitting on her couch. She had had a string of extra vivid nightmares for a few nights and was exhausted. They always left her drained and a little out of sorts; Jamie had obviously picked up on them but had opted not to say anything. She was at least thankful for that. There had been a frosty air between them for a few days since they argued, but she wasn't worried – they always got over it pretty quickly. In all the business with the lab and the sleepless nights, she had completely forgotten the message from Laura yesterday morning and felt guilty as soon as she saw the one tonight. She had half expected their texting to fizzle out considering the nature of their time together – a quick holiday fling was not a terrible idea. But things had continued and Laura had always been a presence in her mind.

This was new to Amy, she had slept with women before but never had they taken up so much space in her brain. Every morning she had a shower, her mind drifted back to the way Laura had felt under her against the cold tiles. She was thankful they had not been to her flat, she wasn't sure she could stand it.

The photo had been a very welcome surprise, and had ignited a fire inside Amy. She moved from the living space to the bedroom and lay on the bed. For the last several nights, she had laid in bed thinking of Laura: how her asleep in the bed next to her had felt comforting – before her mind turned to other thoughts of the woman, her striking blue eyes calling out to her like sirens. Begging Amy to give in and give herself to them.

Amy knew she could be a flirt; but the alcohol was definitely pushing her to say more than she normally would. The direct words from Laura and the photo combined with her active imagination were quickly causing her to need a release. Eyes closed, she imagined what it would feel like to have Laura's hands on her, touching all the places she was touching herself, all the places she craved Laura to touch, her own fingers rubbing across her wet aching clit. It had been a really long time since she had wanted someone to touch her, let alone anyone get under her skin like this. But right now she wasn't going to spiral. She was going to enjoy the thought of Laura fucking her. Here in the solitude of her own bedroom with only the thought of Laura, anxiety couldn't reach her. She was free to fantasize as much as she wanted. Based on the text message from Laura – she was doing the same.

Chapter 22

What Do You Want, Princess?

The next few days were busy for everyone again, but with the promise of the weekend almost here Amy hoped she might get the chance to see Laura in person. They had shared a few texts but nothing like they had that night. The memory was seared into Amy's mind, and it had done very little to dampen her desire to get some more alone time with Laura. Even a brief meet up somewhere public during that day would be nice, Amy had mused to herself. When she had tentatively spoken to Jamie about it, he suggested inviting Laura over to her apartment; the look she shot at him quickly put an end to that idea. They had mostly made up, but it was clear to them both that Laura was a topic best avoided. Amy had never been good about letting people into her space; the fact that Jamie had a key was in itself a miracle. She enjoyed the solitude and the ability to have everything exactly as she wanted it, but it was more than that, her space was safe – she didn't have to mask or play a part for others there. Letting someone in would mean they saw her space for what it was – a carefully crafted structure designed so she could function in the outside world – and it wasn't something she wanted to have to explain to anyone.

Laura was so thankful it was finally Friday. She had limped towards the weekend, with the new team and project finally feeling like it was on track, she was looking forward to relaxing. It was tradition in the apartment to spend one Friday night a month together as a group. They had picked this one long before the holidays – and while she normally looked forward to these nights, today she just wanted to curl up and sleep, possibly for the whole weekend. However, now she was here, sitting on the couch with the other three women had revived her in other ways, she had forgotten how good it felt to just hang out with friends and catch up, she had barely seen anyone over the week with her busy schedule.

In this wider group setting it was easy to hide her continued annoyance with Zoey, the animosity still bubbling away after the mid-week argument. Laura had texted Amy and asked about social media, she hoped in an unsuspecting and casual way. If Amy had any suspicions she hadn't said anything, instead mentioning that she was on a few discord servers and found that was more than enough to get her fix of online interaction while still remaining mostly anonymous. Satisfied with this, Laura thought no more of it.

After a long but fun night of board games where Ali had annihilated them all at monopoly and Laura had eaten her body weight in pizza, she went to bed, opting not to set her alarm at all and letting herself sleep in as long as she needed. Before heading to bed she dropped Amy a message, having not had a chance to see her all week – she was keen to change this tomorrow.

Laura: Hey, hope you have had a good day, Maybe we can catch up tomorrow. X

Amy: I would really like that x

Putting her phone down, Laura went to bed with a smile on her face, a hopefulness prickling at the edges of her lips. As she fell asleep, she absent-mindedly thought about those green eyes that looked at her with such wonder, and how perfectly the red hair had splayed across her pillows. She could swear the faintest smell of cherries lingered on her sheets – even though she had changed them since Amy had been last here. Totally ignoring the flutter in her heart, she drifted off to sleep.

Laura woke up, finally feeling rested. She stretched and rolled over to the cool side of the bed. The pale winter light was coming in from around the curtains sending a dull glow across the walls. Checking her phone she looked over the flurry of notifications. Nothing more from Amy, which wasn't a surprise as it was only ten AM, and she had probably still had to go to the lab. Leaning back she thought about how best to approach her day, and the time she could spend with Amy, she could invite her out on a date – but that felt a little formal, maybe a more casual day time meet up? That would be nice, but it still didn't feel right. Really, she wanted Amy back in her bed, and the easiest way to do that was invite her over to meet the rest of her roommates. But was it too soon? Laura contemplated this for a few moments. She had had people back before and it had been fine, and she suspected Amy would prefer something more low key. Lying back in the bed Laura weighed up the options, finally settling on inviting Amy over for the evening with the heavy implication that she would spend the night.

Opening her messages, Laura sent a quick message to the group chat: she hadn't had Amy around since everyone had got back; they could meet her – it would be nice she thought they would all get on. As per the house rules, she needed permission before inviting her over, not that it was really anything more than a formality. Almost instantly Ali and Munaza said yes, Ali with way more enthusiasm than a normal person should ever have. As soon as Zoey saw the message, Laura would text Amy and invite her over. Getting up, she slowly got dressed as she mused over what she and Amy would be getting up to later. The thought made her smile as she walked into the kitchen, surprised to see Zoey sat at the counter again, laptop out and glasses on.

"Working on a Saturday?" Laura tried to be light in her tone, assuming Zoey hadn't seen the message on her phone yet.

"Yes, but I am stopping at two – I refuse to lose my whole weekend to a commercial law exam." Zoey looked up from the computer, removing her glasses.

"So I was wondering – " Laura started before being abruptly stopped when Zoey raised her hand.

"I saw the text, and I am really sorry but I don't want her here. Maybe you can go to hers or something if you want to spend time with her." Zoey made every effort to keep her voice even. She had seen the message when it was first sent; she knew this was coming and had had time to put her case together before any confrontation could happen.

"Why?" Laura asked, she could feel herself getting annoyed. The rule was that anyone could say no, but in all the years they had lived together no one ever had.

"Because I don't want to see you get hurt Laura, and I think Amy is going to hurt you."

"How the fuck would you know?" Laura didn't bother to hide her anger. She hated people making judgements without facts; she expected better from Zoey who was always a believer in facts.

"Because Laura, she will fuck you like you have never been fucked before, she will make you think you are special, but you will never get to know who she really is." Zoey locked eyes with Laura, almost daring her to bite back. Silence fell over them, Zoey refusing to elaborate, eyes burning deep into Laura, who stood defiantly saying nothing.

"How would you know?!" Laura spat back, hackles up as her arms folded defiantly across her chest.

"How do you think I know, Laura?" Zoey replied, refusing to look away, daring Laura to put the puzzle together.

Zoey had never told any of the women she lived with, or even her sister about her brief encounter with English charmer Amy. It had been a wholly negative experience, and she didn't feel much like reliving it. It had been years ago; at the time she was trying to figure out who she was, having just broken up with her high school boyfriend after they made it all the way through college before he announced that he expected her to just fall into conservative family life with him. Emily had just come out as trans to their parents and Zoey was struggling to hold everything together and support her sister while their parents took some time to adjust.

Amy had felt like a breath of fresh air, someone new and exciting, she was enigmatic and sweet – Zoey developed a crush on her the second she met her. Amy was the first woman she had ever slept with; the sex was still some of the best she had ever had. But she wanted more, to feel a connection and every time she tried, Amy pushed her away. She couldn't remember who ghosted who, but it was fair to say they had not spoken since, and Zoey knew she had grown – she wasn't convinced Amy had.

"Why didn't you just say you had slept together?" Laura finally asked, breaking Zoey's train of thought. "Do you think it will be awkward for Amy to come over because you hooked up like a million years ago?"

"No." Zoey still refused to expand on her feelings, not wanting to go into her innermost thoughts. She had kept them to herself for years – she had no desire to change that now.

"Then what is the problem!?" Laura shouted.

"I don't trust her not to hurt you," Zoey said, trying to sound calm and reserved. A long pause followed, both women looking at each other, Laura with burning fury while Zoey frustratingly kept her cool.

"I am not new to hook-ups or friends with benefits Zoey – I have been a sexually active grown up for quite a while." Laura spat out the words trying to get a hold of her anger, it was rippling over her in waves. The queer community was small, even in a city the size of Toronto, it wasn't exactly an unlimited dating pool – this wasn't a new thing and Laura couldn't understand why it was a problem. Zoey was so calm and matter-of-fact about the whole thing, as if this wasn't the first time she had said no to an overnight guest, or the first time she had ever in all their years of friendship had an issue with someone's night companion.

"Are you honestly telling me that Amy is just a repeat hook-up?" Zoey asked, she knew Laura too well, she knew what it looked like when Laura started to get feelings. More than anything, she knew who Amy was and how she made you feel like the most important person in the world as long as you didn't look too hard or ask too many questions. "The same one that you had stay the night repeatedly? The one you baked cute little cookies for?" she added, trying to drive her point home.

"So what if I did those things?" Laura felt exposed; Zoey was right these were not things she did for a random hook-up, and Amy was fast becoming not a random hook-up or a friend with benefits. "What difference does it make to you?"

"I don't want to have to say 'I told you so' when Amy inevitably breaks your heart." Zoey sighed. She really wished this had gone differently; she wished Laura was less interested in Amy, that this has been a conversation over dinner with the rest of the girls to back her up – to make Laura see sense.

"That is a bit dramatic for someone I have been talking to for less than a month." Laura was stunned at Zoeys persistence on this.

"So you can promise me right now that you're not falling in love with her?" Zoey looked at Laura dead in the eye. She could see how hurt Laura was; she could also see how right she was as a little glimmer ran across her eyes. It was clear in that moment that Laura had no idea about her own feelings; the deafening silence that fell over them only confirmed it to Zoey. But it was too late to undo it. After a few moments, Zoey slid her glasses back on and returned to the computer, the only sound being the tapping of her keys. She could feel Laura's eyes burning into her.

"I hate talking to you when you are in lawyer mode," Laura huffed.

"And yet, you are the one who started the conversation,

again," Zoey said matter-of-factly, not looking up from the screen.

Laura turned on her heels and walked straight to her room. She wasn't annoyed that Zoey and Amy had hooked up in the past – she was never bothered about things like that. It was a stereotype that all queer women knew each other – and it was often true, it was hard to date anyone who had not hooked up with someone in the past. But since when did a random years ago hook-up mean someone couldn't come over? Why did it matter so much that she thought Amy was worth dating properly? And how dare Zoey start throwing around words like 'love'? They hadn't even talked about making their time together more official. Flopping on the bed, she kicked off her shoes and took out her phone. A message from Amy filled the screen, and a smile tugged at her face for the first time today.

Amy: Hope you are having a good day x

Laura: Honestly? It has not been a good day so far,I just had an argument with Zoey again.I love her dearly but sometimes they all make me scream.

Amy: And here was me thinking I was the only one that made you scream ;p

Laura was a little surprised by the flirty nature of the message – not that they hadn't shared similar messages over the last week – but the way Amy just slipped into it was always so smooth. It made her heart skip a beat and all the anger evaporated off her body.

Laura: I mean you DO make me scream

Amy: One of my many talents. Is there anything I can do to make up for your terrible day?

Laura: I think I am just stressed.What sort of things do you have in mind?

Laura didn't want to assume, but she had been trying to get Amy to come visit her tonight – maybe she could ask to go to Amy's place. She had no idea where it was but she wasn't sure it mattered. Her conversation with Zoey had made her even more determined to see Amy.

Amy: Well I'm free all weekend, So why don't you tell me what you want, Princess?

Laura felt a now familiar jolt and ache between her thighs. She had never been one for pet names, but the way Amy said princess turned her to putty. Reading it on the screen she could almost hear the redhead purring it in her ear. This was a clear invitation; she knew she could say whatever she wanted and she would probably get it.

Laura: I would like to see you.

Amy: I didn't ask you what you would like. I asked you what you wanted.

So again - What do you want Princess?

Laura: I want you to fuck me

Amy: That's all?

Laura: I'm aching to have you inside me.

Amy. Consider it done Princess.

Laura was incredibly turned on. The excitement she felt was almost euphoric as the anticipation buzzed across her skin like electricity. The way Amy could turn her mood round so fast was incredible. She had no idea what was going to happen, but she was going to see Amy, and Amy was going to give her exactly what she asked for. Arousal grew inside her, as she let her mind wander to all the things Amy had done to her already. In less than ten minutes her phone buzzed again. She realized she hadn't responded to Amy's last message, she had gotten swept up in her own arousal. The message was simple, just an address and a time – looking at the clock she had about an hour before she needed to leave. An hour for her excitement to grow.

"I'm going out, I don't expect to be back tonight," Laura shot at Zoey as she walked passed. They might be in a fight, but that was no reason not to tell people she was going to be out.

"Be careful," was all Zoey said, without even looking up from her laptop as Laura walked out the door.

Chapter 23

Hotel, Motel, Fuck Me Inn

Amy openly admitted to herself she had been waiting for an opportunity to see Laura again, but didn't want to come across as too keen, so when Laura had directly asked for the physical contact today – Amy jumped at the chance. As the bus criss-crossed the city, she was starting to build a plan in her head. Laura had asked to be fucked, and Amy had every intention of giving the woman exactly what she wanted. Having just arrived at the lab when the messages came, and probably against her better judgment, Amy decided to leave her work and focus on giving Laura what she wanted. The data was being captured automatically again, it would be fine without her for a day. Hopping off the bus, she looked up and the hotel in front of her. It was one of the first places she remembered looking at when she first came to the city, over a decade before. Out her price range then but not now – it was most definitely for tourists and business trips. Perfectly anonymous.

It took Laura most of the ride to the address Amy sent to

realize that she probably wasn't going to Amy's apartment. When she had absent-mindedly copied it into the map, she hadn't bothered to look at the destination, making an assumption it was to her apartment – but she had never bothered to clarify. In her defense she was a little distracted. Amy had given her no further information or instructions, leaving her mind to fill in the gaps. Walking round the corner, she saw the giant letters of the Toronto sign and city hall surrounded by the usual tour groups and tourists; even in the winter the city still hosted scores of visitors. She couldn't remember the last time she had been this far downtown. Checking her map again, she looked at the building that matched the address: the Sheraton Centre. A large 1970s monolithic mega hotel, its 43 stories standing proud against the wintry sky. She was a little surprised by the choice in location, but undeterred, she pushed the doors open and walked into the busy lobby.

It took only a moment for her eyes to find Amy, but when she did, her heart skipped a beat and her breath caught in her throat. She was as stunning as ever, her red hair catching the light, making it dance like fire against the swaths of chrome and marble; a familiar carefree smile spread across her face as she watched Laura cross the lobby. The closer she got the clearer she could see the look in Amy's eyes – it made her body ache and spine tingle. Amy had asked what she wanted, and it was clear she had every intention to deliver.

"Hi," Laura said when she got closer, unable to keep the smile spreading across her face.

"Hey," Amy almost purred back, as she deliberately and slowly looked Laura up and down, causing even more feelings to swirl inside Laura. "Do you want a drink or anything before we head upstairs?" Green eyes locking with blue, they were filled with promises Laura knew Amy was about to keep. Amy reached over and tucked a strand of hair behind Laura's ear, this brief touch sending sparks of electricity through both of their bodies.

Laura was unable to speak, this felt different again; this was nothing like the other times, she opened her mouth but nothing came out. Already completely at Amy's mercy. The redhead raised an eyebrow and left her lazy smile to morph into something far sexier as she closed the space between them and whispered, "Ok princess, follow me."

Waiting for the elevator was palpable agony. The tension between them was so thick it was almost suffocating. Amy stole a look at Laura who was almost vibrating with a mix of feelings Amy didn't care to investigate. This was definitely not the day she had planned; she should be in the lab, but Amy needed to feel Laura again. The urge was almost primal – only growing the closer they were together. Her blue eyes were fixed on the floor, but Amy could feel Laura's anticipation flowing out of every pore. To keep her hands busy, she ran her fingers over the keycard safely tucked in her back pocket. The last thing she wanted to do was overtly stim or give any indication she wasn't one hundred percent in control. The elevator slowed as they neared the floor, something in the mid twenties – Amy had not paid any attention when she booked it or collected the key from reception.

Amy took Laura's hand as the doors opened with a soft swish; even the feel of her hand wrapped around hers made Laura's heart skip a beat – it was so silky soft and delicate but held such power and control. Amy pulled her out onto the corridor setting off down a maze of halls all looking the same, lined with featureless doors. They paused outside a room door. Amy looked at Laura, catching her eyes, holding them in her gaze; it was so intense it made Laura's breath catch in her throat. Amy took out a key card from her back pocket hovering it over the lock on the door, her hand still holding Laura's.

"Are you sure you want to do this?" Amy asked, searching for a final confirmation before entering the room, a point of no return. Laura's eyes flickered to the floor. Amy could tell she wanted this as much as she did, the way she chewed on her bottom lip only made Amy want her more. Rather than reply, Laura took a step closer, putting her hand on Amy's face, tilting her head up to meet hers and carefully brushing their soft lips together. She didn't have the words, her mouth was dry and filled with cotton, the press of their lips together giving more of an answer than any words could.

Amy pressed the key card to the door, pushed it open and led them both inside.

The second the door clicked closed, Amy let her bag slide off her shoulder as she gently pushed Laura against the wall; the movement was fluid and gentle.

As Laura made contact with the wall it was as if something shifted in them. Any hesitation long lost to the world outside this room. In this room, they had no one else to answer to, no distance to keep them apart, for a brief time – nothing was complicated. Amy was a little taller, it was barely noticeable but being this close it caused Laura to keep her head tilted up slightly, as she was pushed against the wall. There was no denying that this gave her an extra rush of excitement. Mouths locked in feverish demand once again, Amy pushing her lips against Laura's, parting them enough to capture Laura's lower lip.

In response, hands came under Amy's shirt and pulled her closer, Laura's hands felt light and warm as they brushed against Amy's skin, her nails lightly digging into her flesh causing Amy's heart to race and her hands busy themselves with undoing the buttons on the front of Laura's jacket.

Within moments both women's tops were discarded on the floor, neither of them taking an interest in where they ended up.

A fleeting thought wandered into the back of Amy's brain. This was not what she expected to happen today and definitely was not 'dressed to be undressed' – her bra was simple black with a lace edge and her pants were as nondescript as they could be. She pushed that thought out of her head as she slid a thumb under Laura's bra and caught her nipple, causing it to become rigid instantly. In retaliation, Laura moved her hands up from Amy's waist and buried one deep in her hair pushing their mouths closer, letting her teeth catch Amy's bottom lip. A moan escaped Amy's throat before she even realized it was there.

"Can I take this off?" Amy asked tugging at the strap of Laura's bra with one hand as the other continued to work her nipple.

"Yes," Laura nodded in return as she pulled at the edge of Amy's and looked her in the eyes, asking if the action could be reciprocated. Amy nodded and moved her hand to unclip Laura's bra with expert ease; both bras joined the other clothes decorating the floor.

Amy pulled Laura away from the wall by gently tugging the top of her jeans. She needed to feel her, she needed to know every inch of this woman's body. It had only been a week since they had last been together and already it felt like too long. Laura responded by kicking off her shoes. It felt like they didn't need words to know what each other wanted; there were no awkward nose bumps or caught hands. They explored each other's bodies without hesitation.

Amy unbuttoned Laura's jeans and bent down as she followed the fabric with her mouth, leaving a trail of kisses across Laura's hips and thighs. Her skin was soft and smooth to touch, warm with a faint hint of vanilla and lavender. Amy stood and looked deep into Laura's eyes; they were swimming with possibilities and yearning. She wanted this, she didn't need to say anything, Amy could see it in her eyes.

Amy pushed Laura backwards onto the bed. She leaned forward to plant a kiss on Laura's lips; they crashed together again. Amy could feel the hunger, the longing building inside Laura. The view in front of her was perfect, the way Laura's body dipped and curved she wanted to commit it to memory so she never forgot it. She ran her hand up Laura's thigh causing a breath to get caught in her throat and goose-bumps to tail behind her fingers. A smile crept on to Amy's lips. This may not be the first time they have fucked, but she was going to take the time to take her in, every inch of her. Slowly.

A niggle of doubt and panic spiked in Amy's mind, her conversation with Jamie still raw around the edges. She chased it away, reminding herself that Laura had explicitly asked for this – to be fucked, for Amy to fuck her. There had been no indication that Laura was expecting to touch Amy the same way. It wasn't like she didn't know how to make people forget about her needs in these situations, taking charge was an easy way to push the scales in the direction she felt safe.

In one swift move Amy leaned forward and took both of Laura's wrists in her hand. Holding them down with a little pressure above her head as she pushed her hips into Laura's warm wet center. Already aching with desire, her pleading eyes begged Amy to give her the release she desperately craved, the one she had so explicitly asked for. A smile tugged at the edges of Amy's mouth, her green eyes locked on the deep ocean blue ones below, snaking her fingers up the inside of Laura's thigh, getting closer and closer, she could feel Laura's back arching trying to get closer to Amy's fingers, pulling against Amy's grip. But she wasn't going to give in that easy, she was in control, and Laura was at her mercy.

"Please," Laura whimpered. She could barely wait any longer; it was almost painful how much she desired the woman on top of her to just touch her. She had never been quite so beholden to others before, this wasn't something she was used to. Laura would have never called herself submissive in bed, but the way Amy again had her pinned and begging was unlocking something deep within her.

"When I'm ready, princess," Amy replied lazily as if she had all the time in the world, she moved her head down to graze her teeth across the exposed flesh of Laura's breasts. The reaction was exactly as she hoped, a moan escaped Laura's mouth as she squirmed against Amy. She continued to leave her hand at the very top of Laura's inner thigh, giving just enough pressure to make sure Laura couldn't forget about it. Her thumb almost touched Laura's clit.

"Please. Amy. Please fuck me," Laura begged, no shame in her voice, just pure unbridled need.

"Oh, you want me to fuck you? Well if that's what you want," Amy almost sang, her voice slow and low; in one fluid motion she moved her hand off Laura's thigh and plunged two fingers straight into her.

Laura let out a high pitched gasp as she pushed her hips forward trying to take in all of Amy at once. This. This is what she wanted and she couldn't get it fast enough, the weight of Amy on top of her, the pull of Amy at her wrists somewhere above her head and the primal need to have her inside her. However, much to her dismay she was quickly discovering, Amy had other plans. The smirk across Amy's face was unmissable and undeniably sexy as hell, she knew exactly what she was doing and Laura was powerless to stop her.

Slowly, Amy pulled her fingers back out of Laura, making sure she could feel every single movement in the woman's body as she slowly and deliberately moved her fingers out millimeter by millimeter. She let her fingers hover over Laura's opening, testing her, teasing her. The wetness now coating her fingers made Amy's mouth water, she wanted to taste Laura again – but she had other ideas first.

"Is that what you wanted?" Amy growled in Laura's ear. She could feel the heat radiating off her; she was enjoying this, possibly too much, acutely aware of her own desire. Watching this confident woman lie here and beg for her was more erotic than she could ever have imagined. Laura let out a small whimper, she couldn't even make the words form in her mouth, but this was all the confirmation Amy needed to slowly push her way back inside Laura's dripping wet center. As she moved her fingers inside, Amy added a little twist, adding a new layer of pleasure that rocked across Laura's body. Her back arched and eyes rolled back in response as she pulled against Amy's hand still pinning her down.

"Don't you dare even think about coming yet, " Amy purred into Laura's ear, it wasn't a question, it was a command. Causing her eyes to snap back open and search for the green pools, a look of panic across her face – there was no way she could stop herself even if she tried. Laura's body was almost vibrating with need, suspended in the need for more – for it faster, but also for this to last forever – she could barely hold it together. Looking up at Amy, it was clear she knew what this was doing to her, the dominating confidence just added more layers of want that made her head spin. The feeling of powerlessness she had in the moment was undoing her, that thought just pushed her closer towards the edge.

Amy continued to slowly push into and then agonizingly remove her fingers from Laura. It was so slow she thought she might lose her mind. Eyes locked together almost in a battle of will – who would give in first? Amy's desire to make Laura scream her name, or would Laura reduce herself once again to begging for more. Both of them could feel every muscle reacting, every electric impulse that rippled through Laura's body, as she tried in vain to gain more from Amy. The blue eyes dark with desire beseeched, oh how they begged for more, but Amy wasn't going to give in; she was in control and she could feel Laura getting tantalizingly close. She ran her teeth across Laura's neck, adding more sensation than the woman could bear. She wanted to watch this woman come, she was going to drink it all in and savor it. Moving herself so she was leaning even further over Laura, one hand still pinning her hands above her head as the other continued rhythmically and agonizingly slowly getting her closer and closer to climax.

Amy paused, her fingers again just millimeters inside

Laura, enough so she could feel them there, enough to make her beg for them once more.

"Please can I come?" Laura barely whispered. It was taking everything in her to get the words out when her brain was so far from in control, her mind was totally consumed with the location of Amy's hands and how they had been moving. Much to her dismay, Amy didn't move, instead keeping her eyes locked with Laura's. Amy smirked, her eyes hooded and dark but full of mischief. She moved in closer, her lips now resting next to Laura's ear, she could feel the warmth of her breath against her neck, another sensation to add to the swirling mix.

"Yes," was all she said, as she moved her fingers back inside Laura. She watched from above as Laura was taken over. The orgasm came fast and hard as Amy was pushing her self back inside, Laura's back arched, her eyes rolled back and she let out a deep moan accompanied by the most perfect "fuck," Amy had ever heard. A sound so primal it almost made Amy go weak at the knees.

Amy moved her hand off Laura's wrists releasing them, giving Laura back full movement. Instinctively she raised them to wrap around Amy's torso and pull her close; the need for Laura to feel the cool pale skin against her own was second only to the need to feel Amy's lips against hers.

Their kiss was deep and long, almost comforting while Laura got her breath back. She had never felt anything like that before, never let anyone take over quite so fully, but now wasn't the time to unpack it; she was content living in that moment with Amy. Far too soon, she felt Amy pull out of the embrace, and shift away off the bed; her disappointment at the end of the physical contact only lasted a fraction of a second. Laura's brain took a little too long to work out what was happening – she realized Amy was now on the floor between her legs just a fraction of a second before Amy's tongue made contact.

Laura's shock was audible as much as it was physical when Amy's tongue found its way to her clit, her taste was sweet and inviting as much as it was arousing. It had taken all Amy's strength to wait this long to taste her. She had spent days dreaming of this, the taste of Laura on her lips again. Amy couldn't deny her own arousal – it coiled inside her aching deep between her thighs. She knew she was wet, she knew she wanted Laura to touch her, taste her, but was she really ready to let go? Could she ignore the looming cliff edge at the back of her mind. Too many what ifs flooded her mind, momentarily she felt like she was drowning in it all. Fortunately the gasp that escaped Laura was enough to pull Amy back into the moment, her thoughts firmly focused on getting her to make that noise again.

The thoughts chased from her mind as she felt Laura getting close to climax again, her hands grabbing the sheets in balls as she clung on to the last remaining moments before her resolve and control were shattered once more. She couldn't tell what Amy was doing exactly, everything was so sensitive but the motion of her tongue as it dragged from her entrance to her clit was making the soles of her feet tingle. From this position, Amy was doing something with her fingers that Laura couldn't begin to describe, but it felt like she was stroking every nerve ending at once. The second orgasm was as all encompassing as the first, her breath caught, her world stopped as she felt the waves of pleasure crash across her body. It felt like she was falling and flying at the same time – nothing made sense and nothing mattered, the only thing she cared about was this feeling of absolute pleasure.

With her eyes closed and her ears full of the sound of

rushing blood, she only knew Amy had moved when she felt the presence of another body on the bed next to her. Amy's skin was warm as she pulled Laura into a tight embrace, her arms wrapped around her as she kissed her forehead. Laura felt so relaxed; Amy had done exactly as she promised. As she floated in a pool of pure ecstasy, Laura didn't even notice as she drifted off to sleep.

Chapter 24

Not Again

Laura awoke with a start, momentarily confused as to where she was, the unfamiliar sheets warm against her naked flesh. She sat up and noticed the blanket that had been laid over her while she was asleep, carefully removed from the other unused bed and placed over her. The hotel room was bathed in dull gray light, the last of the daylight fading from behind the blackout curtains. A smile crept across her face as she looked at the chair and her clothes neatly folded on top. The smile quickly faded when she noticed Amy was nowhere to be seen – in fact there was no trace of the woman at all. It was as if she had never been there.

A heaviness started to form in her stomach as she got out of the warm bed and looked around the room, taking in the space for the first time. A large TV and desk sat opposite the beds with windows taking up the whole wall. It was void of personality – functional and corporate. It just added to the feeling she was alone. Flicking on the bathroom light caused her eyes to strain against the harsh white light and the cold tiles on the floor felt like walking on glass; everything was too much, her senses were still trying to wake up from such a deep sleep.

As she left the bathroom, she spotted her phone next to a scrap of paper on the desk:

Room is paid for including breakfast,
check out is at 11am.
Get some rest. x

The handwriting was long and flowing, but the message left Laura cold. She picked up her phone and moved back to the bed. She had several notifications, emails, and a few other irrelevant alerts from social accounts, but nothing from Amy. How long had she stayed while Laura slept before she snuck out? Why had she left? They hadn't discussed staying the night, but it was a bit of an assumption – why else would Amy have booked a hotel? Thinking back, Amy had said very little. They hadn't talked about anything – no small talk, not even pleasantries in the elevator ride to the room. Laura blushed at the memory of the activities they had engaged in. If she had had the energy her body would have given a more physical reaction – but it was still recovering.

Laura opened the messenger app, thumb hovering over the chat with Amy. She wanted to say something. But what? A flirty message about the sex they had shared? Maybe a thank you? No. You can't thank someone via text for making you feel like that, for doing those things to you the same way you might thank a mechanic for servicing your car. Laura threw her phone down next to her on the bed. An unexpected whirlwind of emotions rising in her chest. She felt used, used by Amy. But then she hadn't been used, in fact, it was firmly the other way round. Again.

Yet again Amy hadn't sought anything physical from their interaction. Didn't she want Laura to touch her? To feel even a fraction of the satisfaction she kept giving her? Laura could feel herself starting to get upset; tears pricked at the edges of her eyes. Refusing to be upset that she had had the best orgasm of her life, Laura opted to feel the second strongest emotion – anger. This wasn't dating, they were not dating, but they clearly were more than a hook-up, you don't fuck someone like that in a random hook-up, it takes trust – trust Laura thought she had in Amy. Worst of all, the only thing that was running through her head was Zoey's comments. Was she really falling for Amy? Could she fall for someone who had remained so distant and aloof? But how could she forget about Amy when she made her feel like that? So completely undone, vulnerable and content.

She flopped back on the bed, pulled the pillow over her face and screamed.

Chapter 25

One Week Since You Left Me

The wind was cold against Amy's cheek. Spring was a long way off, the weather could still chill you to the core given half the chance. She pulled the zipper up on her jacket, offering her a little more warmth from the cold. She regretted leaving her gloves at home, but she had been drawn into a false promise by the clear blue sky.

The weight of her phone rested in her back pocket, occasionally bumped by her satchel, each time a reminder that she hadn't heard from Laura since she had fallen asleep in her arms at the hotel. The way Laura looked curled up in her arms was adorable; even the thought of it made Amy break out in a stupid grin. But it had been a week and Amy had had nothing from her.

It's not that she didn't want to text, she just wasn't sure what to say. It had been such a long time since she had been in this kind of situation, and the rules had changed over the years. Internet dating came with a whole new set of do's and don'ts. She wasn't in her early twenties any more; she wasn't sure how to navigate these waters. But then she hadn't met Laura online; they had met in a club, something even more foreign to Amy. Maybe their connection had come to its natural end, no animosity or upset, just people exploring their physical connection and moving on. It had been made clear to Amy that Laura wasn't looking for more than some fun; the way she had approached Amy in the club and then taken someone else home reinforced that. Laura had been lonely over the holidays and had an opportunity to enjoy her home without her housemates. Amy had been the companion of choice. Then when she was stressed, she reached out to Amy. It was all perfectly logical.

Except Amy didn't feel like that. Yes, there was a physical connection; it was undeniable, no one had made her feel like that in, well, ever. But there was something else, bubbling away in her heart. It was deeper than just the sex and that scared her.

Her mind drifted to places she never let go – past relationships; back to school and the feelings of first love, first heartbreak. It was unlikely that Claire and Amy would ever see each other again – not after the way it ended; as an adult she knew that. At fourteen, they were barely equipped to have a relationship when they were at the same school – let alone one forced to exist across several hundred miles, without the aid of modern smartphones and twenty-four hour internet access. There was no hope for them. She has no resentment for the girl who long ago broke her heart –it was no more Claire's fault things ended the way they did than it was Amy's.

She couldn't lie to herself, the reason she didn't let people get close was because she was worried they would leave. Sure she had had long relationships before; she dated Sophie for several years at the start of university, Jo had lasted for almost two full years and the same for Kate, all lasting long enough to make tight connections and bonds – none close enough to hurt her. They never lived together, Amy never shared too much of herself, and she intentionally kept them at a distance so they didn't need to know too much. They had been relationships full of fun and love, but she always kept a little of herself back, just in case. A way to protect herself from the heartbreaking realization they couldn't cope with who Amy was. In between there had been a few situations, a few one night stands. Several times, Amy and the other person hadn't been on the same page. A wave of shame rippled across Amy as she thought about some of the women she had unintentionally led on.

The beeping of the crossing jumped Amy away from her thoughts, which was probably a good thing – she was dangerously close to letting those forbidden memories rise up to the forefront of her mind, and she couldn't afford to let them. The cliff edge that sat permanently at the back of her mind, deep dark and all consuming – falling off it would be a disaster. She frowned at herself for not paying attention to where her mind was wandering and for nearly missing the University building. She planned to lose today in the lab; there was something soothing about the space, data and equipment, you always knew where things were going – or at least that was the theory.

She pushed the door open to the building and was greeted with a blast of warm dry air; it was enough to make your head spin from the sudden change in climate. Moving towards the stairs, she smiled at security on the desk. Todd was engrossed in his book, something on nutrition and the mind, if she remembered correctly from their conversation earlier in the week. She threw a lazy wave over at him, not expecting him to acknowledge it – she made a mental note to see him for a coffee later. His company had been quite welcome over the Christmas break, and they had definitely transcended to a new level of friendship.

Walking towards the lab, Amy noticed Jamie was already in; he was bustling about in a world of his own. Amy groaned. He was going to ask questions, small ones but pointed like a needle. She could hear it now: 'You been texting Laura much?' He had smirked at her last weekend as she had practically run out of the lab, and relentlessly pushed her for details after. She had kept it to herself, saying they had met up again but left it at that. Every day since he had asked if they had plans to meet up again, every time Amy brushed them off – but it was getting harder to deflect.

Amy knew she was a terrible liar. She could cope with half truths but a full lie always seemed to fall apart before anyone believed her. OK, she thought to herself, she just needed a half truth to survive the day with Jamie – give him just enough information to stave off further questions. With a spark of an idea, she pulled out her phone. She couldn't take it in the lab anyway, but she could text Laura now and put it in the locker. There was no way for him to see the message or even know if there had been a reply. It was a good cover.

Her finger froze over the conversation with Laura. It had been days and they had said nothing to each other. Maybe it had been a hook-up, a casual thing that Amy was about to make really awkward. Maybe the reason Laura had not been in contact is she had found someone else to occupy her bed, and her time. Amy was surprised by the pang of sadness in her chest when she realized that Laura may have moved on. She took a deep breath, trying to think logically. Yes they hooked up but they had been talking for weeks before that, they were friends. Friends could text. Before she lost her nerve she opened the message and typed out a quick casual message before throwing her phone in the locker and walking into the lab.

Amy: How you doing?

Chapter 26

Really F R I E N D S

Laura stared at her phone completely dumbfounded. Nothing. Nothing for almost a week and then just as she had started to let the idea of Amy go, she gets a text, not just any text but a crappy nineties sitcom reference?!

She was mad at herself for the involuntary excitement she felt when she saw she had a message from Amy, the little flutter in her heart and her complete inability to focus on anything as soon as she noticed it was, in short, infuriating. But she was even more mad at Amy. She felt a blush creep across her neck and cheeks. This was ridiculous; how had she got so hung up on a woman she had slept with a handful of times? How could she be so hung up on this woman who left her alone in a hotel? How could she be so hung up on someone who didn't text for nearly a week?

"You ok, Laura?" Jason asked gingerly from across the desk. She had been irritable all week, and more than once bitten his head off over nothing. Now they were well into the new project things had gotten much smoother, yet her mood had darkened every day this week.

"Yeah, I'm fine," she snapped. Realizing her annoyance didn't need to be taken out on Jason, she looked up and sent him a smile. "But I think I am going to work from home the rest of the day." Laura knew she wasn't going to get any more work done sat at her desk in the office; in fact she had barely got anything done at all this week. Another reason to be frustrated. Sex was normally the thing that got her out of a funk, not put her in one. Sex was uncomplicated and fun. She couldn't lie to herself any more – sex with Amy was always fun but it was never uncomplicated.

"Ok yeah no worries, let me know if you need anything, or want to talk or – " Laura put her hand up to stop Jason. He was sweet and he had picked up there was something going on; he was just being a decent human being and friend.

"Thank you, but I really am fine. Have a good weekend," Laura reassured him as she packed her things away into her bag, threw it over her shoulder and left the office.

Laura was staring at her phone again, at Amy's message. On the ride home she had written, re-written and deleted so many replies in her head, running the whole spectrum of emotions from a simple easy-going response to an almost essay about her feelings and what Amy did to her, to just a 'fuck you'. Yet she couldn't bring herself to send any of them. She prized herself on being good with people, knowing how they liked to be treated, spoken to and yeah, even fucked. Yet this woman remained an enigma, a frustrating enigma. Who every time Laura thought she had her figured out, changed again.

As she continued to stare at her phone another notification popped up. It was Emily; she was checking they were still on for tonight. A night out had felt like a good idea earlier in the week: a club, a girl, a chance to forget the hotel, and she would feel much better again. Just like getting back on the horse. She was letting herself get hung up on this one person – that wasn't her style, she liked her life and the way she lived it. She needed to get back to it.

Emily: 10pm at mine or are you meeting me at the bar?

Laura: I'll meet you at the bar,I need to catch up on some work before I can come play.

Even typing the words felt disingenuous. Never had she been less interested in going out as she was tonight. Laura spent the rest of the ride on the metro looking at Amy's message again. She forced herself to put the phone away once she was home. If she couldn't find the words to reply, then she needed to stop staring at the message like a desperate schoolgirl. Laura made the resolve to finish her work, get ready, have a great night out with friends – it was exactly what she needed to do.

The bar was crowded: there was a guest DJ on and they had drawn a slew of new faces into the bar. It was the same one they had come to before Christmas. Ali was still working with the marketing team and it was still one of the hottest places in the city. Laura was starting to feel better – the two cocktails had helped with that – but really it was because she was surrounded by people that she loved. Her friends always knew how to lift her up. Even if she hadn't shared anything with Emily, just being around her was enough to lift her mood – it had been that way since they were kids. If

Emily had picked up on anything off about Laura's mood, she had kept it to herself. But then what would she pick up on – Laura hadn't been very forthcoming on the details of last weekend, opting to let everyone think she had had a very normal night of hot sex with a hot woman, then refused to go into any details. If they had met up before the bar, Emily might have asked how it went, and Laura was not ready to share any details yet.

As they swayed along to the music on the dance floor, Laura caught someone's eye. They had been checking each other out for the last thirty minutes or so, both playing chicken as to who would make the first move. They were cute, shaggy blue hair in a rough bob with several piercings across their face; tattoos sprawled up their arms and disappeared into their tight white t-shirt. It was definitely a look Laura could get behind. She gave them a very obvious look up and down, knowing they were watching, before she turned back to Emily. The look had its desired effect and less than a minute later, they stood next to Laura.

"Hey, you're stunning, Do you have a name, or can I just call you 'mine'?" They had a faint accent, one that was hard to make out in the loud club, and this was a cheesy line if Laura had ever heard one, but still it made her smile.

"It's Laura, and what do I call you?" Laura put out her hand, which they took in a soft handshake.

"I'm Alex. Can I get you a drink?" They let Laura's hand go and motioned towards the bar.

"I'll have a sex on the beach, please and thank you." Laura flashed one of her winning smiles as Alex walked off to the bar. She turned round and looked at Emily who rolled her eyes and giggled.

"How do you make it look so easy?" she joked as she shook her head at her best friend. She had seen this hundreds of times over the years and already knew where this was heading.

Several hours, and several more drinks later, Alex and Laura were heading back to Alex's hotel room. As Laura suspected Alex had come to the city to see the DJ; they were from Melbourne and had been traveling across the world for the last six months. This was all music to Laura's ears, a nice simple easy hook-up that would end as quickly as it started. Just the reset she needed.

Walking into the hotel room, Laura couldn't help but think back to the hotel room she was in last weekend – it was nothing like this. This was designed for travelers on a budget. She hadn't given much thought to the hotel Amy booked. It had been an upmarket chain hotel. She wondered why Amy had picked it; it hadn't been the closest to their location, and definitely didn't have any personality. Laura tried to push any thoughts of Amy from her mind. There was a beautiful person here in front of her, she was going to have a good time with them, then head home. Back to how it should be, how she liked it.

Alex gestured for Laura to come and sit on the bed with them. She obliged and made her first move. She placed a deep kiss on Alex's lips; they reciprocated, tongue tracing her lower lip and Laura instinctively opened her mouth to receive it. This was sexy, this felt good – so why didn't she feel the same surge of excitement that came from kissing Amy? Why was she comparing these beautiful lips to Amy's? Why was she closing her eyes and picturing Amy kissing her?

She tried again to push Amy from her mind, focusing on the sexy tattooed person in front of her, the one she was about to have fun with, the one she could leave in the morning with no sense of guilt.

Clothes started to come off, hands began to explore, this was fun – Laura was having fun, but why wasn't it living up to past experiences? Maybe it was down to the fact Alex had instigated this? Laura was normally the one taking the lead, it was only really Amy that had ever turned the status quo on its head. Alex was talented with their fingers – but it wasn't hitting the spot, falling short of scratching the itch. Laura decided to take a more active role, pushing herself into a more familiar dominant space – this was more like it, this was how it normally went – this way she wasn't reminded of Amy.

Chapter 27

Breakfast

It was six thirty in the morning, and the air was colder than it had been in the middle of the night. The added chill from the wind and impenetrable darkness was haunting. She had a good time last night. They had fooled around and everyone was satisfied, physically anyway. After the activities had come to a natural end and Alex said she could stay the night rather than trying to get an Uber at silly AM, they had both settled respectfully separate in the bed. Laura had laid awake staring at the ceiling, completely unable to remove Amy from her mind, replaying every touch and breath they had shared in a different hotel room. She hadn't intended to be up and out so early, but she was getting more and more frustrated lying there, so she gathered her things and headed out.

Laura braced herself against the wind as she walked the block to the metro station. Her Saturday was looking pretty clear, she really needed to catch up on some work but that could be done from the comfort of her bed while watching nothing on Netflix. If no one had dibs on the kitchen she could even do some proper cooking. She missed cooking but with four other housemates there was not always the space or the time. Plus Zoey used the kitchen for studying a lot of the time, which made it harder to cook around her – not that it was her fault: she shared a room with Ali and there definitely wasn't space in there for exam prep.

As she stood on the platform daydreaming about cooking in her apartment, Laura didn't notice a familiar figure walking along the platform, the red hair tucked away in a scarf and hoodie, the sky still too dark to spot the familiar green jacket.

"How was breakfast?" A voice emerged from behind Laura. It was so unexpected it made her jump; she had been lost in her own world of thought.

"Huh?" She spun round to see Amy. She looked amazing in her jacket and hoodie – such an effortlessly casual look, to match the casual question. Laura stared at her, her brain trying to work out what was going on, while her heart tried to calm itself down.

"At the hotel. How was breakfast?" Amy offered with a shy sheepish smile as she rubbed the back of her head, her eyes cast down to the floor. This was enough for Laura's blood to boil and for her to see red. How could Amy possibly be this casual and relaxed about everything? It was like she didn't consider her feelings at all.

"Really? Really?! That's what you are going to ask me, the first thing you are going to ask me after you walked out on me asleep in bed is how was fucking breakfast?!" she spat at Amy, leaning in, trying not to cause any unwanted attention at the very public metro station that was filling up with early morning commuters. "Actually that's a lie! The first thing you say to me is a *Friends'* reference! And not even a good one!" Laura threw her hands in the air with exasperation, before turning back around, refusing to look at Amy any longer.

Now it was Amy's turn to look confused. She was already regretting going and talking to Laura after spending the last five minutes agonizing over why she was in this part of the city, she knew she didn't live around here. But Amy found herself being pulled towards the woman, desperate to be in her orbit. Confusion and regret didn't sit well with her; her stomach was starting to tie itself in knots, she thought she had been friendly by texting. It wasn't as if Laura had texted her either. Of all the things she could have said, none of them came to her lips. Instead, she focused on the part that she could make sense of.

"I... uh... I actually have never seen *Friends*." Amy smiled and looked at the back of Laura's head, her dark chocolate hair slightly disheveled, as it had looked that morning she had found Amy in her kitchen – Amy tried not to examine why Laura had bed hair. In fact, the more she looked at Laura, the more she realized the woman was probably on her way home after last night. Her clothes were a little too dressy for work with a crumpled edge highlighting they had not come straight off a hanger. Finally Amy noticed she looked cold, wearing only a jacket against the January chill. Amy felt a small pang of jealousy in her stomach, one that she had no business feeling. Laura turned back around, her lips tantalizingly close to Amy's, her blue eyes shone under the dark street lights. She looked mad as hell, which was way sexier than it should be.

"Of course you haven't." Laura threw her hands in the air and turned away again. She couldn't keep looking into those earthy green eyes. They made her want to forgive, they made her want to get to know her better, like they still held all the secrets and promises she could ever want. She sighed, trying to compose herself. "I didn't have breakfast." She took the opportunity to steal a look at Amy's face – it gave nothing away, the confusion and hurt hidden behind a well crafted mask.

"That's cool. I wasn't sure what to do. It's not a situation I have been in before." Amy felt her cheeks flush at the realization she had probably been too forward in getting breakfast for Laura in the first place – she wasn't even sure the woman had stayed the night.

"Oh, and you think it's a situation I am in all the time, do you?" Laura snapped angrily without thinking. She knew that's not what Amy meant, but it had felt momentarily good to see the hurt in her eyes before she managed to hide it. Instantly the guilt washed over her.

Both women stood and stared at each other for a moment, neither one prepared to back down. The metro rattled into the station and people started to file out the doors. This was enough to break Amy's stare, she took a deep breath.

"Are you going to get on that?" The words came out far colder than she had wanted, so she hastily added, "or would you actually like to come for breakfast with me?"

Laura was yet again taken back, unable to keep her mouth closed she let her jaw slack, her lips parted. Amy couldn't help but be drawn to them. Now this woman wanted breakfast, *now*?! Laura wasn't sure she was in the right frame of mind to sit anywhere with Amy – so many conflicting emotions flowed through her – but she was also aware that if she turned this opportunity down, she might not get another. "Fine," she muttered as she crossed her arms in mock defiance.

"Great." Amy beamed at her, either totally unaware or

totally ignoring the passive aggressive tone. "There is a coffee shop down here that's pretty quiet this time of day."

Amy was a few paces ahead of Laura as she led her to one of the dozens of independent coffee houses that littered this part of the city. She wasn't sure why she was doing this. It was clear Laura was pissed off with her for something – and it was also clear she was on her way home from what Amy assumed was a fun night out. She didn't like the way she was feeling about Laura sleeping with others: Amy had no business thinking about it, she had even less business getting upset about it. They were not exclusive, in fact they weren't anything.

Was she doing this to punish herself for not texting sooner? For agonizing over the whole thing for far too long? No, she thought to herself, the reason she was doing this was because she really liked this woman and wanted to make the miscommunication right between them. It's not like Amy wasn't used to miscommunication; it was like she spoke a different language and spent her whole life translating her words for others. Sometimes that didn't always work – this was one of those times. But if she was being really honest with herself, she was hoping this would lead to more intimate moments between them, but she would settle for being friends. Anything to keep Laura in her life.

Once they had their coffee orders and set themselves in a small booth at the back of the shop, the silence between them went from acceptable to awkward in the blink of an eye. It has been a quiet walk from the metro to the coffee shop, but it hadn't felt hostile until they were sitting here opposite each other. Amy began fiddling with the edge of her mug, anxiety building inside her chest, a band starting to tighten. This really had been a bad idea. But before she could get too lost in her thoughts – Laura ripped the bandaid off.

"Do you even like me, Amy?" Laura said in a matter-of-fact way, without even looking up from her own cup.

"Yeah, I mean obviously, I think you're great and we get on really well and –" Amy was cut off by Laura raising a hand and looking her dead in the eyes. The depths of the blue were dangerous like the sea. If she fell in, Amy knew she might drown.

"No, Amy, I mean do you *like* me, in the way you might like someone you want to date, or at the very least want to fuck?" Laura started, trying to keep all the emotion out of her voice as she watched the redhead blush. She reminded herself that however cute she looked blushing, now was not the time to be distracted by it.

"Yes, again, I thought that was kinda obvious," Amy said back, with a little bite to her words that Laura had not expected. For the first time she took her eyes off the coffee mug and looked at Laura directly. "We have shagged, remember?" she added when Laura raised her head and they locked eyes.

"Then, then why won't you let me touch you?" Laura finally asked, all the malice out of her voice. She almost sounded hurt. "I mean if that's not what you want, then why not just tell me?"

Amy's eyes went wide and all the color left her face. This was getting close to things she didn't like to talk about, and Laura had been so – direct about it. People didn't just ask these sorts of questions. "Most people don't complain when they are the center of my attention." Her voice was still ice cold. She could feel her defenses going up by the second. The band around her chest contracted instinctively.

"That might be fine for most people," Laura snapped back, struggling to keep her emotions under control. She didn't want to think about why she was so hurt by Amy's reaction. "You made me feel used, especially when I woke up alone in the hotel." A long pause fell over them.

Amy continued to look like the blood had left her body, brilliant green eyes wide, her chest rising and falling in shallow breaths. "I am sorry you felt used; that was not my intention." Amy tried to soften her voice. She was sorry that she had caused Laura to feel this way; it did explain the week of radio silence. "I thought you would enjoy the peace and quiet, after you had been complaining about your housemates all day. And you look so peaceful, asleep in bed."

"I think I would have enjoyed it more if you had stayed." Laura was surprised at her own words, Since when had she been this honest with someone about her feelings? Especially someone she wasn't in a relationship with.

Another suffocating silence settled over them like a thick blanket. They were saved when Laura's phone rang. She went to get the phone out of her pocket, seeing the name and decided it best to answer. "Hi Al, all ok?" Laura tried to keep her voice neutral.

Amy only had Laura's side of the conversation to go on, and while she tried not to listen, it was impossible given how close they were sat. Based on her expression, Amy assumed Ali was checking in to see where Laura was, giving more evidence to the idea that Laura had been at someone's place last night. Amy hated how that made her feel but before her thoughts could take over Laura ended the call.

"Sorry about that – Ali was worried that I hadn't checked in and I hadn't been home last night," Laura trailed off, realizing that Amy probably already worked that out.

"Don't worry about it, safety first." Amy gave a weak smile. Releasing a breath she didn't realize she had been holding. "I am sorry I hurt your feelings, I didn't mean to." Feeling some of the tension in her chest evaporate, she took the opportunity to look at Laura. Her perfect blue eyes were full of emotion.

"Amy, I think I want to see where this goes between us. I think it's clear we like each other and have a connection. I think I want to explore that." Laura's words tumbled out of her mouth all at once. Then she let them hang in the air, filling the space between them.

"Yeah, I think I would like that too," Amy said back with a half smile.

"But I think you need to be honest with me, and with yourself," Laura continued, ignoring the carefree smile Amy had shot her – a smile that if she looked at for more than a fraction of a second would distract her from everything "If this is something you don't think you can do, you need to tell me. I don't want a repeat of the hotel."

"Really?" Amy shot her a coy look. "Nothing about that you want to repeat, princess?"

Laura felt a jolt run up her spine. If it hadn't felt so good, and hadn't alluded to such promise, she could have been angry at the way Amy changed the tone so fast. She wasn't sure there was anyone in the world that could give her such a whiplash of emotions.

"Well, there are somethings I definitely want to repeat," Laura said in a hushed tone. Taking a moment to clear her head of the images, she pressed on. "But I don't want any more walking out without goodbyes, and I don't want sex to be so one-sided. Unless that is truly what you want."

"It's not..." Amy paused. She felt the air around her get thick, her skin erupt in flames making everything tight, the band constrict like a snake coiled around her chest. "It's not that I don't want you to. It's... it's... complicated ok?" Amy's mind was racing, the black tendrils of unwanted memories were circling at the edges of her mind, threatening to pull her under. This is why she had stayed single for so many years. This is why she had struggled to let people close. It's not like she hadn't been on dates, or that she hadn't had interest from others, but every time they got too close, she ran. She always ran.

"Hey, you don't have to tell me right now," Laura said soothingly as she watched the light switch off in Amy's eyes, instantly replaced by a haunted look, her shoulders slumped. The anxiety, no, the fear, was pouring off her in waves so strong she could almost feel them crashing over her. Laura reached over to touch Amy's hand. Amy jumped at the contact, almost knocking over the empty mug in front of her.

"I... I... I think. I think I need to go," Amy stammered as she moved up from the table, unable to look at Laura. She didn't want to see how she was looking at her, from experience it was going to be confusion, sympathy or anger – and she didn't like the idea of any of those right now. "Thanks for the coffee."

And with that Amy was gone, leaving Laura confused at how things yet again had changed so quickly. She was struggling to put the woman who had just fled the coffee shop and the one that had been so confident and in charge in the hotel together. She swirled the remaining contents of her drink staring intensely at the dregs coating the bottom of the mug rather than the now empty seat across her. It would have been easy to just delete Amy's number and move on.

That would be the sensible thing to do. But there was something about her, something Laura couldn't shake off. Something that felt worth the risk of heartbreak.

She was getting dangerously close to heartbreak.

Chapter 28

Solid Floors

Amy got several blocks over before she stopped to work out if she was even going in the right direction. The band in her chest was making it hard to breathe; the cold air was coming in ragged and sharp. She looked round, realizing she had instinctively headed home rather than to the University. She didn't think she could face anyone right now. She wanted to hide in her own apartment where it was safe. Leaning against the cold brick wall of the building next to her, she composed her thoughts. Taking her phone out of her bag, she sent a swift message to Jamie and headed for home.

Amy: Hi, I am not feeling well today and don't think I can make it to the lab.

Can you check on samples A1 - C42 and record the readings for me? I should be back tomorrow

Jamie: Sure thing! Is everything ok?

I can pop over later and bring you anything you need.

Amy: Thank you but I think I just need to go back to bed.

See you tomorrow

Sliding her phone back in her pocket, she continued towards the safety of her quiet, empty home, all the while wishing she was wrapped in Laura's arms. She didn't know why, but she felt like the woman could make her feel safe. The thought caused her heart to race even more.

Hours later, she was still lying on the floor. Being this close to the floor made her feel anchored; it was a trick she learned as a child and had held onto over the years.

The last three weeks had been a whirlwind of amazement and sheer terror. Laura was worryingly easy to be around; it didn't matter what Amy did, she felt like a moth caught in the flame. She had opted not to think about anything. She didn't want to address the pangs of jealousy she felt the very first night they met or the twinges of excitement she felt whenever her phone lit up with a message from the dark-haired beauty.

The embarrassment she felt for misreading things and leaving the first night felt like it was going to swallow her up, only to be overtaken by the consuming embarrassment she felt for leaving after a few restless hours the following night.

Then at the hotel, Amy really thought she was doing the right thing, giving Laura a night she so desperately needed away from her flat, fulfilling her desires as instructed. All she could see was how peaceful Laura looked asleep in the hotel bed; how good it felt to have her in her arms. Sure, she had known that leaving her asleep in the hotel bed wasn't the best idea, but she was so warm and comforting, there was a risk she would fall asleep right there with her. Amy couldn't risk the nightmares again. But then why had she stupidly texted Laura, when really she should have deleted her number? Yeah, she would have been the whispered gossip for a few weeks before it all blew over, but it's not like that hadn't happened before.

All the thoughts and emotions swam around in Amy's head, making her feel sick. She so desperately wanted to feel the embrace of Laura again. Even thinking about it, Amy could feel the crushing pain in her chest grow, constricting her breath, like an anvil lying on her chest, letting gravity do all the work. The more she thought, the more her mind spiraled. She didn't want these feelings; she didn't want to hurt Laura. She had been stupid in letting things go this far. Why had she intervened on the roof that night? Why had she texted Laura? Why had she fucked her again and again?

"Hey, you ok in there?" A voice from the door sliced through her, like an ice cold knife. It paralyzed her, disconnecting her brain and her lungs. The thoughts swirled and grew heavy, pulling the cliff edge closer. Even lying on the solid cold floor the world started to spin – her breath became short and sharp – she couldn't get the air into her lungs.

"Amy, open the door or I'll use my key, but either way I am coming in." The voice was muffled behind the front door, but it was unmistakably Jamie's. Amy knew he would be inside her flat in a matter of moments and all he was going to see was her pathetically lying on the floor, unable to breathe. She screwed her eyes shut, begging her lungs to work, but the band just got tighter and tighter.

What felt like an age later, a strong and steady hand was wrapped around her fingers interlaced with theirs. Another hand resting on her chest. "Amy, you need to calm down ok," Jamie said soothingly, but his voice was tinged with panic. Amy was breathing, short shallow raspy breaths. He had only ever seen her like this a couple of times and every time it scared him. "Amy, you need to breathe, a nice deep breath ok?"

The sound of his voice rocketed her back to reality; everything became sharp as a pin, where only moments before it was blurry black nothingness. "Come on, Amy, I know you can do it." Jamie applied a little pressure to her chest. The weight gave her something to focus on. Slowly but surely, it felt like the anvil was being lifted from her chest.

Fifteen minutes passed; Amy looked numbly at the ceiling, Jamie still holding her hand and applying a little pressure to her chest. Even though he was directly over her, she avoided his eye contact, instead starting out into the middle distance. All thoughts had left her head, now it was just a vast expanse of exhaustion and emotional hangover.

"You want to tell me what happened, kiddo?" Jamie asked, looking down at Amy, relieved that she was over her panic attack, her pale skin and wide haunting eyes a lingering effect that would fade with time.

"Clearly not," Amy pouted back. She knew he would get the answer out of her in the end, he always did. But right this second she didn't have it in her.

"Ok, but you are going to tell me what happened," he replied soothingly, moving his hand off Amy's chest and repositioning himself so he was lying on the floor next to her, still holding her hand as if she was a balloon that might fly away. "Or do I need to start guessing?" he teased gently, as Amy remained defiantly silent. "Last chance, Amy, or I start guessing."

"Fine." Amy sat up. As everything lurched to the left, she slowly moved back down to the floor, regaining her balance once she was flat to the ground again. "I lied yesterday. I haven't been texting Laura all week. I texted her just before I walked in the lab – but I hadn't spoken to her in days, ever since I fucked her in a hotel room and left while she was asleep." The words came tumbling out. Now that she has started the story, she needed to get it all out. "Then she was heading home after clearly fucking someone else last night and I walked up to her and sort of asked how she was." Amy began erratically tapping her fingers on the floor, the speed increasing to match her breathing as the words tumbled out faster and faster. "But then she was mad and we went and got coffee and I think she likes me likes me but then she said I needed to be honest and I ran away." Amy's chest was getting tight again. She forced down another panic attack. Instinctively Jamie squeezed her hand.

"Ah, I see your intimacy issues have reached a middle," he said with what he hoped was playful reassurance. "And I take it she knows nothing and is probably very confused."

"Probably," Amy muttered. "And she's never going to talk to me again."

"I think you're wrong." Jamie nudged Amy's shoulder with his. "I think she really likes you, and from what I have seen – you look adorable together." Turning his head to look at Amy directly he added, "And, you know, it wouldn't be that awful to let someone in once in a while. You can't punish yourself forever, you know?"

Amy continued to look up at the ceiling, tears forming in her eyes. Maybe Jamie was right, maybe it was time to let someone in – Laura had certainly said she wanted to know what was going on – there was a chance she meant it too. Amy wasn't sure she could ever be vulnerable with anyone again. Jamie knew things about her that no one else did, things that made her put up walls and defenses. She had told Jamie, but that was different.

Jamie shifted off the floor to go and get Amy some water. He noticed her phone sitting on the counter. It was flashing away to itself. Tapping the screen he could see half a dozen messages and a missed call, all from one contact: 'Laura'. Jamie smiled. It was clear that Laura was as into Amy as Amy was into her, if only Amy could for once let someone in she might have a chance.

"Amy, would you like me to read all these messages?" Jamie called over to where Amy was still lying on the floor. He knew she would find these messages both overwhelming and embarrassing to address herself, and if he could alleviate that a little for his best friend he would. "The fact you haven't screamed at me not to, means you want me to!" he sang over his shoulder to Amy on the floor, as he expertly swiped in her passcode and opened the messages.

After a few moments of reading, Jamie smiled to himself. "Well, kiddo, do you want the good news or the bad news?" He headed over to the living room, phone and drink in hand and set them on the table within her reach. "Because the good news is she is mad at you but not ignoring you."

"That doesn't sound like good news." Amy looked over at Jamie, who stood beaming down at her.

Jamie laughed. "Well the bad news – for you – she was mad at you." He sat on the small sofa stretching his legs out, knowing full well this would get Amy up off the floor – and he was right.

Amy frowned, stood up and went to pick up her phone and the water. He could see her scrolling and reading the messages. Her face was expressionless.

Laura: Remember about 2 minutes before you walked out without saying anything we had just agreed to stop doing that?

Laura: What the fuck Amy? What the fuck?!

Laura: Sorry that was unfair. Please let me know you are ok.

Laura: Ok it's been several hours and you haven't even read my messages, if you don't in the next 10 minutes I am going to start calling people.

Laura: Missed Call

Laura: Missed Call

Laura: Last chance Amy!

Laura: Missed Call

Laura: Why has no one seen you in days? Why are you not at the lab? Jamie is a really good liar and said you were sick. You didn't look sick this morning so I assume you lied to him.

Laura: I swear to god Amy! if you go missing and I have to explain this WHOLE messy situation to the police no one is going to believe me! They are going to accuse me of murder or something! I am not going to jail for you Amy! Jamie says he is going to go to your place and see if you are there, which made me realize I have no idea where you live... Jamie said he is going to let me know if he finds you.

Laura: Well Jamie informs me you are in fact ok and at home. I am still mad at you for going MIA again! but I am glad you are safe. Jamie also said I should tell you how I feel. So here goes...

Laura: I have been thinking about you basically non stop since I first met you, that night on the roof when without even knowing who I was you came to my rescue, that isn't something you forget. I just wish I understood you. One minute you are acting all shy and adorable as you fail to pick up on the most basic flirting then the next you are giving me the most amazing orgasm with all this swagger and energy that makes me go weak at the knees. But then you run out on me like a one night stand, but then you take time to get to know me and we text non stop for days. You are just a box of contradictions and I wish I knew what you wanted. I told you what I wanted, I want to get to know you better. Jamie said you would be at Limelight at 8 tonight, and so will I. It can be a date, or just friends or whatever you want, just don't disappear again. Laura x

Amy stared at the message for what felt like an age. Laura's words were all there, plain to see, she wanted a date tonight – and it looked like Jamie had some explaining to do. Her eyes snapped up and looked at him sitting on the sofa, a cheerful look across his face, paying no attention to the fire burning in her eyes.

"Why the fuck did you arrange a date for me?!" she said as calmly as possible, but her rage was white hot. "Why the fuck did you tell her anything at all!" Amy started pacing up and down her small living space, still holding her phone, her knuckles going white. "Why are you even here?"

"I am here, Amy, because you scared me. You scared a lot of people today." Jamie was curt in his response. If Amy wanted to have this conversation this way, then they could have an argument about it. He knew it wouldn't make her feel better. "You told me you were sick – fine, you are allowed to lie to me if you want. But then I had a million missed calls from basically everyone in the queer Toronto phone book because Laura was trying to find you." Jamie stood up, exasperation clear in his voice. "I know you have hang ups about getting close to people. But this woman sounds like she actually cares about you – and all you have done is mess her around. Honestly, Amy, it's a dick move."

"Fuck off, Jamie, I am not messing her around." Amy's anger was boiling over, as she continued to pace across the floor. "She asked me for a hook-up that first night, I said no!"

"Fine, knight in shining armor doing the right thing for the damsel, I am sure everyone thanks you for your sacrifice that night – I know the girl Laura did take home would thank you." Jamie bowed in comic fashion. He could see that last comment stung – it cut through Amy's anger, his words getting more venomous, but Amy needed to hear it. "But I think you lose any hero points the second you start fooling around with her and leaving her in empty hotel rooms." Amy was quiet, the anger still clear on her face. "You are playing with her emotions, and that's shitty. Own it."

"I'm not playing with her emotions! We had amazing sex; we never labeled it, we never called it anything and once we were done, I left," Amy spat back.

"Maybe it's time you realized you are not actually as ok as you pretend to be. A really lovely woman who is not only stunning but also cares about you is unfathomably trying to get to know you, and you respond to her wanting to have sex with you by running away and having a panic attack on your living room floor!" Jamie locked eyes with Amy, anger written all over her face but her eyes had softened. She was thinking about what he said. "Be a better person, Amy, and stop letting past trauma ruin your future." He slowly and carefully grabbed his things and moved towards the door. This was far from the worst argument they had ever had – and what he loved about Amy was that they could fight like this, and it did nothing to affect their friendship. In fact it was better for it. "You ran away from England – that was easy – but it's time to realize you can't run away from yourself." And with that he slid out the door quietly, leaving Amy alone with her anger.

After several more minutes of pacing where she mentally called Jamie every name under the sun, Amy thumbed across her phone, still reeling from Jamie's words. He was wrong, trauma did not rule her life, she was capable of doing anything she wanted. And right now she wanted to prove to him that he was wrong.

Amy: See ou at 8. X

Chapter 29

A Real Date

Amy had never put so much effort into a date in her life. She tried to tell herself it wasnt to spite Jamie and prove a point – but it was. She picked out her outfit specifically to look good – scratchy labels and seams be damned! She could do this. She could do a normal date without her usual amount of worrying and prep. Going with the same black leather jacket from the Christmas party paired with a small white top and a long black skirt with a slit that went her upper thigh; it left nothing to the imagination. Maybe if it was summer she would have gone with heels, but in January, she relented and threw on her Doc Martens again. They went with the look – maybe making it a little more gothic, but acceptable. She would love to say it was all for Laura, but really part of it was to prove Jamie wrong. She was capable of everything he said she wasn't. He had just given her the push she needed to realize it. Standing back she admired her efforts in the mirror, she hadn't had time to put as much effort into the apartment, but she had made it presentable for company, should the need arise.

Waiting outside the bar, Amy realized she knew very little about her date tonight. Sure they had spent time together, they had talked, but not really about anything important. She knew where she worked, who she lived with etc, but beyond that she didn't know what made Laura tick. They had watched movies or pretended to watch movies at least. Most of their time together had been physical – not that she was complaining. Tonight, she was going to change that. They were going to have conversation like normal people did on normal dates. This was a chance for them to take their connection to a deeper level, both emotionally and hopefully physically, if things went well. Her mind wandered to the memories of Laura under her, begging to come, a smile spread across her face as she got lost in memories while she waited. It wasn't long before Laura appeared next to her, causing Amy to first jump and then blush. Hoping it wasn't too obvious she had been caught thinking about all the things she was going to do to the dark-haired woman later that night. Amy shot Laura a well-crafted smile and opened the door for her as they made their way inside.

Amy got the first round: a standard vodka and coke for her and a mojito for Laura. Taking a seat on the same table they had before, Amy took a second to take in the stunning sight that was Laura. She wasn't sure if she had dressed up especially or if Laura just always looked this immaculate. Her dark hair swept to one side, flowing into her lace top that hugged all the right places with a plunging neckline, giving just a hint of what was underneath, not that Amy needed to imagine.

Laura sat across from Amy, her nails absent-mindedly tapping slowly against the side of her glass, she looked expectantly over at Amy waiting for an explanation, an apology, anything. But nothing came.

Keeping her gaze focused down on her own drink, Amy could feel Laura's eyes on her, knowing that if she were to look up she would be met with the intense blue pools. She knew that Laura was expecting some sort of answer or explanation about what had happened, but she wasn't sure she was ready to give it.

More minutes passed in deafening silence. Laura had finished her drink quicker than usual but she had needed something to do to distract from her increasing frustration; she wanted to give Amy space to explain on her own terms, but she wouldn't even look her in the eye.

Anxiety flooded Amy's system, her throat constricted by all the things she wanted to say but that she just couldn't get out. Still focusing on the untouched drink in front of her, the ice now melted she caught the drops of condensation as they ran down the glass. She knew she needed to force herself to meet Laura's eyes or risk her giving up and leaving. She needed to say something, anything.

Noticing that Laura had finished her drink Amy decided to use the excuse of getting her another as a moment to gather her thoughts. Jumping up from her seat and grabbing the empty glass, she said, "let me get the next round," heading off to the bar before Laura could even offer a protest as she looked over at Amy's still full drink.

This evening was not working out the way that Laura had hoped.

The bartender handed her the drinks and she took a deep breath, mentally clicking her mask into place, a slight smirk on her face as she placed the drinks down on the table before sliding back into her seat. Finally making eye contact, she said, "I have to say Laura, I was impressed with your detective work this morning." Amy looked deep into Laura's eyes over her lashes. It might have been risky to bring it up, but she felt that Laura would enjoy the compliment.

"Not really, there are only a few universities in the city, even less with a bio lab like yours, and even without factoring in the side of the city we bumped into each other, it wasn't difficult." Laura blushed a little as she tucked a stray hair behind her ear. She wasn't sure they were ever going to address what happened this morning. "The hardest bit was I didn't know your surname. I still don't actually. I got lucky and a really nice guy called Todd was on security and recognised you from your description – he patched me through to Jamie's office and here we are." She raised her hands in triumph.

Amy looked at Laura with awe and admiration. She was smart and sexy – a deadly combination – and she found it endearing that she had gone to all that effort to see she was ok. She smiled at Laura "Love."

"Excuse me?" Laura widened her eyes at Amy.

"My last name, it's Love." Amy chuckled at the reaction.

"Really? Your actual name is Amy Love!?" Laura broke out in a smile. "I can't even tell if you are joking or not."

"I promise you, my real name is Amy Love. I spent most of my childhood hating it but I grew to like it." Amy had been teased for many things at school, from red hair to being too into books; her name was another easy thing for people to use as a weapon against her.

"That is the coolest name ever, but I can imagine kids being a little cruel about it." Laura continued to giggle. Sipping the last of her drink, she looked over to see Amy had also finished hers. "Can I get you another, Miss Love?"

"Yes, but only if you never call me that again." Amy

chuckled. As Laura got up from the table and headed to the bar.

Amy sank back in her chair. She was finally having a good time; it had been so long since she had been on a date, a real date she had forgotten how much fun they could be to find out about someone else. Not that she was opposed to dating, it just wasn't something she had focused on since the last relationship. Amy felt the pool of dread begin to form in her chest; intrusive thoughts began to nip at the back of her mind. She really didn't want to get in her own head right now, she was having a good time. Laura had been really patient and understanding, but that wasn't going to last forever. Maybe Jamie was right. The more Amy thought the tighter her chest became, threatening to ruin her night completely. She closed her eyes and took a few deep breaths, begging the feelings to go away.

Amy felt the chair opposite move, and a drink slid across the table. Laura was back. She quickly shook her head and pushed everything in her head away. Looking up, Amy saw Laura's blue eyes dancing in the dim light.

Hoping that her momentary shift had not been noticed by Laura, she smiled and proceeded to ask.

Conversation continued to flow with ease. Laura talking about her life, childhood and friends with nothing but joy – Amy artfully dodging questions that probed too much into her life before moving to Toronto. As the night progressed, the conversation moved on to more intimate affairs. They had another drink, the alcohol loosening their inhibitions, both of them now resting their elbows on the table leaning closer into one another. The faint smell of cherries hung in the air between them as Laura reached to tuck a piece of Amy's hair behind her ear. The scent made Laura's mouth water, her eyes flicking down to Amy's lips. Their chemistry was undeniable, as it had been every other time they had been together.

"So...," Laura said, running her finger along the edge of her drink, "four times you have fucked me. Tell me, Ms Love, are you always going to be the one in charge?" She stole a look at Amy, a cocky raise of her eyebrow and smirk spread across her face, but a tell-tale blush spread across her nose giving her away.

"Why, princess?" Amy teased, "I thought you enjoyed it." Flashing her a customary winning smile.

"Oh, I did, as you are well aware." Laura's eyes met Amy's – the tension was heavy and heated. Any thoughts either of them had had about this being a date that didn't end back at someone's apartment was long gone.

"I am a believer in actions over words, so why don't you come back to mine and prove it to me?" Amy hoped she came across as sexy and confident; she could feel her heart beating a million miles a minute in her chest.

To her relief, Laura stood up and began to put her coat on, she walked over and whispered in Amy's ear. "Lead the way, Ms Love."

Chapter 30

My Bed, My Rules

As soon as they stepped outside, the cold January air hit them. Amy regretted picking her leather jacket, a choice in style over warmth that felt like a good idea many hours ago but was quickly proving to be an awful idea now. Making the decision to walk rather than stand and wait on a freezing metro platform helped them both clear their head from the alcohol. The tension between them remained. As they weaved across city blocks Laura felt their hands bump into one another tenderly. Each time, Laura's heart fluttered. After a few moments, she loosely snagged some of Amy's fingers; when the redhead didn't resist she took the fingers more firmly in hers.

Walking hand in hand felt great, Amy decided. Any hint of cold she was feeling now evaporated in the heat emanating from the two of them and their touch. Looking over at Laura, she was taken back by the gentle warmth she exuded, her breath billowing out in cold plumes against the night air as water vapor was starting to cling to her eyelashes. She was perfect. The moment was equally perfect for Amy, the unspoken connection between them strong and certain in ways she hadn't felt before – in a way that made her never want to let go.

Amy paused, causing their arms to stretch as Laura took an extra step, unaware of Amy's decision to stop. Swinging round to look at her, Laura saw a look on Amy's face she had never seen before. She had seen her full of admiration and lust but never this: the way she looked at her now was a look that Laura could very easily mistake as pure love. The innocence shining through her moss-green eyes was almost overpowering in its intensity. A new sensation of anticipation and excitement washed over her. This was quickly becoming more than sex, more than a friend with benefits situation. Which is exactly what she wanted.

With a quick look up and down the street, Amy leaned forward, closing the gap between them and planting a sweet kiss on Laura's lips, so gentle it barely registered as their lips brushed together. Laura held Amy's hand tight, holding her in place as she extended the kiss, pressing their lips firmly together to cement the moment, committing it to memory. They had never kissed like this before, so openly and without expectation. This was not their first kiss, but it felt like their first kiss on the path to forever.

Laura texted her apartment group chat, letting them know she wasn't going to be home. A flurry of encouraging messages pinged away in return; notably none from Zoey. Amy gestured to a tall anonymous apartment block, indicating this was hers. Following her in the door and up the four flights of stairs just made the nerves grow. She hadn't seen Amy's apartment before; according to Jamie no one really did – this was not only unusual but a big step for Amy.

Amy opened the door and moved aside to let Laura in first. The apartment was modest, opening directly on to a kitchen and living space before two doors led to what Laura assumed was a bathroom and a bedroom. It was homey, if a little sparse; Laura couldn't help but feel Amy had avoided putting her personal touch on the place. There was an assortment of frames filled with landscapes, not that she could make out what they were in the darkness. She shrugged off her jacket as Amy clicked the door shut behind her and flicked the light on. It threw a sunset yellow across the room that was warm and calming at the same time.

Turning to look at Amy, she was caught off guard again by how stunning she was, her hair was slightly tousled from the wind and the walk, her cheeks rosy from the cold. But all that went out the window when Laura watched as Amy shrugged off her jacket. The white cropped t-shirt exposed a mouth-watering amount of flesh; combined with the slit in the skirt, it was enough to make Laura dizzy. The air was thick with anticipation; both of them could feel it as Amy closed the distance between them. She pulled Laura closer, her fingers tangling round the soft fabric as she maneuvered Laura's body towards her.

Laura had expected a blazing kiss that rendered her speechless – one that indicated her clothes would soon be on the floor and Amy would be devouring every inch of her. But that isn't what she got. Instead Amy traced Laura's lips with the pad of her thumb, as if committing every contour to memory. Her breath caught at the sheer intimacy of the moment; as their mouths got closer together and they breathed the same air Laura again felt a wave of heady euphoria before taking matters into her own hands and finding Amy's lips with hers.

It wasn't long before they were on the sofa, any cold they felt from their walk long gone. Mouths and hands wandering across each other's bodies with determination and exhilaration. Laura was straddling Amy, taking full advantage of the skirt; her hand was gripping Amy's soft fleshy thigh, the other braced behind Amy's head. Amy buried her hand in Laura's dark hair as she moved her head down and captured a nipple with her teeth. A little pressure combined with the lick of her tongue across the aching peak sent Laura's back arching in response. Amy took the opportunity to snake her other hand across Laura's hip and round to her back, applying just enough pressure with her nails as she did so as to elicit a moan from the dark-haired beauty.

"Am I fucking you here? Or would you rather come to my bed?" Amy whispered against Laura's neck.

"I am entirely at your mercy," was all Laura could say. Whatever fun they could have here could only be expanded upon with more space she thought. Amy moved Laura off her, stood and offered her hand, an action that was both sweet and commanding. Laura obliged instantly, allowing Amy to walk her over to the bedroom.

Laura was a little taken back; she was not surprised to find Amy's bed perfectly made and so inviting. The light wooden posts at each corner and cross beams looked like they were for a lot more than decoration. Her body ached for what Amy could do to her on this bed, what she was hopefully about to do to her. To her relief she didn't have to wait long as Amy let go of her hand and pushed her back onto the bed.

"My bed, my rules," Amy smirked, her eyes dark and hooded as she looked down at Laura. "Rule number one, lose the jeans." Amy gestured down at Laura's jeans, the fly undone long ago. "Rule number two, you take off the rest of your clothes; and finally rule three, put your hands up there and not let go, understand?" Amy nodded to the thick wooden bedpost at the top corner of the bed. Laura looked up at Amy and complied, shifting across the bed she stretched her arms until her fingertips brushed against the smooth natural wood, she shifted further to grip tightly on to the bedpost. Anticipation rippled through her body as she waited for Amy's next command.

Amy knelt at the other end of the bed, looking at the dark amber body stretched out across her bed. She almost couldn't believe that this woman was in her bed. Not that it was the first time Laura had been spread out beneath her, but this time was different, she could feel it. This wasn't just about sex, this was intimate, there was an unmistakable connection. Anxiety coursed through her, only some of that caused by the fact that this was the first person she had ever had in her bedroom – the rest down to the intense emotions growing between them. Pushing those thoughts aside she dragged her fingers up Laura's thighs. Her own heart rate quickened at Laura's reaction. She lowered herself, planting kisses across her inner thighs, alternating between her tongue, her teeth and her lips. Amy could feel the excitement building in Laura, it was coming off her in waves and crashing into Amy, heightening her own arousal.

As she finally reached the apex of Laura's thighs, Amy had to control her own urge to just let loose and give Laura exactly what she wanted, what her body was begging for. No. She needed to savor this, every twitch and breath that Laura made was making her own body react in anticipation. Amy licked her own lips before slowly running her tongue across Laura's opening, ending with a flick on her clit. A deep guttural moan escaped Laura's mouth that made Amy's core pulse with desire.

"You ok up there, princess?" Amy asked moving her head slightly to watch Laura arch her back trying to get closer, without moving her hands off the bed frame. "Don't you dare let go."

"Please," Laura begged. She wasn't even going to hide it; she needed to feel Amy's tongue on her, her fingers inside her – the anticipation was overwhelming. "Please fuck me." Her answer came silently as Amy again dragged her tongue up Laura's core. Laura went dizzy as her eyes rolled back in her head.

This time Amy didn't stop. She kept her tongue in place and applied pressure to Laura's clit, before moving her hand up and resting her fingers outside Laura's opening. Amy smirked when she heard the whimpering coming out of Laura. Stealing a quick look at her, Laura was stretched as far as she could on the bed, her torso elongated to get the maximum amount of pleasure from Amy – the sight only increased Amy's desire.

Laura nearly cried out when Amy momentarily stopped. She was barely holding it together as it was; she had never needed someone so much in her life. Sex was always good, but with Amy she was reduced to a quivering mess of desperation that she couldn't control even if she wanted to. The moment felt like it stretched on forever, and yet was over in a second as Amy pushed two fingers inside Laura while her tongue continued to work her clit. It made Laura buck her hips and arch her back, sending white stars across her vision – but she never let go of the bed. Amy started rhythmically fucking Laura, fingers and tongue working together to ensure she was never left without some pressure or pleasure. Laura responded by rotating her hips, grinding herself into Amy, pushing herself closer and closer to climax.

The closer she got the less Laura cared about how she sounded; the noises she made were almost primal as she felt everything Amy was doing to her, her arms stretched out above her body pulling against the frame, all her muscles tight.

"Fuck," Laura moaned. "Fuck... Amy..." Laura couldn't help herself, she had no control left, she was entirely at Amy's mercy. She felt herself coming, deep inside her radiating out to every corner of her body. Her toes curled as she held onto the bed frame as tight as she could, it was the only thing preventing her from floating away.

Amy could feel Laura tightening, feel the edge of her orgasm approaching; she had fucked many women, but none had reacted like this; none had so utterly given themself over to her. None had made her want to be fucked so badly in return. Right now, that was all Amy could think about; Laura's mouth and hands making her feel the way she was making her feel right now. It was heady and terrifying at the same time, Jamie's words still nagging at the back of her mind.

Amy slowly removed herself from between Laura's legs. Laura lay on the bed panting, still not moving her hands from where Amy had instructed her to leave them. Amy lowered herself and slowly kissed her way up Laura's toned golden brown body, planting a final kiss on her neck.

"You can let go now, princess," she whispered. Laura did as she was told, loosening her grip. Slowly bringing her hands down, running one over Amy's cheek, cupping it and drawing their faces level.

Chapter 31

Role Reversal

"Now it's your turn." Laura dragged her eyes over Amy's naked body. She could happily come again, the mere thought of Amy's mouth back on her clit was enough to make her bite her lip in anticipation. But that was going to have to wait; now, it was her turn to undo Amy. She shifted their weight around so she was on top of Amy, her own dark hair falling like curtains around them, mixing with the red on the bed. Looking down into Amy's eyes, she saw anticipation and hunger staring back at her; Amy didn't need to say anything, it was written all over her face how much she wanted this. Moving a hand to Amy's breast, she ran her nails gently over her hard nipples, Amy's eyes rolled back as electricity coursed through her body. Laura leaned in for a kiss, her mouth pressing against Amy's; she could taste herself on Amy's lips, it was so hot she could barely keep her focus.

As their mouths fought each other, passion crashed over both of them. Laura moved one hand, slowly tracing it down Amy's milky skin watching every twitch and movement she made. A moment of nerves flooded Laura; she never got nervous when it came to fucking someone, but this – this was different. She liked Amy, she more than liked Amy, she wanted more than to just fuck Amy. It was unusual for her to be so close to someone for so long before sex – it added a layer of complexity Laura normally avoided. What if they didn't have sexual compatibility? What if she didn't touch Amy in a way she liked? She knew she definitely wanted to fuck Amy; she wanted Amy to know how much she desired her. Leaving her trailing hand resting at the top of Amy's inner thigh, pushing the thoughts to the back of her mind, she returned her mouth and attention to Amy's erect nipples.

Laura could feel her body moving against her, pulling her fingers in closer. Her hand buried deep in her chocolate hair, the other pulling Laura closer, her eyes closed. This was all she wanted, to be able to show what the last three weeks had meant to her. Slowly, carefully, Laura slid her fingers into Amy. Her eyes widened as her breath caught; Laura wasn't sure she had ever seen something so arousing. Bringing her mouth to meet Amy's, their lips fitted together as if they were always meant to be; this wasn't just sex any more, this was different and Laura wasn't going to fight it. Their bodies moved in unison, finding a rhythm and pattern instinctively.

This felt amazing, Amy thought; this was everything she had dreamed it would be. The feel of Laura's skin against hers, their mouth and the way Laura was moving her fingers felt unimaginably perfect. It had been years since she had let anyone this close to her, and for a split second, she couldn't remember why she had denied herself this feeling – not that she thought it had ever felt this good before. But slowly, the dread began flooding her brain, the panic settling at the bottom of her lungs like ice, making it hard to breath, making her unable to keep her mind in the moment – her brain screamed at her. Loud and deafening, a dark vortex of fear clouded her mind.

She tried to keep her eyes close, to focus on the feeling of Laura inside her – focus on how good it felt, how right it was, how much she wanted it to continue. It was perfect, almost too perfect, it had never felt so good, their bodies pressed together this was almost tender and loving and, and and...

"Please, stop!" the words came out of her mouth before she could stop herself, whispering almost like a plea. Her body was still reacting, moving, enjoying the sensation, her words and her actions did not match up. So why was she asking Laura to stop? Laura was puzzled; she lifted her eyes to try and meet Amy's searching for clarification. "Laura, stop," Amy said forcefully, moving out of Laura's arms and across the bed, bringing her knees up to her chin. A cold sweat started to form across her exposed skin.

"I... I'm sorry. You caught me by surprise." Laura's head was spinning. Five seconds ago she had been fucking Amy; she had given the impression she was enjoying it. Now, she was as far across the bed as she could be, her face ashen and eyes blurring with a complex set of emotions Laura couldn't begin to decipher. "Are you ok?" Laura reached out with her hand, but fell short of touching Amy's leg.

"Yeah, yeah, I'm fine," Amy said slowly blinking, before putting on the fakest smile Laura had ever seen her wear.

"I said before, Amy, if you are not into sex then we don't have to – you don't have too. Asexuality is nothing to be ashamed of." Laura tried to keep all the conflicting emotions out of her voice. She was feeling hurt and confused, but all she wanted to do was reach over and hug Amy. Everything has been going so well. What changed?

"I know it's nothing to be ashamed of, but I'm not ace." Amy tried and failed to sound casual.

"Then if you don't like what I am doing, you can tell me to do something else, I am not offended by being given direction." Laura tried to sound confident, like it was no big deal she might actually be terrible at fucking another woman.

"No, no, it felt amazing." Amy smiled, a genuine smile, more to herself than Laura. She wasn't lying: it had felt amazing, and she wished it was still happening, now the ice in her chest had thawed she was feeling much better. Or at least she was until she met the look in Laura's eyes, a mix of worry and sadness that she had never seen in the blue depths before.

"Then, what is going on?" Laura pleaded.

A long silence fell over them, a long painful silence. Before Amy looked down at the sheets and started to talk.

"I'm not ace, I like having sex. I was like, really enjoying having sex with you," Amy started, picking at the corner of the sheet by her foot. She had never felt so exposed in her life, but she wanted to open up to Laura – she needed to. "I'm just not very good at letting people in..." Amy trailed off, she wasn't sure where she was going with this, how much she could tell Laura -- how much she wanted to tell Laura. "As you may have noticed," Amy gestured around the room, "I am a bit of a control freak." Daring a look up at Laura, she could see the woman watching her intently. She could also see she was cold. Rooting around under her pillow she dragged out a baggy shirt and tossed it at Laura. A moment of surprise crossed her face before she threw it on: the sight of Laura in one of her t-shirts wasn't something Amy had prepared for. It sent a bloom of warmth across her chest, and a pool of desire to grow much lower, a swirl of intense feelings she wasn't ready to unpack. She distracted herself by getting another shirt from the draw to her side.

"I don't think you're a control freak," Laura whispered as a smile tugged at the edge of her lips. She couldn't get over how easily Amy had just thrown her a top, like it was nothing. She was sitting wearing one of her shirts. It smelt of cherries.

"I have never had a partner come to my flat." Amy nervously chuckled at the absurdity of it.

"Ok, so? You like your space?" Laura wanted to keep her tone even. She knew better than to ask the question really on her mind – *'then why am I here?'* It was on the tip of her tongue before she swallowed it. "That's not a crime, Amy."

"I dated someone for almost two years, and she never saw the inside of my home. I have never had a hook-up back here, never had friends over for drinks and movies. There is one spare key with Jamie, and that's it." This admission by Amy did nothing to quiet the burning question in Laura's head. She desperately didn't want to read too much into it, but it was getting increasingly hard not too.

"Having boundaries is healthy." Laura wasn't sure where she was going with this, but Amy opening up had to be a good thing right? It wasn't as if she hadn't noticed that Amy had carefully avoided many questions over the last few weeks.

"I'm also, like, really really bad at people." Amy shuffled and rubbed the back of her head. "As you may have noticed, I don't pick up on stuff and I kinda get the wrong end of the stick sometimes."

"So?" Laura shrugged.

"Somctimes it means I end up in situations that are not always that healthy or..." Amy paused. How could she possibly say anything to Laura. The ice had been steadily building in her chest again and was starting to prick at the bottom of her lungs. "I have been in some pretty fucked up relationships."

"And people have hurt you?" Laura asked, trying to encourage Amy without her feeling pressured. She could see the turmoil written across her face.

"Yes, and no. I hurt others as much as I hurt myself – probably more" Amy couldn't look at Laura; she could feel her blue eyes watching her. The silence stretched out between them.

"Have you thought about forgiving yourself?" Laura asked, desperately wanting to take Amy's hand in hers, but resisting. Amy clearly needed to get something off her chest, and she didn't want to distract from that.

"I'm trying," Amy said softly, head still bowed to look in her lap.

"And this is why you won't let me really get close to you, to touch you?" Laura asked, she was putting the pieces together but something was still not adding up. It went some way to explaining why Amy was apprehensive about a real relationship with Laura now, but she suspected it wasn't the root cause.

"No..." Amy squeezed her eyes shut, really wishing this was over. A cold detached edge coming into her words. "I mean, yeah, I guess." She could feel herself detaching, shutting down to protect her own emotions. However much she wanted to tell Laura, the words just wouldn't come out. There were so many things she should tell her, maybe about why she really came to Canada, or how she really got the scar on her eyebrow. Even just being honest about her boundaries. But nothing would come out.

Laura studied Amy. This was probably the most raw

she had ever seen her. Sat here in her bedroom – a space that no one else had ever seen – she looked small and vulnerable. She found it difficult to imagine anyone ever saw Amy like this. The feeling of intimacy was almost as overwhelming as the silence that stretched over them again.

"I understand if this... between us ends here." Amy sounded detached and deflated, it almost broke Laura's heart. The silence continued to settle between them, after a moment Laura looked up catching Amy's eyes with her own.

"I am going to touch your face now." Her voice was barely more than a whisper, gently and lovingly as she reached forward and picked up Amy's chin, tilting it towards her. The big mossy green eyes stayed looking at the bed. "But that is not what I want," she added, trying to offer her reassurance as Amy dropped her eyes, avoiding Laura's intense loving gaze. "I am still interested in seeing where this goes, Amy – and as long as we communicate and act honestly then I don't see the issue."

No sooner were the words out of her mouth than Amy's arms were wrapped around her in the biggest hug imaginable. It took Laura by surprise at how fast she had moved across the bed and flung her arms around her. Laura responded with an equally big embrace.

They sat like that for a long time. Laura felt like she was getting to finally see the real Amy, and it just made her feelings grow deeper. This display of honesty and vulnerability just added another layer of humanity to Amy. A dawning realization settled across her: she was falling for this woman, and falling fast.

Amy felt Laura's warmth against her. It was so comforting, so honest. It made her want to tell her everything, to really let her in. But as she opened her mouth, nothing came out. The words died with her bravery. With a sinking feeling of shame, and regret, Amy knew however much she wanted this, she should stop it. But she felt powerless to do so.

Laura was destined to be another mistake, just like everyone else.

Chapter 32

New Dawn, New Day

Everything felt different, and it took Laura a moment to realize why. This wasn't her bedroom and she wasn't wearing her pyjamas. Refusing to open her eyes in case it was a cruel trick of her mind, she stayed deathly still, wrapped in the warm soft bed. Amy's bed.

She couldn't feel the weight of the redhead next to her, but she wasn't worried. They fell asleep together last night, Laura curled up under Amy's chin, still wearing her shirt. Rolling over, she pressed her face into the pillow, the scent of Amy's shampoo surprisingly strong, and undeniably comforting. Feeling around on the bedside table for her phone, she dragged it under the covers with her, checking the time. It was a little after nine AM – considering how late they had stayed up, she felt it was still reasonably early.

Her mind drifted back to last night. Amy had yet again fucked her within an inch of her life, and she had yet again melted into it. But more than that, Amy had opened up. She had been honest with Laura – she had admitted she wanted this. A warmth spread across her chest. She could deny what it was – but there was no point any more. Her feelings for Amy were growing and she wanted to explore them.

Reluctantly, Laura slithered out of the bed, finding her clothes in a neat pile on the chest of drawers. She threw on her underwear and opted to keep the baggy top on – if she had her way, she was going to claim it as her own. Padding out the bedroom, she saw Amy wrapped in a blanket asleep on the sofa. Her face was peaceful, a calm Laura never thought she could possess was etched on her lips. A dog-eared book lay open on the floor, clearly having fallen out of her hand. The whole picture made Laura smile as she silently walked over to the kitchen, checking her phone as she went.

There were a few notifications from the group chat: she had messaged on the way to Amy's last night to let them know she wasn't coming home. She hadn't seen the replies last night but they were bordering on pornagraphic from Ali – she really needed to see her partner again soon, Laura mused to herself as she filled up the kettle. Zoey yet again had left her and the group chat on read. Laura rolled her eyes in frustration at her friend. she was going to have to get over this at some point. Taking the initiative, she messaged Emily; the three of them were going to have a girls' evening soon, and Emily would shut Zoey down lighting fast. Putting her phone on the counter, she busied herself with hopefully finding coffee, praying to herself Amy wasn't so English that she only had tea.

Amy awoke silently with a jump. She wasn't planning on sleeping at all last night, but at least she managed to extract herself from the bed without disturbing Laura. God, it had felt so good to have the woman wrapped in her arms; she was warm and smelt of lavender and vanilla. It was heady and heavenly at the same time. It was also dangerous.

No sooner had they curled up together than had Amy felt the pull of sleep, her body finally relaxing with the weight and warmth of another person. She couldn't ignore the way Laura fit in her arms, or how good she looked in her shirt. Which was the sight she was greeted with when she opened her eyes. Laura leaning on her kitchen counter, scrolling on her phone, her long bronze legs disappearing into the faded black oversized cotton. Amy wondered for a second if it was appropriate to just go and take her there in the kitchen, but thought better of it – Laura looked like a woman that needed her coffee first thing in the morning. A pang of fear struck Amy's chest as she ran over the activities of last night. Had she really spoken that openly to Laura? And despite it all, the woman was still here. Maybe she wouldn't fuck this up like she did everything else after all.

"Please tell me there is coffee in here," Laura lamented from the kitchen. She had spotted Amy wake up a few minutes ago and wanted to give her a moment before making demands. "You can't tell me you have lived here forever and only have tea!" she wailed into a cupboard.

Amy chuckled and sat up before pushing herself off the sofa "Don't worry, princess, I definitely have coffee in there somewhere – I cant promise it's any good – Jamie drinks it." She rested her hand on the small of Laura's back, leaning over her to grab the glass jar from the top shelf. It did nothing to dampen her desire for Laura. She lingered for a moment before her hand and moved it down to her ass. Laura responded by leaning back into Amy's hand.

"Can I help you, Ms Love?" Laura practically purred as she leaned into Amy.

"Walking round my flat wearing my shirt makes you rather distracting." Amy tried to sound confident and cool; she suspected she sounded like neither.

"Flat?" Laura giggled as she raised an eyebrow up at Amy.

"Apartment," Amy retorted with a mocking thick Canadian drawl, but she couldn't stop her face cracking into a smile. Laura twisted round so she was pressed chest to chest with Amy, whose hand was now on her hip.

"Oh, so you like what you see?" Laura flicked her eyes down to Amy's lips before capturing them with her own. Forgetting about the kettle and her quest for coffee she pulled Amy in closer. This was going to be a better start to her day than any coffee could provide. "Also never do that accent again."

"Make me," Amy teased her eyes and flashed a wicked smile as she moved her hand back round to cup Laura's ass again. Laura pushed against Amy, pressing their chests together. With only the thin cotton between them she could feel Amy's nipples taught against the fabric. She couldn't help but feel more turned on than she already was; knowing Amy felt the same way added a new layer of desire she hadn't had before. Burying a hand in her hair she held took a fistful of Amy's shirt, holding her in place. She was rewarded with a thigh between her legs as Amy leaned forward, providing just enough pressure on Laura's core. Laura's eyes rolled back, as she deepened the kiss. If Laura wasn't careful, she was going to end up being fucked in another kitchen. She wasn't sure she could cope if Amy fucked her here as well. Taking action, she pushed Amy lightly. She backed off slightly and as Laura continued pushing – while refusing to move her hands – she guided Amy carefully to the living room.

Laura pushed Amy back, forcing her to sit on the couch. Without moving her hand from her chest, she sat straddling her lap, the shirt riding up just enough to expose a tantalizing amount of upper thigh. Amy couldn't help but run her hand up the toned leg, her thumb grazing the inside apex of Laura. The look Amy gave her was a mix of desire and hesitation; she wanted to make sure this was what Laura really wanted before going any further. That hesitation was something Laura was beginning to realize was just part of who Amy was. The searing kiss Laura planted on her was all the answer she needed.

Amy slid her fingers between Laura's folds; her center was slick as she pushed her way in. Amy's heart skipped a beat. Looking up into the oceans of blue, Amy felt something tug in her heart, quickly chased away by the deep kiss Laura planted on her lips as she moaned in response to Amy's fingers.

It was a slow and lazy orgasm that Amy pulled from Laura as she rocked her hips straddling Amy's lap. They kissed and entwined their free hands until Laura arched her back and came, a delicious smile forming on her lips. Satisfaction.

"I am going to be honest," Amy said as Laura caught her breath, leaning her forehead against Amy's. "I don't really have anything for breakfast, and the coffee is pretty bad." She ran her fingers lightly over Laura's ribs, she was so soft and warm.

"This doesn't surprise me at all," Laura sighed as she peppered Amy's neck with kisses. She was going to need to eat something eventually, but if a morning of sex with Amy was on offer, she would take that over breakfast any day.

"So what do you say to showering and then heading out for brunch?"

"I think that's acceptable, on two conditions," Laura mused, her fingers finding Amy's and curling their hands together.

"Oh?" Amy cocked her head.

"One – you fuck me in the shower." Laura blushed a little, she wasn't sure she had ever been quite so forward. "Second, you don't question where this shirt has disappeared to." She was surprised that the second request made her more nervous than the first.

"I think I can agree to those terms." Amy chuckled as she leaned forward to plant a kiss on Laura's lips.

It was several hours before they managed to leave Amy's apartment, having both worked up an appetite after Laura's request for sex in the shower extended to a few more orgasms back in the bedroom. Laura hadn't pushed to touch Amy – not that she didn't want to, but yet again, Amy artfully took just enough of the lead to keep her mind occupied. It wasn't until after a lunch date and they had kissed goodbye at the metro station that Laura really had time to look back on the whole night. It had been almost perfect: they had connected on a new level, and she knew they had both felt it. Amy had opened up in ways she hadn't expected, and while it definitely explained a lot of her actions over the last few weeks, Laura couldn't shake the nagging feeling that something was missing, like Amy was hiding something from her.

Chapter 33

Girls Night

It was another week before Laura managed to get Emily and Zoey together for a girls' night. Opting to spend a Saturday night with Emily eating junk food and watching rom coms made Laura reminisce about college. The addition of Zoey was normally a good thing, but tonight was definitely strained, mainly because the conversation had yet again fallen on Laura and her love life.

"Urgh," she huffed. "We could talk about *your* love lives?!" She waved a hand in front of her at the two, before grabbing another slice of pizza off the coffee table; *Sister Act* 2 played forgotten in the background.

"Well, we all know mine is DOA, and Zoey over there I think is still a virgin," Emily teased, shooting a look at her younger sister. The look Zoey sent back could kill. Laura was still hoping she never saw Zoey in a courtroom – she imagined someone would die with that ice stare.

"Fuck off, Emily," Zoey pouted, crossing her arms. "You know full well I am not a virgin. Relationships are just not my priority right now."

"Yeah, they are *never* your priority." Emily mimicked

her sisters tone; Zoey clenched her jaw. "Plus, I am pretty certain you have left it so long you are basically a virgin again anyway."

"That is not how that works!" Zoey almost shouted back. Laura decided to step in before they killed each other, but inside she was smiling. She loved seeing the relationship the sisters had – especially after some rocky years.

"Now, now, children," she started. "If you can't play nice then I will have to put you both in a time out."

"Ok ok ok!" Emily pleaded. "Then tell me about your girlfriend. The loveable Amy Love." Zoey rolled her eyes and let out an exasperated moan. Emily ignored her. "When do we get to meet her?"

"Well, for a start, she is not my girlfriend." Laura couldn't help the smile that formed

across her face. It's true they hadn't put a label on it, but they texted every day and she had no interest in seeing anyone else. "And you have already met her!"

"That doesn't count!" Emily wailed and pouted. "It was months ago and it was a busy night. There were loads of people there! Plus Zoey has met her!" Zoey shot Laura a pleading glance; she didn't want anyone knowing about her past situationship with Amy. Laura was happy to keep that detail to herself as well.

"Trust me, Emily, she is nothing special," Zoey retorted. "And we were thrown out after like five minutes, it doesn't count."

"Ok, fine! But I want to meet the woman who is making my best friend have a 'just fucked glow' that lasts for days!" Emily nudged Laura with her foot as she wiggled her eyebrows.

"I have already told you, Emily, I am not going to give

any details." Laura blushed – even the mention of sex with Amy made her act like a schoolgirl – it was embarrassing.

"Good. Please don't tell us, now or ever," Zoey interjected. "I never want to hear about the two of you having sex."

"Do you have no joy in your life, Zoey?" Emily sarcastically drawled at her sister.

"No!" Zoey protested a little too fast and loud. "It's just Laura is like a sister to me. It would be like hearing about your sex life – I just dont need to think of either of you like that!"

"I swear you are adopted sometimes!" Emily rolled her eyes as her little sister. "There is nothing wrong with sex you know!"

"I know!" Zoey shouted. "I just dont need to hear about it." With that she stood up from the floor and took the empty wine bottle. "I'm getting another drink." She headed to the kitchen.

"Now grumpy has gone, tell me everything!" Emily beamed at Laura, her expression full of wonder and excitement. Laura knew she wasn't going to hear the end of it until she gave some details.

"There isn't much to say that you don't already know. We have fucked a few times." Laura paused, blushed and smiled. "Maybe more than a few times. But we have also been on a few dates where we just chatted and I had a really good time. I kinda really like her."

"Duh!" Emily looked dumbfounded at her friend. "Anyone with eyes can see that you are head over heels about her!" Her gaze shifted to something more serious before adding, "You're falling in love with her. I am really happy for you, Laura." She reached over and grabbed Laura's hand and gave it a squeeze.

"Yeah, I really really like her. She's different, like she listens to me and I think she really hears what I am saying, but then she's a clueless idiot but also, like *insanely* sexy at the same time." The smile kept spreading across her face. She wasn't scared of falling in love with Amy, not after last weekend.

"When are you next seeing her?!" Emily was practically buzzing with excitement.

"I don't know, we haven't arranged anything." Laura looked sheepishly at her hands. She had wanted to see Amy every day this week but refused to look like a lovesick stalker. It would have been so easy to go to her apartment after work – she could have cooked or they could have ordered in. Laura was getting lost in the idea of a life with Amy again.

"Earth to Laura!" Emily shouted as she waved her hand in front of Laura's face. "Stop daydreaming about her and make a hot date with her!"

"I was not!" Laura lied, as Zoey came back in. The unimpressed look on her face deepened when she realized they were still talking about Amy. "Fine... maybe I was." Laura sheepishly shrugged.

"Oh!" Emily almost shouted. "You should invite her to Life Ball as your date!"

"No," both Zoey and Laura replied in unison, before glaring at each other. Laura instantly changed her mind the second Zoey vocalized her dislike of the idea.

"Actually, I changed my mind." Laura looked straight into Zoey's eyes, daring her to have an issue with it. "I think it's a great idea, Emily!"

"Urgh, whatever." Zoey rolled her eyes and picked up her phone, willing herself to get lost in some doom scrolling. She was so done with talking about Amy, hearing about

Amy – it was as if no one else could see where this was going.

Laura froze for a second. Her change of heart had gotten Zoey to shut up, but now she would have to invite Amy for real. Her stomach started to tie in knots. She wasn't sure a big club night was really Amy's scene; in fact, she was willing to bet money it wasn't. Add to that the pressure of it being the big Valentine's dance, it would be a pretty public display of their relationship. But then the idea of spending the night with Amy, having fun, dancing, introducing her to friends -- it all started to feel very right. The knot started to uncoil and was replaced by something far more pleasant blossoming in her heart. She pulled her phone out her pocket and opened her messages. It was no surprise to see Amy at the top of her contacts – she had quickly risen to Laura's number one contact.

"What do I say?" Laura felt the nerves reappear.

"You say, 'Hey sexy lady that I am falling in love with. Please be my date to the biggest queer event of the year so I can show you off to all my friends. Then come back to mine so I can ride your face until dawn'." Emily went to snatch the phone out of Laura's hand but she was too slow as she lunged forward. Laura shifted back, causing Emily to fall in a heap.

"Emily, stop being a dick," Zoey dryly spat at her sister. "And Laura, you absolutely cannot send a message like that." Her eyes bored into Laura. They were so dark that they looked black. Laura had always found them intimidating even as a child; as an adult they were deadly.

"Why not?" Emily whined from her slumped position on the floor.

"For a start, you are not bringing her back to our home." Zoey raised her finger as if counting to a child. "Second, you know full well that there are at least three different things in the message that would cause Amy to run away. Lastly, it sounds fucking desperate and you should never lower yourself to that."

"Fine, what should I send – and don't think I am ignoring the fact you won't let me have her over," Laura huffed. Zoey was as usual right about most things, but not about Amy staying over.

"Yeah, Zoey! Let Laura have her booty call! Don't deny her a night with her lady love!" Emily fluttered her eyelashes at her sister. "Plus you could always stay here after the ball – I will even give you the big bed!"

"Fine. Invite her to stay over. I will stay here with Emily," Zoey relented. "But you still can't send that awful text."

"Then what *do* I say?" Laura groaned, the nerves that had been growing steadily, but not unpleasantly. It was a tense apprehension that only comes with anticipation of something good.

"Keep it simple. 'Hi Amy, wanna go to the dance with me?'" Zoey said over the top of her phone, her attention back on whatever video she was silently watching.

Laura took out her phone and typed a message, and before she had time to worry about it – she hit send.

Chapter 34

Be My Valentine

Laura: Hi, wanna come to the Life Ball Dance?

Laura: To clarify I mean with me as my date.

Amy stared down at the message. She wasn't sure what to make of it. And to make matters worse, Rachel and Jamie had noticed her reaction to the message – there was no chance she could ignore it and leave it until later to reply. This was about to become a thing.

A wave of mixed emotions flooded her, so fast she didn't have time to control her reaction: excitement that she felt every time she received a message from Laura; the anxiety of such a big event; and the panic that pinched her chest at the idea of being Laura's 'date' and what that meant socially. Closing her eyes for a second she got everything under control. This was something she should have expected sooner or later, and she was genuinely excited to spend more time with Laura. She was going to the ball anyway, what difference did it make if she was going as Laura's 'date' or with friends?

"You gonna tell us what made you go all pale and wide-eyed?" Rachel nudged her ribs. She could probably look over and see what was on Amy's screen, but she wanted to respect her friend's privacy.

"I bet you ten loonies that it's a message from Laura asking her on a date," Jamie interjected from the other side of the booth. He was sipping a giant extravagant coffee that Amy couldn't name even if she tried. It was their bi-monthly coffee catch up, something Rachel had insisted on when she stopped working at the university. It worked for Amy, a clear set time and day to keep up with friends – but right now she was regretting it.

"No dice, Jamie! We all know the only three people who message our Amy are me, you and her new squeeze." Rachel shot a smile over her shoulder at Amy. They all knew she was right – she was the only one prepared to say it. It's what Amy loved about Rachel. Her unabashed honesty was refreshing and blissfully easy to understand.

"Her name is Laura," Amy retorted, instantly regretting giving away who had texted her. She sighed, resigned to the conversation they were going to have. "And she asked me out on a date – I think."

"What do you mean 'you think'?" Rachel asked, making a swipe for the phone, but Amy was too quick, shoving it in her pocket and out of reach.

"I mean she asked me to go to the Valentine's dance."

"Well, you go anyway, with us, so no big deal, right?" Jamie added, leaning across the table, his voice becoming far more serious than before. Things had been left a little jagged when it came to Laura; neither one of them had apologized for the argument, or acknowledged it at all.

"Well, then she clarified that she wants me to go as her date." Amy rubbed the back of her neck. She loved the fact she didn't need to hide herself with her friends.

"And that is a problem because?" Rachel raised an eyebrow as she twisted in her seat to look at Amy.

"Because she is falling in love with Laura but hasn't told her a single thing about herself," Jamie teased.

"I am not!" Amy snapped back, her cheeks heating at Jamie's words. "And she does know things about me!"

"Whatever, kiddo, I am not going over this again." Jamie sighed and leaned back in his seat. "But you can't deny that you have a connection with her. You might not be ready to call it love -- but no one looks at their phone like that for just a friend."

Amy pouted, shuffling on her seat uncomfortably she knew he was right. "Fine, but what do I say to this message?" She took her phone out of her pocket again and threw it on the table, the message still illuminating the screen. As expected, Rachel jumped for it, grabbing it and to Amy's horror she started to scroll up the messages. "Rachel, please don't do that!"

"Why, what am I going to see?" she sang as she continued to scroll with big theatrical motions through Amy's phone.

"Nothing! I just. Those are private!" Amy stumbled over her own words, she desperately racked her brain for the last time they had exchanged some very private texts. Hoping it was further back than Rachel's attention span.

"Does she always send you little kisses goodnight?" Rachel jokingly pointed at the screen still holding out of Amy's reach.

"Urgh, shut up, Rachel!" Amy tried again to grab the phone, looking over at Jamie for support. He just laughed, threw his hands in the air and leaned back in his booth, watching the chaos.

"Wow, Amy!" Rachel stopped scrolling, looked over at Amy, who was starting to go a deep shade of red. "I never thought you would send those kinda texts! You go, girl!" Amy leaned forward, her head resting on the cool wooden table as she let out a groan. This was beyond embarrassing. "But in answer to your question, you say 'Yes'!" Rachel placed the phone next to Amy's head.

"Did you really need to go through my messages to give me a 'yes'?" Amy moaned into the table refusing to look up.

"No, but it was fun!" Rachel laughed back. This was how their friendship had always worked, Jamie and Rachel pushing Amy to be a little bolder – to take risks. A lot of the time that came with some necessary joshing and hazing – today had been no exception.

Amy sat up taking her phone back, she was going to say thank you and that she would think about it. To her horror, while she wasn't looking, Rachel had taken the liberty of replying to her.

Amy: I would love too. x

Chapter 35

Control

Laura finished fixing her hair in her vanity mirror. She wasn't afraid to admit she was nervous. A proper date with Amy felt wonderfully normal and yet like something only a privileged few ever got. The annual Toronto Life Ball was only a few hours away, and it was one of her favorite events of the year. She and the rest of the apartment had their tickets booked months ago. Ali's partner was coming over and Emily was also joining them – it was a big group tradition. Looking over her shoulder to the bed, she saw the dusty blue suit ready to be worn, complete with the sexy underwear she expected to show off later that night.

Laura had picked out a tux on a whim, then spent weeks persuading Ali to work her magic to take it from the drab and boxy to a magnificent gender bending suit that hugged all Laura's curves. When she got this, Laura had assumed she would use it to turn a head or two and have a good night in bed with someone; now all she wanted was to feel Amy's eyes rake over her. The thought of Amy undressing her had been firmly in her mind since she took the suit out of the bag days ago. It made her insides ache and twist with anticipation.

It was fair to say she had to do some groveling to Munaza and Ali; after all this was an event they always went to as a group – this year they had agreed the theme of blue, and Laura had made sure her underwear continued the same theme. But they were understanding enough: this was love right? And neither of them wanted to stand in the way of that – plus Laura had offered to do the cooking for the next three weeks.

As she finished curling the ends of her hair, she returned her attention back to her eyeliner, more thoughts of a certain beautiful redhead filled her mind. She had taken up so much of her thoughts over the last few weeks; from their physical encounters to the times they had spent getting to know each other through texts and a few calls, it had been a surprise that Amy was open to voice calls, but Laura wasn't going to complain – especially when more than one had resulted in her masturbating to Amy's voice.

They haven't managed to spend any time together since Laura had asked Amy to the ball, something her body was acutely aware of, her dreams kept reminding her in vivid detail. Amy had even promised to stay the night, which Laura took as a sign she really had accepted Laura was someone she could trust and let in. She had easily gained permission from the rest of the women she lived with for Amy to come over, with a swift promise from Ali to be chill about the whole thing. Zoey had decided to stay at Emily's tonight – which was as close as Laura was going to get approval from Zoey.

Checking the clock, she realized time was slipping away from her and she needed to get dressed. Quickly picking up her phone and sending a text to Amy before she got dressed, a smile tugging at her lips.

Amy froze, ice filling her lungs as her eyes blurred, no longer able to read the text on her phone.

> Laura: I can't wait for everyone to meet you later.x

She attended the Life Ball every year, it was tradition. She went with Jamie and Rachel and it was one of the few social events of the year she endured – it was for a good cause after all. This year she was also looking forward to seeing Laura, for their first pre-organized official date. At some point over the course of the week she had agreed to go back to Laura's and stay the night, which was a normal thing normal people did. Ever since she had agreed to this, her mind was filled with terror. Going back to Laura's meant definitely seeing the housemates. It meant defining what they were not just to themselves, but also to others. It felt like everything was becoming very solid very fast; then soon, there would be expectations.

Amy couldn't deny her want for Laura. She ached for her touch. She desperately wanted to keep feeling the way she was – the bubbling of desire, the excitement – but ever since she had agreed to spend the night, the nightmares had been getting worse, waking her up in a cold sweat several times over the last few days. She was now exhausted and paranoid of what might happen when she fell asleep, let alone what might happen if she tried sleeping in the same bed as Laura. Every avenue open to her felt like it was closing. She wanted to be with Laura more than anything, but the suffocating dread in her mind was growing.

All these thoughts swam in her head at once, the text message sealing it all together – this was not just agreeing to something between the two of them, tonight was going to be a declaration of their official courtship, publicly.

The world tilted left. Amy felt faint, sick and full of pulsating energy all at the same time. She knew what this was. She knew she was powerless to stop it happening.

She fell to the wall, pressing her back into it to stabilize herself. She slid to the floor, her head in between her knees. Focusing on her own breathing. In. Out. It was all she could do, just focus on getting her lungs to function, trying not to let the dread consume her, not to let the ice in her lungs drown her.

No one was going to come and rescue her this time. Jamie was meeting her at the ball with Rachel. No one was going to fix this for her. She had to get her head straight.

In.

Out.

In.

Out.

She had to get this under control. The screaming and roaring in her head; the dread looming from the shadows.

In.

Out.

In.

Out.

The darkness clouding the edges of her vision.

In.

Out.

In.

Out.

It took Amy thirty agonizing minutes to get herself together enough to get up off the floor. Exhausted and unsteady on her feet, she flopped on the sofa. Fumbling around for her phone, she found it, almost lost to the underside of a rogue cushion. She was dizzy, all the weight from the last week had finally caught up with her. She looked over at her outfit hung on the back of the door. The black tailcoat with union jack lining, tight black shorts and fishnets were a bold look, more punk that she might normally embrace publicly – but she had foolishly wanted to show off. Be someone Laura might want to be seen with. Even the thought of getting dressed and heading out the door made her lungs falter, her breath getting shallow and fast again. No. There was no way she was going to make it out of the flat.

Her finger hovered over the message from Laura. She should text her and let her know – but what could she say? She didn't want to ruin the night for Laura, she had been talking about it for days. Instead she opened her chat with Jamie.

Amy: I can't come tonight. Please tell Laura I am at the lab

Jamie: What's wrong?

Amy: Nothing, I just can't, ok.

Jamie: Amy, I don't like this. What's going on?

Amy: Nothing is going on, please just tell her I am at the lab.

Jamie: Fine, I will tell Laura.

Even if you don't want to tell me the truth, you need to tell her the truth, Amy. Before this gets out of control.

Amy looked at the last message. This was already out of control. She was falling for Laura, and there was no way to stop it. Turning her phone off, she laid back on the sofa and stared up at the ceiling. All she could think of was how much she wanted Laura here with her, and how much that scared her.

Chapter 36

Life Ball

The music was loud and Laura had to shout to be heard by anyone, even standing next to each other. The large mid-twentieth century building was decorated in swathes of silky material and glitter balls. The organizers really had gone all out this year, and it looked spectacular. The group had already christened the dance floor; not the first people and definitely not the last. Before long they headed to the bar for much needed refreshments. Zoey had said she would get the first round of drinks in – she was really trying to play nice, but she was on edge with Amy's impending arrival. Taking her phone out to pay, Zoey noticed a message from Emily. She looked momentarily puzzled, forgetting the reason she got her phone out in the first place. Reading the message was even more confusing. She turned to Laura who was fiddling with her own phone. She suspected Amy was either uncharacteristically late or had said something stupid.

"Emily is looking for you."

"Why?" Laura looked equally confused. "Text her back

and say I can meet them in the smoking area?" It was far too loud in the main room for a conversation. Laura pushed herself away from the bar and her friends before beginning to head to the small outdoor space.

It was cold outside; winter still had a choke-hold on the city. Sunny days led to clear cold nights, and she regretted leaving her coat inside. As she turned to look round the empty space, she could see Jamie, Rachel and Emily walking towards her. Her heart sank a little not to see Amy with them. As they got closer, she could see the expression on Jamie's face was of forced neutrality, while Emily looked pained – whatever they were wanting to talk to her about, it didn't look like good news.

"I'm sorry, Laura. Amy isn't coming," Jamie said softly, touching her arm as soon as he was in reach. The look of upset and betrayal that flashed across the woman's eyes didn't surprise him. He was all too aware of how quickly people fell for Amy, even if Amy wasn't. She had this intoxicating way that drew people into her orbit, and by the time she realized they were too far in, people's feelings got hurt.

"Oh," Laura started. "Is everything ok? I haven't had anything from her." She gestured to her phone, still in her hand.

"Something came up at the lab, and she had to head over," Jamie lied. He was not great at lying, but he hoped the woman in front of him would be satisfied with that answer. He was, of course, wrong.

"OK, but why didn't she tell me that?" Laura narrowed her eyes. She felt like the three people in front of her knew something she didn't, and while she didnt know Jamie or Rachel at all, she did know Emily and could tell when she was lying. "Because I don't believe you."

"Laura, please just trust me?" Emily stepped forward putting her hand on Laura's upper arm and giving it a reassuring squeeze. "There are plenty of other people here who you could be having a great time with."

"Yeah, but I don't want to be having a great time with them." Laura shifted away from Emily's hands. She hated feeling like she was being left out of something, especially when it concerned her. "I wanted to spend time with Amy. Where is she?"

The three of them stood in silence for a moment. Neither Rachel, Emily nor Jamie wanted to lie to Laura; she so clearly cared about Amy deeply. Jamie let out a sigh, of defeat and exasperation. They had spent some time discussing Amy's message; none of them believed the redhead, but only Jamie had any idea what was really going on – he suspected she had had a panic attack. But the last thing she would want is anyone in her personal space, especially Laura. Emily in turn was frustrated by Amy's actions and was going to focus on looking after her best friend; Jamie didn't blame her for it. But here in this moment, the look in her eyes he had seen on countless women before, when it came to Amy.

"You love her." It wasn't a question, it was a statement and he directed it squarely at Laura, his soft eyes catching hers. She didn't need to say it out loud; it was written across her face.

"No," Laura shot back, her resolve failing instantly. "Well, not quite yet." A hollow feeling fell in her chest, a chasm opening exposing her very heart to the world. No one had said it aloud yet; she had barely let herself think about it, but she knew she did. The second she said, "no," she knew it was a lie. "I mean, we haven't talked about it," she added. All these weeks of people joking about her falling in love, the little moments she felt like she was lighter than air... it was all a lead up to this: the moment she realized she was hopelessly in love. Laura bristled with anger, that this was the moment her feelings showed themself to her. She quickly shoved them back down, not willing to think about it.

"You won't be the first to fall for Amy before you catch yourself." Rachel said, a sad smile across her face; if Laura didn't know better she could have sworn that sounded like the voice of experience.

"Where is she?" Laura asked more forcefully, folding her arms across her chest.

"She said she is at the lab," Jamie stated, matter-of-factly. It is what Amy had told him; he didn't believe it for a second. No one did.

"I think you need to stop wasting your time with Amy," Emily said, her big expressive eyes directed at Laura, practically willing her to see sense.

"Funny, because a few days ago you were all for me seeing more of Amy!" Laura scowled.

"My opinion has changed," Emily stated flatly. She hated seeing her best friend so upset over a woman. "I don't like how she is messing you around."

"Nothing to do with your sister then?" Laura shot back, instantly regretting bringing Zoey into it. It was clear from the look on Emily's face she had no idea about Zoey and Amy.

"What has Zoey got to do with this?" Emily narrowed her eyes, stiffening slightly. It was one thing to mess with her best friend, but to upset her sister as well... that was a dangerous move.

Sensing the tension and tempers rising, Jamie stepped

in "Laura, Amy is my best friend and I love her dearly – but she's not treated you well at all." This was an oversimplification and Jamie knew it. Amy hadn't done anything intentionally but that didn't stop her actions. "I think Emily is right."

Laura looked at the trio in stunned silence. This had gone from them passing on a message that Amy couldn't make it, to them telling her to stop seeing Amy. They had no idea who Amy was when they were together, how sweet and caring she was under the layer of aloofness and charm. "Whatever," she snapped at them eventually. "I get it, she's not coming. Thanks for passing on the message." With that, she stormed back inside the main room.

Laura tried to occupy her night with dancing. She loved moving to the music; it was such an escape. Emily had come and danced with her several times, choosing not to discuss the argument earlier. Laura was sure it would come up again at some point, but not here and not tonight. The large group had snagged a table close to the dance floor, an assortment of bags, coats and drinks adorned it, usually with a person or two when they took a break from the dance floor. As the song shifted from an upbeat pop number to something slower, Laura took it as her cue to head back to the table for a drink.

A beautifully manicured finger tapped her on the shoulder. For a split second she hoped it was Amy, before the thought fell out of her mind as she turned to see a tall slender woman standing in front of her, the pink hair standing in contrast to her elegant silver dress that hugged her body.

"Hello," the woman purred at her, her big silver eyes traveling up Laura. Her voice was unmistakably tinged with a French accent.

"Hey." Laura cautiously smiled back. She couldn't place this woman, so it was unlikely they had met before. Laura would definitely remember this woman: she was statuesque and beautiful.

"I would like to dance with you." The woman fluttered her eyelashes, her words offering so much more than a simple dance. She stepped a little closer to Laura, causing her to have to tilt her head up to maintain eye contact.

"Thanks, but I am not dancing at the moment," was all Laura could stammer out, shocked by her own refusal. There was no reason she shouldnt dance with this woman, it was only a dance after all – but somehow it felt like a betrayal nonetheless.

"Maybe." The woman moved her hand to Laura's chin, tilting it up to make eye contact. "We should do something else then." Her lips lightly brushed against Laura's in one of the sexiest moves she had ever been subjected to. Yet Laura's body gave no reaction.

"Thank you," Laura said more firmly, as she took a step back giving them both more space. "I am here with friends tonight and not interested in anything."

"Pity," the woman purred, giving one last look up and down at Laura before disappearing into the crowded dance floor.

"That woman was not only stunning but ready to jump you right here!" Ali buzzed with excitement as Laura returned to the table "*Please,* tell me you got her number."

"No, I didn't get her number," Laura waved her hand dismissively. "I wasn't interested in what she was offering." It was unexpected for her to turn down someone that was that attractive, but her heart wasn't in it – her heart was with Amy, wherever she was. Even though she knew she wasn't coming, a small part of her heart was holding out hope that she would turn up any moment now. Within seconds, her mind was once again full of images of the woman who had stood her up tonight. Without warning, she felt tears pricking at the edge of her eyes; was she really that upset about Amy?

"Stop thinking about her, she isn't here." Zoey spoke from her seat across the table. She had clearly seen the whole interaction.

"Don't give me that fucking look, Zoey." Laura choked back tears. She had had an awful night and the last thing she needed was Zoey to rub salt in the wound.

"What look, Laura?" Zoey snapped back.

"The 'I told you so' that's written all over your face." Laura waved her hands around, trying to keep her voice low so as not to make a scene.

"Well, I did, Laura. I told you she would do this to you." Zoey was exasperated, she had tried to give Laura a warning about Amy and her flighty attitude before – but her friend hadn't wanted to listen. "I thought I was really clear about how Amy operated. But you didn't want to listen."

"I," Laura started, all of a sudden feeling deflated and exhausted. "I thought she was different with me. I really like her, Zoey, I like her a lot. I..." Laura trailed off. She very nearly said she loved Amy, but thankfully caught herself. She didn't need the pitying look from Zoey. To her surprise, Zoeys face softened; she recognized the look in Laura's eyes, she remembered how it felt. She was genuinely sorry her friend was suffering like this over Amy of all people. The English wallflower had some power over people – to make them feel like they were the most important thing in the world to her – only to drop them once she got bored. She held her arms out for a hug and the dark-haired woman fell into it. Zoey could feel the sorrow in Laura.

"Would you like to go home?" Zoey asked, stroking Laura's back soothingly.

"Please," was all the muffled response she got back.

Chapter 37

The 3 Stages of Acceptance

It had been almost twenty-four hours since Jamie had told Laura Amy wasn't coming. Laura had heard nothing from Amy. Her messages hadn't even been delivered, the single tick tormenting her every time she checked her phone. Laura wouldn't admit it, but she was getting desperate.

After leaving early from the ball, she spent the rest of the night silently crying on the sofa with her head in Zoey's lap – who had been a true friend and said nothing more about Amy. Her head was a wash of emotions: new feelings and deep heart-aching sadness. Shock was the first thing to consume her. The feelings had come from nowhere, her heart working independently from the rest of her. Laura didn't believe she could feel so strongly about a person, and for them to feel nothing in return. It simply didn't make sense.

After shock came the denial, trying to convince herself and Zoey, who had listened to her ramblings for hours, that this wasn't love, it was infatuation, lust – just a response to great sex. Unfortunately Zoey had shut that train of thought down with a stare that bore into her soul. Now she was firmly angry with Amy. She loved Amy. Letting that realization hit her was like being run over by a bus. How dare Amy treat her this way? How dare she not text or call to tell Laura herself she wasn't going to make it?

A large part of her wanted to go to Amy's place, knock on the door and confront her. But she knew deep down that was the quickest way to get Amy to close up – possibly permanently. She knew what she should do: she should take everyone's advice from last night and delete Amy's number and walk fast in the other direction. Amy had caused her almost as much hurt as she had joy. She owed her nothing and yet all she wanted was to talk to her, to understand what was going on.

As she continued to pace, an idea flickered across her mind. It wasn't the worst idea, and it would hopefully give her the answers she desperately needed. Grabbing her phone she thumbed across her contacts until she came to Emily's. They still hadn't talked about last night, but she knew her best friend would help her, even if she didn't want to.

Laura: Hi, please can you give my number to Jamie? I need to talk to him asap.

Emily: I don't like this, she's not good for you.

Laura: I know what you think, and I love the fact that you are looking out for me. But I am not prepared to give up on something that could be amazing that easily.

Emily: I don't know, I don't want to see you get hurt

Emily: Correction. I don't want to see you get MORE hurt

Laura: Please Emily, trust me?

Emily: Fine. you know I am always I am here for you x

It wasn't long before an unknown number flashed across her screen. Assuming it was Jamie she answered with a curt, "Hello."

"Hi Laura, it's Jamie." A smooth soft voice came from the other end of the line. "I guess you want to talk about Amy." She didn't know the man well, but she already enjoyed his directness, and his loyalty to Amy was admirable.

"I do." Laura kept her voice even and neutral; nothing here was Jamie's fault and she couldn't take her frustration out on him. Silence fell over them, as Laura waited for Jamie to say something.

"I promise she won't have done anything to hurt you deliberately. She will have thought she was doing the right thing. But that doesn't make any of it ok," Jamie started. He wasn't sure how much he was going to say to Laura, but the woman sounded desperate, upset and at her limit last night. Jamie didn't want to admit he was frustrated with Amy. She so clearly felt for Laura probably as much as Laura felt for her. Amy was being an idiot, letting her past rule her present, and if he could help – he was going too.

"She wasn't at the lab, was she?" Laura asked, trying to sound as neutral as possible while feeling anything but.

There was a long pause on the other end of the line, before Jamie let out a sigh. "No, she wasn't, but I have no idea what she was actually doing – she lied to me as well."

Jamie wanted to trust Laura. "I think she was, and probably still is, at home – she has an apartment north of –"

He was cut off abruptly by Laura. "I know, I've been there," Laura said flatly, somehow more annoyed knowing that Amy was AWOL rather than just hiding from her. Her gut twisted in a knot, she had resigned herself to a conversation where Jamie told her Amy wasn't ready for dating or she was sick – hearing she had lied to him as well made her feel angrier.

"Wait! You have been to Amy's place?!" Jamie couldn't hide his shock, even if he wanted to. This was a huge deal for Amy; he had never known anyone to go to her apartment. "Actually been inside her living space?!"

"Yeah, only once, but I stayed the night after a date...," Laura tailed off. She didn't want to tell Jamie all the details of her and Amy; she didn't know the man and it was clear Amy was private, even when it came to her best friend. If she hadn't told him, she needed to respect that.

"Fuck, she must really like you," he blurted out without thinking. "I have never known her to let anyone in her apartment – let alone stay the night." He paused. "That's a really big deal. I know it may not feel like it – but to Amy, that's massive." A silence fell over them. Jamie didn't know what else to say; Laura sounded like she had been up all night – you could hear the sleep pulling at the edges of her mind. You could also hear the hurt and anger – both justified as far as Jamie was concerned.

"Amy's brain works differently from most other people's," he said slowly, gauging the reaction down the phone.

"Yeah, I am starting to get that impression." Laura almost smiled. She hated the fact she was happy that she was the first person Amy had let see her apartment. It had to mean something right? A secret part of her that had been reserved just for Laura. "Where do you think she was last night?"

A long silence followed again, she could almost hear Jamie thinking before he finally answered, "She was at home, probably having a panic attack." He exhaled. If Amy had let this woman in her home, she clearly meant more to her than Amy had let on. Letting her know where she probably was didn't feel like the worst thing in the world.

"What?!" Laura almost shouted down the phone, an icy panic spreading across her whole body. "Is she ok? Have you checked on her?"

"She's fine," Jamie said, trying to adjust his thinking to take in all the new information. Amy had clearly kept things from him, and this was now uncharted territory. "She knows how to deal with them, and if they get past a stage she can manage, she knows what to do." He paused again, but Laura didn't fill the silence. "As I said, her brain kinda works differently."

"So why didn't she come out last night?" Laura pushed "Why didn't she tell me she wasn't coming?" Her voice grew small as she pictured Amy alone, scared and struggling. It made her heart ache. "Why didn't she tell me about the panic attack – I could have helped."

"Laura, I know Amy hasn't told you..." He swallowed. Was he really about to break one of the secrets he held for Amy? No, he couldn't, that was for Amy to tell. But he wanted desperately to help both these women sort it out – they were both mad for each other. "She hasn't had an easy life – Amy is just trying to protect herself from being hurt again."

"She sorta told me about how she's not had the best relationship experiences," Laura said, rubbing her own eyes, the lack of sleep and upset catching up with her. "But I'm not an idiot; she never talks about family or home or England. In fact she talks frighteningly little about herself. I know something is going on and she doesn't feel she can tell me yet."

"Interesting," was all Jamie could manage. He was again shocked that Laura knew as much as she did – the woman was clearly observant to notice how little she knew about Amy. "You know she has never had a girlfriend come to her apartment, right?"

"Yeah, she said." Laura felt the knot ease; at least Jamie was saying the same things Amy had. "I don't want you to think I underestimate how big a deal it must be that I stayed the night in her bed."

"Did she stay in bed with you?" Jamie couldn't help himself, the question slipped out before he could catch it. Laura didn't answer; he could feel the silence stretching between them, thick and heavy.

"There's something else going on isn't there?" Laura ignored his question, they both knew the answer – her lack of answer was all the confirmation he needed.

"Yes," was all Jamie could manage. "Laura, you need to understand that the fact you have been in Amy's home means she really really cares about you. I have never known her to care for anyone as much as she does you."

"I know," Laura started before she was interrupted.

"No, I don't think you do. " A flare of anger in Jamie's voice; Laura had no idea how monumental this was. He cursed his best friend for not telling him all this. He would never have suggested Laura and Amy stop seeing each other if he knew. "She will be panicking, she has no idea what happens once you tell people the things about you that make you damaged. But the fact she even told you in the first place... I can only assume she loves you, even if she doesn't know it yet herself." This was a bold thing to say. He had no idea if Amy did love Laura, but she had never acted this way before. It was the only logical conclusion; plus he had a gut feeling he was right.

Laura's breath caught, everything stopped, she went dizzy and slid onto the bed to steady herself. Did Jamie just say that Amy loved her? The fire and heat that spread across her body at the mere thought of her feelings being reciprocated was enough to thaw even the coldest winter day. It threatened to extinguish the anger she was feeling.

"I'm sorry I told you to forget about her," Jamie's voice cut across Laura's thoughts. "Amy doesn't often keep things from me, but clearly how close the two of you are was one of those things she didn't feel she could share. So I am drawing my own conclusions from that." He felt sheepish, for his actions last night, the conversation with Emily and Rachel had been abrupt and unpleasant. All three decided that Laura deserved better – but now he knew Laura had gotten closer to Amy than anyone ever had. He knew this was special. He needed to try and get the two of them talking and to get Amy to open up.

"I need to see her." The words came out in a whisper; Laura was barely able to get her thoughts straight.

"Yeah, I think you do." Jamie let a smile hit his face that followed his words down the phone line. Maybe there was hope for these two women after all. "Name a place and time and I will make sure she is there."

Ten minutes later, Laura hung up the phone and flopped back on her bed; all she had to do now was wait for Jamie to confirm he had Amy. She wanted to be happy: Amy had feelings for her, she had let her in way more than she had ever let anyone else in – and these actions came from a place of love. Love for Laura.

The puzzle that was Amy Love was starting to fall into place for Laura. All her shyness and double-checking didn't come from anything other than trauma. The leaving after sex, the nightmares... it all painted a picture of someone trying not to let themselves get hurt again. This beautiful intelligent woman lived her entire life in closed-off solitude as protection. It made Laura's heart break for her, ache for her. She wanted nothing more than to pick Amy up and hug her until all the sadness was gone, and even then – she wasn't sure she ever wanted to stop.

With a renewed sense of hope, Laura finally let herself go to bed. Shaking off her clothes, she threw them haphazardly on the floor, before digging in the bed for her sleep shorts and Amy's faded t-shirt, the one she had stolen for Amy's bedroom. The bedroom no one else had ever been allowed in. She drifted off to sleep with the faintest smell of cherries.

Chapter 38

Second Chances

Laura sat in what she hoped was a secluded back corner of the coffee shop. It was neutral ground for both of them. She didn't know how Jamie had planned to get her to show up – she didn't care: as long as Amy was open to talking, it didn't matter. Once she had a few days' space from the raw emotion, she couldn't say she was feeling better, but she at least felt human.

She loved Amy, or at least that's what Zoey thought. Zoey had commented it was embarrassing how fast Laura had fallen – but what if she was misreading the situation, misreading Laura? It was stupid to even consider the idea she was in love. It had been barely months since they first hooked up – love didn't work that way. Waking to the smell of Amy's shampoo had reminded her, sure, had it made her smile? Yes – but that didn't mean she was in love. Laura groaned and pushed the conversation with Zoey out her mind. Right now, she couldn't deny the anger she was still feeling towards Amy. Just proving she wasn't in love.

This wasn't a coffee date to throw herself at Amy; this

was a chance for both of them to talk – honestly and openly. Love could come later, if at all. Right now, it was fun lust.

Looking at her watch for what felt like the hundredth time since she arrived fifteen minutes ago; it was still another ten minutes before the agreed time. Loading the coffee shop app on her phone, she placed the order for both their drinks, still saved in her phone from the last time they got coffee together.

The drinks arrived a minute before Amy was due. The butterflies in her chest only increased, their wings feeling like razor blades. A mix of anxiety about the talk they needed to have, but also excitement for the chance to see Amy again. Closing her eyes, she knew she had it bad for this woman – and she just wanted to make it work.

Less than five minutes later the door opened and in walked a familiar green jacket. Laura saw Amy before Amy saw her, and predictably her heart skipped a beat. Even at this distance, the woman took her breath away. Green eyes looked around the coffee shop, seeking out Jamie, until they settled on Laura, a small smile flickering across her face before Amy walked over.

"Jamie set me up, didn't he?" Amy asked, her voice showing no sign of annoyance, her carefree smile tugging her lips up at the edges as her eyes met Laura's. Amy pulled out the chair and sat in front of the drink. "This for me?"

Laura was shocked with how at ease Amy was acting, as if she hadn't stood her up and then ghosted her. It made the anger flare inside her: this was the person she was told to avoid, the charming smooth talker who would steal your heart and leave you for dirt. Laura took a deep breath before starting. She wanted to remain calm and measured – she wanted answers – and shouting at Amy wasn't going to get them.

"Why did you stand me up?" Laura said in the most neutral tone she could manage, but she could feel her jaw clench. "We made plans, official plans. People were expecting to see us."

"You still went and had a good time with your friends though, right?" Amy tilted her head to the side, as she stirred the steaming mug in front of her.

"I did, for the most part." Laura was hesitant, unsure of where this was going – this was not the conversation she expected to have, she expected Amy to be upset, or at least apologetic. "But I was meant to be there with you. I go with my friends every year, and this year I wanted to go with you. I wanted my friends to see me there with you."

"You want people to see us together?" Amy looked bemused at Laura. She tilted her head to one side again, once more stirring the mug before her.

"Yeah. They know we have been doing... whatever it is we are doing and they wanted to meet you." Laura was losing the battle of trying to keep her voice neutral. Amy was so frustrating to talk to sometimes. "In fact, most people thought it was weird that you were not there with me. You know, after I told them you would be." Laura looked directly at Amy, really looked at her. Something wasn't adding up. Why was she so casual, like she had canceled a lunch with friends rather than stood up the woman she (according to Jamie) loved.

"I just. I didn't feel like it." Amy shrugged and looked away, avoiding eye contact. Her resolve was starting to fail her. After being tricked to come here and meet Laura, she had been taken back. Her feelings were twisting inside her. She desperately didn't want to tell Laura the truth: it was embarrassing that she had such bad anxiety she couldn't leave the house.

"And you couldn't pick up the phone and let anyone know?!" Laura snapped, trying to keep her voice down.

"I didn't think it was a big deal," Amy trailed off, her carefree demeanor falling as she picked at the edges of her jacket.

"Are you ashamed to be seen with me, Amy?" Laura asked, not managing to keep the anger out of her voice any more. "Because if you are, then I am really not interested in this."

Amy snapped her head up. Their eyes met for the first time in weeks; Laura instantly felt the connection between them, it was undeniable. Moss-green eyes that held all the answers, that pulled her in, that made her want more. Under everything, Amy looked tired, like she hadn't been sleeping. Like something was on her mind, and she was hiding it all behind this carefree exterior.

"Why would I be ashamed to be seen with you?" Amy asked, sounding genuinely puzzled. "You are literally the most beautiful woman I have ever seen." Amy blushed a little at the admission. But Laura wasn't going to be distracted by the compliment or Amy's blush.

"I don't know, Amy, but it's weird that you had Jamie tell me you weren't coming rather than replying to my text yourself." Laura didn't want to drag others into this argument, but she was at a loss. She was always at a loss when it came to Amy. It was becoming clear Amy wasn't going to tell her the truth about why she wasn't there, and Laura wasn't going to rat out Jamie.

Deafening silence fell over them, the tension so icy, deep and thick; it was crushing and suffocating in equal measure. Amy squirmed, picking at the edges of her jacket, refusing to look at Laura – who sat with her arms crossed, waiting for Amy to offer something truthful, something tangible. After what felt like an age, Amy's shoulders slumped – finally giving up the mask she had adopted to get her through these sort of situations.

"I'm sorry." Amy's voice changed; she sounded tired and upset, like she had let go of whatever mask she was holding. "I don't know how anyone could be ashamed to be seen with you: you are stunning, amazing, and insanely hot." Her green eyes softened, as she looked deeper into the brilliant blue pools across the table from her.

Laura hated the fact her body reacted to the look Amy gave her. It was full of longing; it called to her. She didn't want to forgive Amy just because she gave her puppy-dog eyes. She wasn't ready to forgive Amy.

"That doesn't answer my question, Amy." Laura kept her eyes on Amy. A long pause fell over them before Amy slumped her shoulders even further and let her eyes fall. "What happened?" Laura pushed.

"I was... I *am* scared of how much I like you," Amy almost whispered, her eyes firmly looking at the mug in front of her. "It's been a really long time since I cared so much about anyone. I know I am not the easiest person to like in that way. I think I was scared that you would realize I am not really worth the trouble and not want to see me anymore."

"And rather than talk to me about it, you decided to just run away? Again." Laura found it easy to slip back into a more neutral tone, now Amy was finally showing some emotion.

"I... I'm sorry," was all Amy said.

"Jamie said I should give you another chance," Laura stated as she lifted her coffee to her lips. "But my friends are a lot less convinced." She took a sip of her coffee, giving Amy time to speak.

"What else did Jamie have to say?" Amy didn't take her eyes off her mug, a hint of annoyance seeping in – she was uncomfortable with the idea of Jamie telling Laura anything.

"That you are different, and your brain just works in a different way."

"That's a very diplomatic way of putting it." Amy let out a cold half chuckle, trust Jamie to be diplomatic about her misgivings. She pulled her eyes up to meet Laura's, chewing on her bottom lip.

All the world stopped, frozen in time. Was she about to tell Laura she was autistic? Was Laura going to understand or just see her as a freak? Her insides continued to twist with anxiety. Jamie had done the groundwork for her, gauged her reaction with his own brand of diplomacy. Was Amy ready to admit she picked clothes based on texture, or cut the labels out of them before she could wear them? That she couldn't stand to eat some foods because of the way they felt in her mouth regardless of taste? That she had no idea how to read people naturally and it took decades of practice to even get this far? That she couldn't stand being around large groups of people for long because everything was always so overwhelming? That she could hear the electricity in the walls at night? These things made her different, made her something most people didn't want to understand.

She took a deep breath. If she didn't tell Laura now, she was going to lose her nerve, and then her chance to salvage anything would be lost.

"I have a disability," Amy started.

"Do you?" Laura couldn't help but exclaim. She hadn't seen anything, and she was normally pretty observant. "Sorry, I hadn't noticed."

"I'm autistic." Amy let out a breath. This was new territory for her – she had no idea how Laura was going to react. "People call it a hidden disability, so you can't see by looking at me." Amy didn't sound at all confident. In truth, she thought that you could see just by looking at her; there were clear signs if you knew what to look for. "But it affects my life every day."

"That...," Laura started before pausing to take the information in. Like dominos falling into place, it all made so much sense now. "That explains a lot, not everything, but a lot. Why didn't you say anything?"

"Because people make awful stereotypical statements and treat me like I am somehow less of a person because of it, or like a project that needs fixing." Amy winced, she remembered all too well how people would treat her differently as soon as they found out. Every time it hurt to see someone forget who she was in favor of how they thought she was because of her disability. "I am not the greatest when it comes to communication. I upset people by being too blunt or honest. I don't react the way people want me to react to things, then they get upset." Amy trailed off. Laura sat quietly looking at her. The way she instinctively raised her hand to rub the back of her neck; it was endearing, and clearly a nervous habit. She wondered how many people Amy had told in the past; if she had tried to tell others that she was disabled, only for them to disappear on her.

"I wish you had said something sooner, Amy." Laura reached over and took Amy's hand in hers, electricity sparking at the contact. She quickly ignored it in favor of a genuine moment of honesty between them. "I could have adapted my communication style to fit with you. I still can."

"Really? Why would you do that?" Amy finally looked up into Laura's eyes, and saw nothing but acceptance and longing in them. There was even a smile across her face; a small one but it was there.

"Amy – I work in tech, neurodiversity is accepted and embraced. Also one of my house mates is on the spectrum. It's why we all agree not to have people over unannounced; it's why I don't bake often – as the smell can be overwhelming. We love her, and want to adapt to make her life easier." Laura paused for a second. "Is that why you don't have people over to your place?"

Amy winced. She didn't want to lie to Laura; she was trying so hard to be truthful. Laura had taken this revelation much better than she could have ever hoped. Maybe there was still hope they could be together, or at least be friends after this. But then the dread came back. In the back of her mind she knew this was never going to happen – she had already thrown so much at Laura. How much more could one woman take before she realized she could do so much better elsewhere? With someone less damaged.

"Erm.. yeah, that's it." Amy felt the crushing dread build, as her chance to be fully truthful passed.

"What happened between you and Zoey?" Laura asked, without waiting a beat.

Amy was thankful for the shift in conversation topic; what happened with Zoey was regrettable but not the worst thing in the world. She knew there were way worse mistakes behind her. "We... I... Were not on the same page when it came to what we were doing." Amy felt Laura's fingers curl round her own, a feeling of comfort and understanding radiated off the tanned woman. "I don't think Zoey was in a great place. She was exploring her identity, and I was probably the wrong person to do it with. I wasn't clear that we were just casually hooking up. Zoey thought it was more than that."

"I can't imagine that was easy for either of you," Laura said soothingly. She wasn't going to chastise Amy. It took two people to communicate and she knew Zoey was equally bad at it at times – especially when she was emotionally vulnerable.

They sat in silence for a while, Amy watching Laura circle her thumb over her hand. It was such a small thing to do, but it made Amy's world shift. It was more than the sparks she had always felt touching Laura, this felt deeper, more solid.

"What now?" Amy asked, her head was swimming with everything. She hadn't exactly slept well in the first place and she was feeling exhausted.

"That is up to you, Ms Love." Laura smiled at her, squeezing her hand once more, before retracting it and leaning back in her chair. She desperately wanted Amy to understand how ok she was with all of this, how she was willing to make changes in her communication and expectations to fit with Amy. "We are going to finish our drinks here, and then I am going home to sleep. Then I am going to text you tomorrow to invite you over to stay the night." Amy's head shot up, a look of confusion fixed across it. Laura found it adorable and amusing. The smile on her face got larger. "And I suggest you take this opportunity to get a lot of sleep, because I don't expect you to be doing much at mine." Laura watched the blush race across Amy's face. Her eyes widened as she nervously rubbed the back of her head. This was the Amy she fell for and it made her heart swell seeing her again. Laura knew she could fix this; just adapt the way she interacted with Amy a little and it would all work out.

All Amy could do was nod. She couldn't understand why Laura was still here, still entertaining the idea of any sort of relationship with her after this, after all the mistakes she made. But she wasn't going to argue. Not now.

Chapter 39

Nothing Else Matters

Somehow between the coffee and Laura's bed, they ended up in a bar; Laura couldn't remember how – and right now she didn't care. The heady mix of want and alcohol swirled inside her head.

This was not love, this was sex. She was horny, and Amy made her feel good.

Mouths and tongues clashed in a heavy mix of emotion, passion and desire. How they had gone from a reluctant coffee meeting to a bar and cocktails, then to her bed, Laura didn't know. All she knew was how much she was enjoying Amy's lips on hers.

Amy reached down and pulled at the edges of Laura's shirt. It was almost amusing to her how even after the last few months, Amy still waited for permission before going any further, as if the making out and the heavy petting wasn't an indication enough to her that Laura wanted things to continue. The cool air hit her nipples, making them even more sensitive, drawing them up into peaks, which Amy quickly took advantage of, rolling her tongue expertly over one. Laura let out a hiss from between her teeth as she looked down at the redhead, her moss eyes peering over her lashes, almost into her soul. Laura should have been unnerved by the intensity but she was too distracted by the sensation of Amy's mouth on her chest and her nails running down her back.

Amy flipped Laura over, so her back was exposed to the cool night air. Grabbing Laura's hands in one swift movement, she stretched them to above her head, pinning them away from her. Amy's other hand moved down Laura's spine, trailing fingers and dragging nails slowly down each vertebrae, ensuring Laura felt everything. Laura wanted to turn her head and look at Amy, to see the look in her eyes as she teased her – but if she moved there was a chance Amy would stop – and at this moment the only thing worse than not being able to touch Amy, would be the idea of Amy stopping.

As her fingers reached Laura's ass, Amy dug her nails slowly into the flesh, feeling Laura's breath catch as she did. Laura bit down on her lip so as not to let out a moan any louder than the sounds she had already been making. The tightening of Amy's hand on her wrists only made her core ache more – this woman had a hold over her than she had never experienced before. She could ask her to do anything in this moment and Laura would. The slight pain of Amy's nails pressing into her soft skin subsided as she trailed her fingers lazily down between her thighs; Laura automatically spread them allowing Amy fingers to trace her wet outer lips, the sensation caused Laura's body to shiver from head to toe.

"Please," she begged, no hint of shame in her voice. "Amy, please." Her breath lost, words muffled by the bedding, still stretched and pinned by Amy's arms.

"Well, seeing as you asked so nicely, princess." Laura

could hear the sly smile pulling at the corner of Amy's mouth when she spoke. It momentarily pulled her focus away from Amy's fingers hovering at her entrance. Slowly, agonisingly slowly, Amy pushed herself inside Laura, her two fingers hard and firm against her wet, sensitive core. She pushed herself all the way in, the feeling of Amy's fingers inside her was enough to make Laura cry out in ecstasy. She was being undone at a microscopic level by nothing other than Amy's touch. It was somehow the most vulnerable and erotic thing she had ever experienced.

Laura desperately wanted to provide her own friction and movement by gently rocking her hips back and forth. Amy, to Laura's dismay, kept her fingers rigidly still – the small amount of movement she was providing herself wasn't enough to do more than increase the tension building inside her.

With another whimper, Laura let go of any sense of control she had. Tears almost in her eyes, she begged like she never had for anyone's touch before, the words tumbling out in a barely audible whisper, her voice dry and husky. "Please, please, please." As if she was praying to a deity.

Amy looked down at the expanse of perfect skin, the only light coming from the streetlights outside and the faint glow of the string lights hanging in the room. Laura's moans and pleas were doing things to her, giving her feelings that had laid dormant for a long time. All she wanted to do in this moment was take the woman in front of her to places she had never been, to undo her utterly and completely. To show her how much she had missed her.

The rocking of Laura's hips into her hand was hypnotic, the desperation clear in her voice, the complete trust she had in Amy in this moment to give her everything she desired. Amy wasn't going to disappoint. She slowly twisted her fingers round, feeling Laura clench around them, her body silently begging for the friction, until she curled her fingers forward. She couldn't help the smile that spread across her whole face as Laura all but screamed her name as her fingers brushed against her g-spot. There was no going back now, even if she had wanted to: the sounds escaping Laura's lips were like a spell on Amy, all she wanted was to keep hearing them – to find out how long she could make those sounds for, before she couldn't take any more.

Slowly, Amy slid her fingers in and out of Laura, taking a moment to press lightly on the small patch of tissue that made Laura swear she was going to pass out with pleasure. Her rhythm didn't change, but the need in Laura for more burned deep. She couldn't work out if she had made an audible sound, but her wish was answered when Amy removed her fingers and went to push them back in, adding a third. The extra friction pushed Laura even further to the edge of pleasure, the impending cliff at the edges of her conscious mind.

Her body shook. She strained against Amy's hand on her wrist, stretching herself out, pulling out the fireworks erupting from her skin. Amy's fingers pressed inside her; Laura couldn't even begin to work out what movement they were doing, but she was sure she had never experienced a release like this, where the world faded away and all that was left was the two of them and the fragile unspoken connection between them.

Until it broke, the build up and fireworks all crashed at the same time, sending her body into feelings she couldn't describe. A scream of pure pleasure ripped itself from her lungs, as she swore she touched the heavens, unable to breathe, too enthralled to care – she floated in euphoria. A euphoria caused by Amy, the woman who had the potential to leave her heart broken in a heartbeat.

Time lost all meaning. It could have been minutes or days that Laura laid there trying to catch her breath, trying to recenter herself into reality, though she felt her reality may never be the same again, knowing she could feel like that – and Amy was the one to do it to her. Slowly, she felt the hand binding her wrists above her head move. The pressure of Amy's hands and warmth of her body disappeared. Laura missed it instantly, but before she had a second to try and get her disappointment out, she felt Amy's hand on her shoulder, gently encouraging her to roll over. Laura obeyed the command, rolling into the middle of the bed, once again feeling the warm presence of Amy against her. She couldn't help but draw herself into it, her hands reaching out to pull her closer. A hand came to cup her face, soft and tender – so unlike the way she had just been fucked.

"You ok there, princess?" Amy breathed into Laura, the feel of her comforting, warm breath against her face. She couldn't talk, not yet. If she spoke now she was liable to say something she shouldn't. Instead, she leaned forward with the last of her energy and captured the soft pink lips with hers. Laura knew she had missed Amy, but she had no idea how right the world felt with this woman in it. She vowed at this moment she wouldn't be spending any more of her life with anyone else, it was clear – her future was Amy Love or nothing.

Zoey was right.

Chapter 40

Do Over

Laura: Hey, would you like to come over tonight? x

Amy sat on her bed unable to take her eyes off the text.

It was exactly as Laura had said it would be. She had sent the text like nothing had happened. Amy couldn't believe it, she almost didn't. After they parted ways yesterday, a sense of calm washed over Amy, a sense of hope flickered in her chest, one she had never felt before. Laura knew so much more than anyone else ever had and she was ok with it – more than ok with it, she was embracing it. This was her shot at a second chance to get it right, and she really didn't want to blow it.

As soon as the text arrived, thoughts started to creep into the back of her mind, memories she never let surface. Shaking her head she pushed them back.

No, not tonight.

Tonight, she was going to give herself over to Laura as she had dreamt of since the first night they met. She was going to feel all the things she wanted to feel. Laura had accepted her as she was, more than anyone ever had before and this was her chance to show Laura how much that meant. How much she trusted her.

Thumbs flying across the screen she replied to Laura. A confirmation quickly followed and she sat smiling at the screen once more. Tonight was going to be the start of something with Laura. She was determined.

"You promised to be on your best behavior." Laura looked straight into Zoey's eyes, her glasses providing a barrier she knew Zoey hid behind. It was as infuriating as it was obvious. Her arms were folded as she leaned against the kitchen counter. This was becoming a battle of wills.

"I said I would try," Zoey clarified. She still wasn't a fan of Amy; she was probably never going to be a fan of the woman. Having Laura cry in her lap for hours only a few days ago had done nothing to help Amy's case. But Laura had spent several exasperating hours trying to convince Zoey that Amy was a decent person and how now everything made so much more sense. She hadn't told her how it made sense, but she was convincing. Right up until she said they were more similar than she knew. This had made Zoey's blood run cold — what had Amy told her? What did Laura know? Zoey had worked hard over the years to curate her outward personality.

"Please, Zoey." Laura was pleading, and while she was acting like it was a joke, Zoey could see in her eyes that she meant it.

"Fine, I will be civil – but don't expect me to be happy she's staying over." Zoey rolled her eyes as she turned back to her seat.

"Oh don't be such a grump!" Ali sang from across the room "It's just you that doesn't want to see Laura all loved up, you ice queen!"

Zoey shot Laura a look. She hadn't told anyone else about her past encounter with Amy, and she wanted Laura to shut down the conversation before she said something everyone regretted. Laura looked like she understood and went to sit on the sofa with Ali and Munaza, distracting them from their teasing. Zoey returned to her laptop; she would have to finish up sooner than she originally planned – somehow Laura had convinced them all to go out so she could have some time with Amy, and then she was staying the night. The idea of Amy being in her home was, for Zoey, complicated. She had reluctantly shared her history with Laura in the hope it would convince her to ditch the woman. Unfortunately, it looked to have only made them stronger, or Laura's feelings stronger at least. Zoey still wasn't convinced Amy was capable of love. It's not that Zoey hadn't wanted to give Amy the benefit of the doubt, but every time she made an effort to forgive her, she did something else to hurt Laura. Looking over at her housemates on the sofa giggling about Laura's love life Zoey wished she could join in. But there was nothing on this earth that would make her trust Amy Love.

Laura leapt up from the sofa, clutching her phone in her hand. There hadn't been a knock at the door, but the soft ping of a text meant she had arrived. The smile across her face was intoxicating and solely for Amy. Her face started to go a little red, blushing as it dawned on her – she was actually nervous about Amy meeting her roommates. Walking to the door, she wondered what Amy she would see today: how much masking would she be doing. She had done a little reading and masking was one of the phrases that came up. Laura was hopeful Amy would feel comfortable enough to let her guard down a little, even around the other women in the apartment. Resting her hand on the door handle Laura took one last deep breath. This was it. This was the start of her and Amy, for real.

The smile across the redhead's face was effortless and carefree, the warmth in her eyes was genuine as she laid them on the woman of her infatuation. But Laura couldn't help but feel there was a distance between them, as she opened the door wide. Amy had her hands firmly in the pockets of her green jacket. She looked like she didn't have a care in the world – and Laura couldn't help the mixed feelings of desire and disappointment spread across her body. She was excited to see Amy. Every inch of her body reacted to the mere sight of the English women – but she couldn't help a tinge of disappointment in the carefully curated smile she wore.

"Hey," Amy said through her smile. She looked so casual, it was at such an odds to how she had been most of yesterday. Laura was quite unnerved. She moved back from the door so Amy could walk in. As she walked past, she planted a soft kiss on Laura's lips. It caught Laura off-guard; she hadn't expected physical contact in front of the others. But she couldn't escape how perfect it felt, the way Amy's soft lips felt bushing against hers was enough to make her insides stir, hungry for more.

"Hi." Ali had bound up from the couch, and was first in

line to greet Amy. Zoey stayed firmly on her seat, ignoring the proceedings – but they both knew she had seen the kiss. "How do you feel about hugs?" Ali asked, her voice full of sunshine.

"Hugs are good." Amy smiled back, holding her arms out ready to receive Ali's energetic greeting. She almost fell back with the force the woman jumped at her. Both giggled and separated, as Munaza came over and stretched her arms for a hug – Amy obliged, keeping her smile even and controlled. Laura suspected Amy was, in fact, not as ok with hugs as she was pretending. But it just made Laura's heart flutter; Amy was prepared to embrace her housemates to make Laura happy.

This was going really well, Laura thought, but Ali and Munaza were not the ones she was worried about. Zoey got up from her seat, slowly she walked over to Amy with a neutral expression, her arms folded. Amy held her arms out a little sheepishly for a hug, mirroring the action with a little less certainty than she had for the previous women.

Zoey walked in closer, making sure her head was on the other side of the redhead's face to Laura. She got in close enough to whisper and not be heard by anyone else.

"If you can't love her, you need to leave," was all she whispered before breaking the hug. Standing back, she caught the faintest flicker of panic in Amy's green eyes. Good. "Come on ladies, let's leave the lovebirds to their evening." Zoey smiled sweetly before grabbing her coat off the peg and heading out the door as Ali and Munaza followed, not even offering a second glance to either of them.

"That went better than I expected." Laura sounded relieved as the door clicked shut behind the trio. Zoey had kept her word to Laura and now they had the apartment to themselves. She stole a look at Amy. The carefree smile was gone and she now looked nervous as she shuffled her feet and rubbed the back of her head with her hand. Laura closed the gap between them and placed her hand on the back of Amy's neck, pulling her in for a deep sensual kiss. A small moan escaped Amy's mouth as her tongue searched for Laura's, and her hands moved to her waist taking fistfuls of material in her hands.

The heat began to build and coil like a spring in Laura's center as the kiss moved from sensual to something more needy and urgent. It was clear Amy was feeling the same pull. Laura broke the kiss for a moment. Seeing the pout in Amy's eyes made her giggle. "I love kissing you in the doorway, but could we move this somewhere more comfortable?"

"Yeah, that sounds like a great idea, princess, lead the way." Amy moved back so Laura could walk past, a wicked glint in her eye as she followed Laura straight to her bedroom.

Chapter 41

Right in the World

This was not their first time, not even close, but it felt new; it felt different. This was the first time Laura was going to have sex with Amy when she knew she was in love, not just suspected love, but full blown head-over-heels unabashed love. She wanted to remember this – all of it. Leading the way to her room, Laura was filled with all sorts of anticipation. She had spent far too long dreaming of all the things she wanted to do to Amy, and all the things she wanted Amy to do to her. It looked like tonight she finally got to make some of those fantasies a reality and she wasn't going to waste any more time.

"My bed, my rules – remember," Laura teased Amy, as she tugged at her jeans by the belt loop. "And I want these to come off; in fact, I want all your clothes off." She had never been this bold with Amy before, but she liked it, returning to her usual rhythm.

Amy obliged and stripped all her clothes off without hesitation, folding them neatly in a pile, a move that made Laura smile. Laura drank in the woman in front of her. They had been naked before, but this was the first time she really got to look at Amy, and she really liked what she saw. Every curve was perfect as it led into the next, while her milk skin stretched unblemished across her body. Amy bit her bottom lip as a blush crept across her nose. She crossed her arms, unexpectedly shy given her past boldness. Laura realized she was still fully dressed and it probably made Amy feel uneasy. Laura took her shirt off with one hand, loving the emotions that played out on Amy's face. As she licked her lips, a blush crept further across her cheeks, but her eyes grew dark and hungry.

Laura closed the gap between them, keeping her eyes locked on the hooded green ones in front of her. It felt like there was more of a connection between them, the something deeper she had been feeling was already dancing around them, ready to ignite the second they touched. There would be no going back from here, the final piece of her would belong to Amy.

As she peppered kisses down Amy's neck, feeling the tension build, all she could think was how much she loved this woman. How much it all felt so right like it never had with someone before.

She had felt love, sure. But never like this. This was love deeper than anything else. Amy was the other half of her; she completed her in ways she couldn't express even if she wanted to. She was going to spend forever with this woman. She knew it, like it was written in the stars. Amy's breath caught as Laura's lips found the base of her neck. She committed the sound to memory, and the spot that caused it.

Pushing Amy back slightly until her lower legs hit the edge of the bed, she placed her hands on Amy's sides, gently guiding her down to sit on the bed, before she swung her leg over and sat straddling Amy, giving her a few extra inches in height. The heat radiating from her core was overwhelming. Now she was almost naked and exposed, it would take nothing for Amy to reach forward and touch her. If she did, Laura wasn't sure she could hold her resolve. Amy's hands snaked around her, the warmth of her palms and the cool feeling of her fingernails sent every part of her skin ablaze. Laura buried one hand in Amy's hair, pulling just a little to get her to look up. The sight of her lips parted and eyes gazing up at her sent a new wave of anticipation to her apex. The whimper that caught in her throat at the same time was about to undo her. She occupied her other hand to massage Amy's breasts, letting her fingers linger over and graze her firm, erect nipples.

Using this new control over Amy's body, she pulled them together for a passionate kiss, hot and deep as lips and teeth and tongues danced together. Laura was a little distracted and taken back when her bra suddenly became loose and fell to the floor. She broke off the kiss for a moment to look at Amy, who shot back a smirk so ladened with promise Laura almost lost her willpower.

God, she couldn't wait to taste Amy; feel her body give in, but she needed not to rush it, she reminded herself. This wasn't a quick fuck; not that it ever really had been with Amy – it had always been something more, like it was always destined to get to this point. This was her time to explore every inch for the first time, to commit it to memory. To find all the places that made her moan and whimper and beg. Anything to get her to make that noise again.

Taking the opportunity of Laura's temporary waver, Amy moved one hand to Laura's final remaining item of clothing, running her thumb on the inside of her black lace panty edge. Laura took in a sharp gasp. Arching her back to give Amy more access was instinctive, a primal need to have the woman touch her took over.

Amy could feel how wet Laura was for her, and she knew she was the same. With someone else, she might have been embarrassed at how fast her body had reacted, how quick she had submitted to her. But not here. Laura made her feel things no one ever had before; she just needed to embrace it and let Laura in, all the way in.

Laura regained her resolve and removed Amy's wandering hand. She was greeted by an indignant pout that made her laugh – maybe a submissive Amy would be a brat. She hoped to find out. Putting both hands on her warm shoulders, she pushed them back onto the bed, her back hitting the mattress with a soft thud. Now Laura could see how beautiful Amy really was, her hair spilling across the bed as her moss eyes looked up at her, still filled with wanting.

"You ok with this?" Laura asked keeping contact with Amy's eyes, a small nod and half smile were all the encouragement and consent she needed. She started laying kisses from the top of Amy's neck while placing one firm hand on her hip. She could feel Amy's breath catch as she moved across her sensitive skin, the goosebumps rising under her lips and tongue as she traveled across her chest, capturing a nipple in her teeth gently. It caused Amy to moan and arch her back. This was a side to the woman she had never seen before, vulnerability tied with anticipation; it was like a drug and Laura couldn't get enough of it. She never wanted to get enough of it. Drifting her hand lazily from Amy's hip to the top of her thigh, she could feel the heat radiating out of her, the yearning, the primal need for her touch. Laura couldn't resist any longer; weeks of anticipation and fantasy were here in front of her and she was going to drink it and savor every last moment. She ran her thumb over Amy's wet warm slit and the desire caught in her own throat as Amy let out the most delicate of whimpers – a wordless plea for Laura to satisfy her.

Amy could barely string a coherent thought together. From the feeling of lips and tongue doing circles around her tight nipples, to the firm grip Laura had on her hip, her grip on reality was falling away. The hand on her hip moved further down, deliberately but gently stroking across her core, not pressing deep enough to give any release, but with the promise of so much more to come. An overwhelming urge to kiss Laura came over Amy. She pulled Laura up with a hand on the back of her head and leaned in to force their lips together; they came back at her with equal feverish need. Laura shifted her weight to encapsulate Amy with her body. Her hair cascaded down around them like a dark waterfall, eyes dark as midnight burned with the embers of desire. Amy could swear she might fall into them, and in this moment, she wanted to. Drowning in the idea of Laura, the idea of them – nothing had felt more right.

Her thoughts got pulled away from Laura's eyes as a thumb made contact with her clit, slowly pushing in between her folds, causing her legs to involuntarily spread wider, welcoming her in. Taking the invitation, Laura slid two fingers inside. Amy did nothing but roll her eyes back in unfettered desire.

It felt amazing. There was nothing that could ruin this; she was totally giving herself over. The slow circles her thumb was mapping across Amy's clit felt like electricity building, slow and deliberate, as their mouths continued to dance together. Amy's hips started to move involuntarily, matching the pace of Laura's hand. A smile crept across Laura's lips, pulling them tight as they continued to kiss.

"I want to taste you," she whispered into Amy's mouth, causing green eyes to focus on blue, no longer rolling back in ecstasy; they gave everything away – and what they didn't, the moan that escaped Amy's lips did.

"Yes!" The faintest whisper, almost inaudible, escaped. Laura moved her body away from Amy's lips; a fleeting moment of sadness that they were no longer kissing. That thought was quickly replaced by far more devious ones as she started trailing kisses down Amy's torso, trailing all the way down across her hips, until they met the spot her hand was working.

The first drag of Laura's tongue across her clit was something Amy could never forget – the fireworks, the pressure and the promise – it caused her back to arch further, one hand jumped up to cover her mouth capturing the scream that threatened to escape while the other moved to bury itself in Laura's hair. She wasn't going to last long, and they both knew it.

Laura couldn't get over how sweet Amy tasted. It was like ecstasy on Laura's tongue. She wanted nothing more than to keep doing this forever. Maybe it was all the waiting – maybe it was the fact she was finally seeing Amy for who she actually was – there were so many reasons why this was borderline perfect. But none of it mattered. What mattered was that Amy was close, and Laura was the one to take her over the edge. She stole a look up at Amy, her pale skin almost glowing in the dim light, one hand across her mouth, holding in whatever sounds she didn't dare let out – Laura would let her keep them a secret this time, but next time she wanted to hear it all. Amy's other hand was buried in her hair, keeping her mouth working where it was. Even in this moment, Amy couldn't completely give over all her control, something else Laura would rectify in the future.

Laura wanted to keep Amy suspended like this forever, in this singular moment of pleasure. Moving her hand from its resting place on the inner of Amy's thigh, she pushed two fingers back into Amy. The hand covering her mouth was unable to hide all the sound that escaped, a sharp high gasp emanated deep from within the redhead. The sound itself made Laura's core clench with its own need. But she was too busy focusing on this moment. She wanted to remember everything, from the rotating of her hips to the tighter grip as she balled up a fistful of Laura's hair, the way her body tightened around Laura's own fingers.

She felt Amy come. It was hard and fast; after weeks of pent-up frustration she expected nothing less, but the continued waves that followed were a pleasant, and undeniably sexy surprise.

Once she was satisfied Amy couldn't take any more in that moment, Laura slowly removed her fingers. She trailed and kissed back up her body, now covered in a cool layer of sweat. Their lips met again, Laura getting even more turned on as Amy tasted herself and her own climax on Laura's lips, feverishly kissing them, sucking them – like she also never wanted to forget this feeling.

Laura flopped back on the bed, rolling to the side of Amy to catch her breath. She was feeling heady and like she was floating all at the same time, and she hadn't even been touched. Yet. Amy's eyes were wild, as she propped herself up on one elbow, the look of pure release still thrown across her face. Laura could drink this in, but before she got a chance to collect her thoughts, a wicked smile spread across Amy's lips.

"Your turn," was all she said before pushing herself on top of Laura, hands wandering and lips meeting once more. The last thought Laura had before she let go completely was how sexy Amy sounded. There was a huskyness that hadn't been present before, a reminder of her recent muffled screams.

As Amy's lips made contact with her entrance and her tongue danced inside, Laura lost all her control – giving herself over to the absolute pleasure of being fucked by the woman she loved.

Laura gazed over at Amy. She was asleep, her red hair spilled across the pillow like a mane. She looked peaceful curled around Laura, with her head resting on Laura's chest, and an arm over her torso. Laura loved the way she looked; the way they looked together here at this moment, Amy's pale skin caught in the small shaft of light creeping from the streetlight outside. She could get used to this; she wanted to get used to this. Nuzzling her head down into Amy's hair, she caught the hint of cherries. Laura drifted off to sleep with the easy feeling that everything was right in the world.

Chapter 42

Drowning

Amy was drowning – or at least what she thought drowning felt like. Her lungs were heavy and refused to fill with air. Everything was black and cold. Ice cracked and fractured inside her chest, splintering and piercing her organs.

The more she tried to call out, to take a breath, the harder it became. Her head was spinning or was her body spinning? She couldn't tell: it was too dark, the expanse of nothingness making her feel more alone than she ever had. Trying to open her mouth was impossible. Her mind screamed. Trying to open her mouth was impossible, held shut by forces she couldn't see.

She was sinking. Drowning.

Out of the darkness, she felt a weight on her chest. The spinning stopped instantly as the warmth grounded her.

Thawing the ice. The roaring in her ears was pierced with what she thought was someone calling her name – but there was no one here, no one to call her name, no one to save her. There was never anyone to save her.

"Amy." A voice came from somewhere around her; it was panicked and distant. "Amy, you need to breathe."

She couldn't breathe, her lungs were full of ice, but the pressure on her chest was warm, spreading across her body, preventing her from falling any further.

"Amy!" The voice was loud; it was close. "Amy, you need to open your eyes and breathe. Please." Open her eyes? Could she do that? Were they not already open? She thought they were, staring into the black nothingness. Then there was a heat on her cheek. She could feel it, a hand – a warm hand – on the side of her face. Maybe she could open her eyes.

Amy's eyes fluttered open. They looked wild and scared, her pupils darting around, searching. They locked with Laura's blue pools, barely visible in the dim night. They were full of worry , fear, and a hint of something else that Amy couldn't place.

"Amy, you need to calm down!" Laura hoped she sounded less panicked now Amy's eyes were open, but she didn't feel it. The fear and haunting in Amy's eyes made her blood run cold. She wasn't sure she ever wanted to know what made someone look like that. But it felt like whatever she was doing was working, a hand on Amy's chest to help her breathing and the other on her cheek. She could feel the wet tears on her hand. All Laura wanted to do was hold her tight and never let go.

"It's ok, Amy, I've got you," Laura said soothingly. Amy's breathing was returning to normal. Her eyes were fixed on

Laura's, almost pleading for this to be over. Amy moved her hand up to the cover Laura's on her cheek. The feel of her hand was so delicate, fragile. Laura felt herself ache for Amy even more. Leaning closer and planting a soft kiss on Amy's forehead, Laura felt how cold Amy was. "Amy, I am going to step away for a second. I am going to get you a top, ok?"

Laura moved to the pile of clothes they had discarded a few hours ago. She grabbed Amy's t-shirt and threw her own on, hoping it would make Amy feel more at ease. By the time she had turned round again, Amy was sitting up with the sheet pulled close to her chest. Her eyes had a vacant look and even in the dark Laura could see the faint blush across her cheeks as her chest rose and fell in deep relieving breaths. Sliding across the bed, she passed Amy her top, the redhead quickly put it on, without taking a second to look at Laura.

"You don't have to talk – but can you let me know you are ok?" Laura looked at Amy's profile, holding her breath, hoping Amy was not going to slip into another panic attack. Jamie had said she had them, and now retrospectively, it was clear that is what Amy had had the first time they had tried to spend the night together. But what Laura could not get her head around is why Amy was having them in her sleep. What nightmares could be so bad they cause such a violent reaction? Her thoughts were interrupted when Amy gave a small nod, turning her head towards Laura and giving a weary hollow smile. Laura leaned over and squeezed Amy's hand, a move which Amy reciprocated.

They sat in silence, holding hands in the dark for several minutes, Amy recentering herself as Laura tried to catch her own brain up with what had just happened. It felt like it had lasted forever but equally been over in less than a minute – her mind was racing. She had been asleep when she jolted awake, woken by Amy thrashing in the bed next to her, face etched with pain and panic. She hadn't been breathing; it had terrified her.

"Thank you," Amy whispered after the longest time. She didn't turn to look at Laura, instead keeping her gaze fixed on the bed sheet covering them both.

"It's ok. I hope I did the right thing; this is new to me," Laura said honestly as she brought her knees up to her chin, somehow feeling vulnerable herself.

"It's never happened when people have been around before," Amy mumbled. "Well, not like that anyway." The guilt and shame was starting to eat her up inside. She had hoped that telling Laura everything she had would mean this didn't happen, that opening herself to Laura would prevent this reaction. Clearly she was a fool to hope.

"Can you tell me what it was?" Laura asked gently as she moved her thumb in circles on the back of Amy's hand, trying to comfort herself as much as the other woman.

"No," was all Amy said. It was cold and distant; she pulled her hand away from Laura's. The comforting movements felt like someone was rubbing sandpaper on her skin.

"Do you know why it happened?" Laura pressed. She felt a jolt of anger at Amy's coldness; she just wanted to help.

"No," Amy responded in the same cold tone.

"Maybe we should try and get back to sleep?" Laura suggested. She just wanted to feel Amy in her arms again. It had felt so good to fall asleep the way they had; she wanted that back.

"I don't think that's a good idea," Amy stated, as if it was fact. "Maybe I should go."

Ice fell across Laura as if she had been thrown in the harbor. How could Amy possibly suggest that in this state? After everything how could she even contemplate just leaving? "Well I don't think that's a good idea!" Laura retorted. "I would like it if you could give me some idea of what just happened – so I know for next time."

Amy turned to look at her. Her eyes were blank, they gave nothing away, no hint of emotion. Laura didn't like it. "It doesn't matter."

"It does to me, Amy. It matters a lot to me – if you are going to be sharing my bed then I need to know!" Laura tried to keep her tone neutral, but it felt like Amy was being intentionally obtuse.

"No one cared before," Amy said, shifting away from Laura slightly. Still unable to fully look at the woman. Something in Laura snapped.

"This isn't about your fucked-up past relationships Amy. We all did stupid shit in the past; it's what makes us less shit people now," Laura almost shouted in exasperation. She calmed herself down before adding, "The look in your eyes tells me it's deeper than that. And fine you don't have to tell me – but don't treat me like an idiot that can't see you are hurting." Laura spun round; she didn't want to look at Amy any more. "I really wanted to give this a go with you, Amy. I am crazy about you. I feel an actual deep connection with you that I haven't had in a long time. But the way you have acted is kinda fucked up. And I don't think it's because you're autistic." Laura felt her emotions bubbling up, the clash of relief a few minutes ago replaced with anger now. "Something else is going on, and you need to tell me or you need to leave me alone."

Silence. A long protracted deafening silence fell over them.

"I was outed at fifteen." Amy's voice was small, weak. She continued to look down. She couldn't believe she had said this much already, and all she had said was five words. "I lived with my dad at the time and he wasn't the nicest man in the world. I was normally pretty good at staying on his good side – you know being out when he was drinking, making sure I didn't get in the way at home etc. But when he found out. He got really nasty." Tears began to prickle at the back of Amy's eyes. She hated that she cried thinking of this. "I uh... he didn't take the news well. He got violent... not for the first time, but it was definitely the worst time." Amy paused. She couldn't believe she had uttered the words, spoken aloud things she had never told anyone other than Jamie. It had been a secret for almost fifteen years, buried so deep she didn't think she would even be able to say it aloud.

"Amy..." Laura's hand slid over and took one of Amy's in hers; at the same moment silent tears started falling from Amy's face. It made sense: the last bits of Amy Love were finally slotting into place. Her avoidance of talking about her family, her fierce independence, her reluctance to commit.

"I had to move across the country to live with my mum; I lost everything I had. My friends, school, everything I owned that I wasn't wearing that night." Amy took a deep breath. "The next few years were lonely. I didn't make friends, I shut myself off completely. I was living in a strange place with strange people, and I have never felt like I fitted in again."

"Amy, I am so sorry that happened to you," was all Laura could say. The pain was evident across Amy's face, the haunted look had returned. "You know none of that was your fault, right?"

"I know." Amy waved Laura's statement away. "I spent a lot of my late teens and all of my twenties making bad choices, bad relationships and in bad situations. Even when I was dating someone and in the most stable place I ever had in my life, I couldn't even be happy with what I had." Amy sat silently, feeling Laura's eyes burn deep into her – searching for something, more answers? Amy wondered. Silence descended like a fog resting heavy in the air. Amy continued to look at the floor and avoid Laura's gaze. She had no idea what came next; she always left before she had to tell anyone, never let anyone get close enough to need to know.

"I think I understand now," Laura said slowly, moving her hand up to Amy's chin – pulling her face so she could see her eyes. "I understand why you won't let anyone in."

"That's, that's not it." Amy could feel her chest tightening in a vise, but if she didn't say it now she may never be able to again. She had never felt so vulnerable in her whole life. "He... ah, I – I thought I was going to die, I felt like I was going to die." Her eyes shot up to meet Laura's; they were so beautiful and blue, so deep you could get lost in them. " He said that people like me don't deserve to live." The words hung in the air.

"Amy, you know that's not true right?" Laura felt the need to say something – anything to end the silence. Amy's eyes were ringed red making the green look like it was on fire, almost inhuman.

"Yeah, so then I ended up living with my mum." Amy moved on as if she didn't hear Laura. "She wasn't the greatest, we didn't really know each other, and I was not exactly in a good place, mentally. Our relationship is better now, not great but better. I think the ocean between us helps."

Laura had so many questions burning inside her. But

she didn't know how to ask them. She just continued to hold Amy's hand and study her eyes, big green pools glazed over like ice on a lake – hiding what was going on behind them. There were a thousand questions running in her head, so loud she wouldn't be surprised if Amy could hear them.

"You can ask me anything. I have nothing to hide from you any more." Amy sounded deflated.

Laura was torn between craving more information to just wanting to reach over and make all the pain go away. "How did you get outed?" she finally asked, trying to put a timeline together in her head, trying to ask the right questions to help her put everything together.

"My best friend wasn't really my best friend. One sleepover she fell asleep in my bed; we both did. We weren't careful. We got caught by my stepmother the next morning. She told my dad that night and the rest is history." Amy waved her hand dismissively, as if this was something so normal it barely warranted a reaction. The reaction was more chilling to Laura than the story; how nonchalantly Amy brushed it off, like it was normal. Like any of this was normal.

Laura gave Amy's hand the smallest of squeezes, hoping it conveyed everything she wanted to say. Hoping it was conveying a feeling of encouragement and support. No wonder she never stayed the night; It was all so strikingly simple now. Laura could relate to the best-friend-come-secret-highschool-girlfriend story, though she suspected few ended as badly as this one.

"What did the best friend have to say about all this?"

"I don't know, I never saw her again. I guess to her I just vanished." Amy shrugged. She had thought many times over the years about reaching out, but she never knew what to say. What do you say to a woman that you shared everything with one day and then just disappeared on the next?

To Laura's horror, Amy started to stand up. Her body stiffened as she let go of Laura's hand. She let it fall to the bed. A wall grew instantaneously between them the second they lost contact, the moment lost forever. "Amy, what are you doing?" Laura asked slowly, unable to hide the panic seeping into her voice; dreading what was about to happen, powerless to stop it, the all-too-familiar pattern of behavior returning. A pattern that now made so much sense.

"I need to go," Amy stated, as if it was a fact. She slid on her sneakers and picked up her jacket.

"I don't think you do, Amy." Laura sounded desperate, she felt desperate. "You don't have to leave."

"Goodbye, Laura." Amy's voice was a hollow whisper as she started to walk away. Laura couldn't take it. The rage that filled her was explosive and out of nowhere, searing white-hot anger.

"Don't you dare disappear on me Amy. Don't you dare fucking walk off and expect me to just be ok with it!" Laura had stood now too, reaching out and tentatively resting her hand on Amy's shoulder. She felt Amy tense and freeze under her jacket; recoiling as if bitten by a predator.

"This was a mistake," Amy said coldly, not bothering to turn around.

"No, Amy, it wasn't a mistake. Nothing about us is a mistake," Laura pleaded. "You don't have to be like this, you know, you could let someone in." She paused, all the anger vanishing from her voice. "You could let me in," she almost whispered. Amy moved her shoulder out from under Laura's grasp and continued to walk away.

Amy glanced over her shoulder at Laura, her own tears streaming down her face. Laura was rooted to the spot. She had come to care so much about Amy, she couldn't picture her life without Amy in it in some small way.

"Don't make me beg you not to leave," Laura pleaded, but it was too late. Amy was already on the other side of the door. She slumped to the floor, tears she had been holding back finally erupting from her face.

"I love you," she sobbed into the dark empty room.

Chapter 43

Goodbye

The sun was still rising as it chased the last of the night's sky away to the west. Laura stood at the entrance to her building, wrapped in a thick coat, protection from the cold night air. Late February still had its fingers deep in winter. But the mornings were getting lighter; spring wasn't going to be far away.

It had been days since she had had anything from Amy – nothing, and all she had done in response was mope around her apartment, doing the bare minimum amount of work before returning to her duvet and mindless scrolling. Then out of the blue last night, Amy had texted her asking if she could come and see her before eight AM. She should have said no, or ignored it – but she couldn't. She hated the way her heart warmed and her soul sang when she heard from her. She hated that all she had wanted to do since they last spoke was to wrap her up in her arms and tell her it would all be ok. Amy had promised to explain everything. So here she was at seven AM in the cold outside her apartment, waiting for Amy. Because that's what you did when you were in love.

Amy rounded the street corner. She had asked Jamie to park a block away; she didn't trust herself to come otherwise. She had spent all night going over what she was going to say to Laura, and no matter which way she said it – her heart always came away broken. She looked up to see Laura standing in the doorway, her dark brown hair tied back in a French braid. Getting closer, it was evident that Laura had not been sleeping much either: her skin was a little pale and her eyes were glazed over in the way they do when you cry for hours, until you run out of tears. Guilt riddled Amy: she was the one to cause this, it was another mistake she could add to her ever growing list.

They both stood in silence, neither one wanting to start. Laura felt a yearning towards Amy she had hoped had lessened over the last few days, but it had just grown stronger – the desire to reach out and pull her close, to have anything from her was almost inescapable.

"Amy, I –" Laura started, reaching out for Amy's hand, but Amy took a step back, expanding the distance between them, cutting Laura off before she could talk. Before Amy lost her nerve. A single touch from Laura and her ice thin resolve would shatter.

"I am going away for a while," Amy said, with confidence she could only pretend existed. "I think I need to deal with some things before I can really be myself, my real self." The words all came out too fast, like she was forcing them out. "I need to go back home." The word got caught in Amy's throat; it had been ten years, it wasn't still home, it hadn't been for a long time. "I think I need to go back to England," she clarified as much to herself as anyone else.

The words hit Laura with all the force of a freight train.

After all of this. After all their times together. After everything they had said to each other. Everything they had felt – this is how Amy was ending things.

Amy looked at the floor, fearing looking into Laura's eyes, those beautiful blue eyes that made her want so many things, so many things she couldn't have. They could persuade her to stay, and that was the scariest thing of all. They made her believe they could be together, but she knew it would never work, could never work.

"I could come with you?" Laura choked, knowing already in her heart that that wasn't going to happen, she wasn't thinking clearly. She was throwing out the first thing that came to her head; it was desperate. She was desperate. "You shouldn't do this on your own, Amy."

"Actually, I think I need to do this on my own." Amy's voice was hollow, the idea of ever returning had always filled her with dread; now it left her numb. "My flight is booked for this afternoon. Jamie is taking me to the airport."

"No." Laura reached her arms out to try and touch Amy, but she moved back, avoiding even the delicate edges of Laura's fingers. "Please don't walk away from me again, Amy." Laura almost sounded like she was begging as tears caught in her throat. Emotion curling and suffocating her.

"I'm sorry," was all Amy could muster. Her resolve broke and the tears began to prickle the edges of her own eyes. "I never wanted to hurt you. In fact, that was the last thing I ever wanted to do. As soon as I started getting any real feelings for you, I should have backed off – but I couldn't. You made me feel things and want things that I am not capable of having."

"You could have those things. You could have me." Laura begged. Her mind was racing; how had this all happened so fast? How had she gone from butterflies at the idea of seeing Amy again to finding out she was going away, potentially forever?

Laura loved Amy and there was no denying it. How had she gone from not even knowing this woman existed to being in love with her in such a short space of time? How had she let herself get so close to someone who was so incapable of loving her back? Feelings of anger mixed in with heartbreak prevented her from crying, or maybe that was the dehydration from shedding so many tears over the last few days.

"You don't want me like this, Laura. You deserve someone so much better than who I am." Amy gave up trying to stop the tears and let them flow down her face. "And if I am ever going to be someone worthy of a woman like you – I need to go."

Laura leaned over and wiped away a tear on Amy's cheek, her red hair catching in the wind and sticking to the wet trails left behind. Laura moved to face Amy directly, pulling her close. She didn't resist this time. She couldn't bear to be apart from her.

As their lips met for the final time, Amy felt the warmth in her chest, the warmth that came from being this close to Laura. Her whole body screamed at her not to do this – to just give in to the easy option and stay. Laura broke the kiss off first, the tender softness of Amy's lips burnt into her memory forever. She rested her forehead against Amy's, not wanting to ever forget the cherry smell of her shampoo, or the skip her heart made when she was so close to the woman she loved.

"I will wait for you," she whispered tenderly. "I will be here when you get back!"

"Please don't, Laura." Amy said firmly, through her tears. "I can't be doing this for anyone but myself." Even though she wanted nothing more than to know Laura was here waiting for her, she couldn't ask this from anyone. It was the quickest way to ensure they could never be anything to each other again. Amy took Laura's hands in hers and removed them from her waist, breaking their contact felt like pulling apart two magnets. "We had fun, but that's all it was, fun. We never defined anything, we never made big plans. It was just an extended fling."

"No, Amy, I don't think it was that at all. And neither do you." Laura flushed with anger. "I refuse to believe that this all means so little to you that you are prepared to just walk away."

"You deserve a person that can stay the night in your bed. You deserve a person who won't leave you asleep in hotel rooms because she's too busy running from her own problems. You deserve a woman who can give you everything you want. That isn't me," Amy finished. She had spent so long rehearsing this last night so she could deliver it with the needed lack of emotion.

"You don't get to tell me what I deserve, Amy. I am the only one who gets to decide how I feel," Laura said bitterly. "How long do you think you will be gone?"

"I don't know," Amy said, rubbing the back of her neck. "In fact, I have something for you." Amy remembered as she dug in her pocket.

"A leaving gift, how lovely," Laura said sarcastically, the softness of her voice giving away her hurt.

Amy pulled out a single silver key and placed it in Laura's hand, she looked at it with confusion, not understanding what this was supposed to symbolize. "The rent is paid up for the next six months, and fixed for the six after that," Amy stated. "It's nothing fancy, but it's yours if you want it. Jamie has all the paperwork ready for you."

"What?" Laura was dumbfounded. Amy had just given her her apartment. She didn't have to live in a shared house anymore, she would have her own space. She couldn't even find the words to thank Amy. The excitement of her own place was almost enough to make her forget how she was getting it. She would finally have somewhere she could bring people back to she thought – only to have the crushing realization that the only person she wanted to bring back was Amy. "You don't have to do this," she started, unable to put a sentence together. Everything was happening so fast.

"It's already done. If you don't want it, I understand, I left all the furniture, but changed the bed." Amy was so formal and business-like, this side of things was easy to detach from.

"What about all your things?" Laura was still looking at the silver key in her hand, still processing the gift.

"The advantage of always running is I got really good at traveling light." Amy chuckled. It was hollow and made Laura's skin crawl. "I donated everything to the shelter, they will pass on what they can or sell it."

"Wait!" Laura almost shouted, snapping out of her daze "What about your work at the university? How are you going to continue your research?" Suddenly remembering, she allowed herself a moment of hope that Amy had also forgotten and was about to change her mind.

"I have set up automation for the last few readings, and Jamie is going to monitor it locally for me. The testing phase is nearly over anyway, so it will only be for a few weeks." Amy had spent time over the last few days talking everything over with Jamie. He was the one who had suggested she needed to deal with things if she had any hope of a relationship – with Laura or anyone else.

"Guess you have thought of everything then." Laura's

voice was dejected, the realization that this was really happening starting to wash over her as she stared at the key to Amy's apartment – her new apartment.

"I won't ever forget you, Laura," Amy said finally, looking into the big deep blue eyes. She never wanted to be apart from them; they pulled her in like sirens calling to ships at sea. Before letting herself fall into the pools, Amy stepped back again, letting go of Laura's hand that she hadn't even realized she was holding. "Goodbye, princess," she whispered, flicking her one last careless smile, that she had spent so many years practicing.

Laura crumpled finally letting go of anything she was holding back. She loved Amy. Amy was the person she was destined to love forever; it was etched into her soul with such certainty. This was a crushing pain she had never experienced. Every inch of her wanted to scream after Amy, crawl on her knees and beg at her feet not to leave. But she couldn't move, like a wounded animal she bled tears in the doorway. She had always said she would rather love and have lost than never love at all, but in this moment she felt like Love was nothing more than a barbed dagger ripping her insides apart – never to recover. Never to love again.

Walking away from Laura felt like the biggest mistake Amy Love could possibly make. And she knew she had made some big mistakes. Her chest was heavy. It felt like the cold air in her lungs was stabbing her deep in the chest. Her heart was breaking more with every step she took in the opposite direction of the woman she loved. A part of her heart was always going to belong to Laura, even though the other woman would never know it.

Amy Love Will Return

Acknowledgments

First and foremost I want to thank you, the reader. If you had told any past version of me that I would have not only written something, but then had the guts to publish it – she wouldn't have believed you; and in truth I am not sure I quite believe it now. So the fact that you are sitting here and reading this is mind-blowing, terrifying and humbling, all at the same time.

When I started writing this it was on a whim, with no direction or plan and it was only with the love and support of my best friend and editor Paige Gadsby (yes that is her real name) who listened to me fumble my way into getting the words from my head onto the page – even the sexy ones. Other very deserving thanks go to my wife, who had no idea I wrote a book for four months until I blurted it out to her one Sunday afternoon. Her continued love and support across all my ridiculous ideas warms my heart. I also want to thank the countless members of the indie author community who have been both funny and utter dicks in equal measure. They really did put up with my stupid questions and were an immense help in navigating stormy waters.

More personally I want to thank the following people for knowing exactly what they did – fuck you all very much: Loren, Stacey, Chris, JayDell, Sabrina and lastly my all-American cheerleader, Shelby. I can no longer imagine my life without you all in it.

Growing up as a girl with undiagnosed Autism and ADHD, I never felt like I fitted in and I retreated more to stories where things made sense and people went on amazing adventures; when the real world didn't make sense, I always had books that did. I always resonated with the outcast and the misfit more than the lead character, and the edgy, never-grown-up goth in me still does. It was important to me to write a character that felt these things but ultimately found who she was, and in turn found a family and love.

This book series has been written in airports and train stations, McDonalds and shopping mall food courts – all stolen moments when I should have been doing other things. I have had the immense privilege and the ability to go to these places and take up space. Many of us are not that lucky and it's why we should continue to fund and support our local libraries – the last free public space you can go to.

Lastly I want to thank Leia and Tilly, the best four-legged companions I could ever ask for. They are the best listeners and foot warmers.

The Many Mistakes series continues with:

The Many Mistakes of Zoey Andrews
The Many Mistakes of Laura Miller

Coming Soon!

The Many Mistakes of Zoey Andrews - Preview

The Straight Girl

Laying in bed with her first college boyfriend was where Zoey first realized she was probably gay, and that she was probably in love with Laura, her sister's lifelong best friend.

It was here, looking up at the water-stained ceiling in the rundown frat house, that she finally let those feelings exist for what they were – not pseudo sisterly love, but raging-hot passion and lust that she had carried for almost her whole life.

Shit.

Joe was a nice guy, well as nice as any sophomore finance major could be. He was on some sports team that Zoey could never remember; his parents and hers knew each other from the business arena. They had set them up the summer before she left for college, stating how he could show her around and get her settled in. It was the most obvious setup Zoey had ever seen, but considering she had never managed to get a boyfriend in highschool she couldn't see the harm.

There had just never been any passion, no spark – Zoey just assumed this was just the way things were, that movies and books had lied about romance. Kissing Joe had been like kissing a fish that was desperately trying to grow a beard: wet and smiley with far too much tongue. But nonetheless, she had gone through the motions of dating and parties, and now coming up to Thanksgiving, she had finally given in and had sex with him. Not that he had been particularly pushy. He had taken her out for a nice meal and been really caring, Zoey mused to herself, as she listened to his breathing next to her in the bed. But when she tried to conjure up the passion and romance she should have felt, all she could think was that he had probably not changed his sheets since his mom put them on the bed at the start of the semester.

No, she desperately tried to focus on the physical events of the night before. Candles had been lit and sexy music had played from a bluetooth speaker slightly too close to the bed. As Joe was putting the most minimal effort into foreplay, haphazardly pawing at her breasts and trying to finger bang her in something akin to a cardio warm-up routine. It hadn't hurt; she had expected it to, based on books and teen magazine accounts. She was just totally ambivalent about it. He was mercifully quick in his thirty seconds of furiously uneven thrusting – the lack of rhythm had totally thrown her off any sense of enjoyment.

Rolling out the bed, Zoey's foot landed with a squelch on the cold slippery remains of the condom Joe had thrown on the floor last night, the reminisce of his good time seeping into the carpet. It was at this exact moment she decided that she was done with men and having sex with them; there were enough data points here to make an informed choice after all.

Without waking Jo, she gathered her things that had become part of his room over the last few weeks, got dressed and left. She would text him later that day and tell him they were over.

Walking out into the crisp November morning, Zoey turned her attention to the other realization of the day. Laura. She had known her since she was five, when Emily, then Eric had started in the same kindergarten class; they had become instant friends and remained that way ever since. Zoey had been the annoying younger sister for most of their childhood and early teens, but when she skipped a year in high school, the three of them had become inseparable. The assumption had always been that Eric and Laura would marry one day; that was, until Zoey caught Laura at Homecoming, making out with one of the cheerleaders. At the time, Zoey couldn't understand why she had cried in her bed that night, but now it was all becoming painfully clear: the jealousy, the need to spend time with her, be close to her. It wasn't about being left out; it was because she had a giant, huge lesbian crush on her. Shit.

Zoey groaned as she swiped her card to enter the halls building and trudged up the stairs. She wanted a hot shower and to flop in her own bed before having to go to class later. She hoped Ali would be out, the pink-haired art major had been a surprising roommate allocation and Zoey still wasn't sure about her yet, but they only had to share a room for the first year – after that she was free to go where she wanted. Maybe to share with some of her Law major peers or at least someone on a less liberal course, hopefully someone with the same work ethic.

Walking down the corridor, Zoey could hear the unmistakable sound of Ali having sex. Loud, unabashed sex with the RA; fortunately it sounded like they were not in her room and instead making use of the RA's single room. Retreating into her space, she was pleased to see Ali had at least tried to keep to the new cleaning chart. Her bed wasn't made but at least her clothes were not all over the room. After a hot shower, Zoey crawled into bed hoping to get a few hours of sleep. Unfortunately that was the exact moment Ali burst back into the room carrying her bra like a trophy.

"Ooooh you were out all night!" she sang as she flopped onto her own bed. "Did you finally give Joe the handjob he has been asking for?" Zoey shifted further down into her sheets. The last person she wanted to talk to about any of this was Ali, her abrasive, extroverted roommate.

"No," Zoey muttered from under the sheets. She could hear Ali laughing from the other side of the room, laughing at her for not giving her boyfriend what he wanted. It made her blood boil. "Actually we had sex, and he was terrible, not only because he couldn't find my clit with a GPS, but also because I think I am gay!"

Silence hung in the room for a few seconds as Zoey waited for any reaction from Ali at all. This was the first time she had said the words out loud. In her own defense, she had only come to this conclusion in the last few hours.

"Finally!" Ali screamed from the other side of the room. "I was worried I was going to start giving really unsubtle hints soon."

"You knew?!" Zoey exclaimed, throwing the sheets off her face and sitting bolt upright in her bed, looking over at Ali. She still had her shoes on and was swinging her legs off the edge of the bed, propped up on her elbows. "Who else knows?!"

"Chill out, Zoey. I am pretty sure everyone knows now – you being the last." She bobbed her head from side to side, humming a tune. "Well maybe second to last to know – unless you have already told Joe?"

Zoey groaned and flopped back on the bed before throwing the cover back over herself. Why did being yourself have to be so complicated?

The Many Mistakes of Laura Miller - Preview

Laura's Choice

Laura had never regretted drinking before, but after her night of whiskey with Jamie, she was starting to see how easy it was to regret her life choices. The hangover had lasted days. It was the worst Laura had ever felt; the combination of mental, emotional and physical pain fueled with far too much whiskey had taken almost a week to go. Jamie had stayed with her until Emily had arrived, taking care of her in ways she had never expected from a man she barely knew. Laura couldn't help but feel a new sense of friendship with the lab tech; he was always going to be Amy's friend, but the way he had looked after her was more than most would do.

Since that night, she had allowed the new information to wash over her, mingled with the grief and heartbreak she was already feeling. It had done nothing to dampen her feelings towards Amy; if anything it had only made her heart yearn for the woman more. Now knowing all the reason behind her actions, the horrors she had experienced, this made Laura realize she wasn't weak but the exact opposite. Amy Love was the strongest person she knew.

She threw her head back in a groan. This was not what she needed to be thinking about right now. After a few days off work, she really needed to get her head in the game before she got behind. Jason had covered for her but he couldn't keep doing the work of two people. But no matter what she did, her mind was still full of Amy Love. Laura rubbed her eyes and looked back at the computer screen. The lines of code blurred in front of her. In a moment of anger, she slammed the lid of her laptop closed, causing Jason to jump opposite.

"Woah!" he feigned a yell at her, throwing his hands up in defense. "What did that poor computer ever do to you?" His shaggy dirt blond hair, combined with his athletic frame and heart of gold, made him a real catch. He just struggled keeping hold of them past the first few dates.

"Existed." Laura crossed her arms and pouted.

"Ah, that age old problem of inanimate objects just existing." He let out a small chuckle. "Could there possibly be another problem here?"

Laura cracked a small smile. Jason was such a goofball, but he always knew what to say to cheer her up. He flashed her a sympathetic smile in return. "You know there is." She sighed and threw her head back again, hoping this time the tears wouldn't betray her. "I just can't get her out of my head."

"Maybe you're not meant to." Jason shrugged as he dug around in his desk drawer before pulling out a Wunderbar and throwing it over the desk at Laura. "Like what if she *is* The One."

Laura looked Jason dead in the eye as she unwrapped the candy bar. She couldn't quite believe he was saying this to her after the weeks of crying at her desk; weeks of talking about nothing but Amy and most recently the failed sexual encounter with a literal goddess – this was his big answer. "Fuck off, Jason," was all she managed around a mouthful of chocolate and peanuts, before opening her laptop and attempting to return to work.

It was at least another hour before either of them spoke, Laura mentally accepting the candy bar peace offering, inwardly admitting that it had made her feel a little better. But it was going to take a lot more than a Wunderbar to get her to forgive Jason's next move, as an email pinged in her work inbox – the shrill chime pulling her out a moment of concentration. Before she could gravitate towards her inbox Jason started apologizing.

"Now before you get mad, I have already finished QAing the code for today. Secondly, think about it before biting my head off ok?" He once again had his hands up in apology as Laura narrowed her eyes and found the email.

From: Jason.B@globtech.org

To: Laura.A@globtech.org

Subject: Flights to SNT London

Laura scanned the email. It was a list of flights from Canada to England: times, changes and prices, all laid out next to a booking link. Her eyes shot up to meet him again – anger bubbling inside her.

"What is this?"

"Look, Laura, you are miserable," Jason started, his tone measured like he was laying out a business case. "Amy is the woman for you, and if I was in your position, there is nothing I wouldn't do for the woman I love – I wouldn't let her go." Jason rolled his shoulders back, a faint smile settling on his face, wistfully thinking about his perfect fictional woman. He was going to make someone the happiest in the world one day.

"She already left." Laura sighed, her heart still so heavy.

"Then go get her". Jason beamed as if it was the most obvious thing to do it the world.

"What?" Laura couldn't quite put together what he was suggesting here.

"Get on a plane and go get her back." He pointed at the back of her laptop, where the email was still open detailing all the flight details she needed.

"I can't do that," she stuttered. It was absurd to even think like this. No one just got on a plane across the world for love! Especially not Laura.

"Why not? What have you got to lose?" He crossed his arms in defiance. "You have the money for flights. Ok, not business class but you can slum it in coach." He was frustratingly right, she could afford it now she wasn't paying rent. A flicker of hope caught in her chest, the first hope she had felt in weeks. Allowing herself to look in detail at the email, there were four options, the cheapest left from Hamilton Airport in thirty-six hours. Could she really do this?

"What about a return flight?" She tried to let logic form some part of this. She would need to find out where Amy was and travel across a foreign country and then what? Knock on her door and tell her everything she had wanted to tell her? Hug her? Cry at her.

"Book it when you are over there. Say you are visiting a

friend for the holidays. Hey, maybe you will choose to stay out there and not come back," he joked. "Please come back because I need you here with me to fix this awful code."

Laura looked back at the screen. Was it really that simple? Could she just go?

Printed in Dunstable, United Kingdom

77703261R00201